I0626634

THE LAST FULL MEASURE OF DEVOTION

Sam Everson Biehl

Copyright © 2019
All rights reserved.
ISBN: 978-1-7331673-1-4

To R., my one-and-only.
My hands would be empty without yours.

AUTHOR'S NOTE

My first trip to Gettysburg was in 2014. My boys and I toured the visitor's center and walked through the cemetery. Four years later, I returned, but this time with a new purpose: to conduct research for portions of this novel. I toured the battlefields. I hiked to the top of Little Round Top. I visited Cemetery Hill. I studied the monuments - especially the one that commemorates the actions of the 73rd Pennsylvania in repelling the Confederates. I sat beneath the shade of the lone tree on Cemetery Hill which overlooks the fields below. I thought about that night, the night of July 2, 1863.

There were between 46,000 to 51,000 total casualties at Gettysburg. 11,000 of these soldiers would not return home. The remainder either licked their wounds and continued on with the war or were sent home - often with a missing limb or two. Some undoubtedly suffered from PTSD, though undiagnosed, as doctors did not have a word for it at the time. When these survivors arrived home, they adapted to civilian life in all sorts of ways, but most never forgot the war, though they may have tried to.

My great-great-great grandfather, "Civil War John", fought in the Civil War. John, a Swiss immigrant and farmer, had joined the 17th Wisconsin regiment in 1864 as a substitute for a family member. He was captured during the Battle of Wyse Fork - along with most of the 15th Connecticut Infantry - and marched for 16 days and 190 miles to the infamous Libby Prison. He spent two days there before being traded for some Confederate prisoners at Fort Monroe. When the war ended, John finally returned to his Wisconsin farm where he lived a long, full, and happy life.

When later interviewed about his capture and brief soldiering experience for the local paper, Civil War John describes the march as mostly positive: "Union war songs rang out constantly from the little troup as it marched along, and the members of the party continually 'joshed' their captors and the civilians with whom they came in contact."[1]

Later in the article, however, Civil War John reveals that the journey was "not as happy in every respect." Rations were low and the captives marched almost 12 miles a day. Furthermore, upon his arrival at Libby Prison, famed for its overcrowding and horrendous conditions, he began to plot his escape.

Family lore also paints a curious dichotomy of his experience. During his first draft in 1863, John paid a substitute to go in his place to avoid going to war, but then willingly became a substitute in 1864. Finally, when Civil War John arrived home, he constantly carried a cannon ball in the pocket of his overalls. Everyday, he walked his fields with that metal ball as his companion until the day he lost it somewhere in those acres of rich farmland.

To me, that cannonball symbolizes the darker side of his experience, the part that remained hidden away from even his family and closest friends. How could he describe the hunger or the endless marches? How could they have understood what he went through in the thick of battle? How could he describe the brutality of the aftermath? Perhaps he did not suffer from PTSD, but he did remember the war. For both the good and the bad, it affected him.

Civil War John's experience is not unlike the 3.8 million veterans in the United States today who have been disabled - either physically or mentally - in the line of duty[2]. These men and women, upon their return from battle, face many of the same difficulties as their Civil War counterparts. They may struggle to find a trusted, sympathetic ear to listen as they put into words the horrors they have seen. They may be unable to adjust to the fluidity of life outside the military or the safety of being home. They may also struggle to find adequate health care and

---

[1] "Greatest Sport of All, Civil War Vet Recalls." *The Fond du Lac Daily Reporter.* March 24, 1925.

[2] "Veteran's Day 2015: November 11, 2015." United States Census Bureau. November 4, 2015. https://www.census.gov/newsroom/facts-for-features/2015/cb15-ff23.html

housing.

For these reasons - and others unmentioned - **50% of the profits of this novel will be donated to the Fisher House Foundation** so that more veterans will be able to get the care and services that they need to live a happy, fulfilling life with the support of their families.

And so, readers, while this story is fundamentally about two people meeting, falling in love, and facing issues which challenge them as a couple, this story also contains elements of coping with loss, discovering a new purpose, and fixing mistakes.

PROLOGUE

The civil war over secession and plate slavery raged on; men and women of both the Union and Confederacy perished for their beliefs, both insistent that they were right and that the other was wrong.

Logic dictates, however, that both cannot be right and after two bloody standard years of battle, neither the Confederacy nor the Union had accomplished their intended goals.

Half-way through the war, the Union government settled on a bold shift in their intended objective with the passage of the Declaration for the Support of Inner Planet Extractions and Freemen Enlistment, more popularly called the "Extraction Edict". This sweeping legislation proclaimed two new laws: first, that cybernetic extractions were now legal within the rebellious Inner Planets, thus providing Cyborn citizens an opportunity to become Freemen, should they choose; and second, that all able-bodied Freemen were allowed to enlist in the Union army.

Outer Planet Abolitionists and Freemen claimed victory, for it was the first time the Union government openly admitted that this vicious civil war was not just about reunification, but also over extractions. As a result, patriotic Freemen joined the Union army in droves, citing not only their desire to fight for their system, but also a need to prove that they were capable to do so.

But recruited Freemen expressed disappointment upon learning that their military service would amount to nothing more than the jobs that Cyborn soldiers refused to do. They voiced their resentment as they were paid less than their Cyborn counterparts. They reluctantly swallowed their frustration when their struggle for citizenship and equal rights would continue long after the war was over. The Extraction Edict was a beginning, certainly, but not the end of the Freemen's fight for equality.

This civil war touched the lives of everyone in the United Systems: from the dock merchants of the Border Settlements to politicians in the District, from Union sympathizers on Virgis to the soldiers and generals of both armies. The stakes had grown ever higher and as a result, both sides continued to employ strategies to encourage success.

The Union's blockade of the Inner Planets prevented trade with sympathetic systems far from the United System while the Confederacy expanded its fleet of runners and merchant raiders to cripple the economy of the Outer Planets. Orbital forts exchanged hands with startling regularity, as the Confederacy - and then the Union - recaptured planets the Union - and then the Confederacy - had to abandon.

Though most Union soldiers viewed it as a moral and ethical duty to bring the Inner Planets back from secession - using due force as was needed - it was the Confederacy that tasted victory after victory, one battle after another on their own lands. The Inner Planets rejoiced, while Union morale plummeted.

Both armies suffered devastating losses as the war progressed. Some soldiers, both Union and Confederate, returned home in the metal box of the suspended - their bodies forever gone but their plates still intact, celebrated for their ultimate sacrifice. More unfortunate soldiers returned home Broken - alive, but bearing wounds too severe for even a Fixer to completely heal. These soldiers lived in limbo between suspension and normalcy, some choosing to hide their missing limbs with cybernetic implants and others not, but neither were able to completely mask their mental anguish and trauma.

Through it all, the Confederacy would not yield, and the Union furthered its offensive, but despite their superior numbers and equipment, they seemed no match for the hero of the Confederacy, General Edelli of Virgis.

A brilliant strategist and elegant military leader, he and his Army of Virgis seemed invincible, able to push back the invaders with fewer soldiers and barely enough critical supplies. Yet the Union devotion to their cause did not waver, and despite their inability to completely subdue the Confederacy, they stubbornly pressed onward.

Tired of always being on the defensive, General Edelli crossed the Kluane Cluster and invaded the Outer Planet of Nova Penn, sending the planet's civilians into a panic and the nearby generals into a hasty scramble to repel the Confederates from their lands.

On his journey to Nova Penn's capital, General Edelli camped his army near Gerin-Bue, a quiet community that would unwittingly become the chosen place for the two grand armies to confront each other. The residents of this tiny place waited with bated breath as Union reinforcements met Edelli's troops upon the rolling hills and grassy fields surrounding their town, the ultimate outcome hopelessly unclear.

~ Excerpt from <u>Habitation of the United Systems: A History</u>
by Jorroll F. Shren, Historian and Politician

CHAPTER ONE

Fact: Your tears solve nothing. His plate is
infinite.

I know this. I know this with all my breath and mind, but the tears
threaten to fall anyway. I fight them back and fail.

It's all a blur, everything's a blur - voices and sights alike - everything
but the metal box stamped with the star and the crescent - the seal of
our great Union - that he carries in his outstretched hands.

The box is set into my hands. It's heavy, weighted down from the
familiar energy inside.

I am then ushered to the transport, the transport that's taking me
back to Nova Penn. I do not recall the soldier who handed the box to
me. I do not recall saluting when I turned to leave. I do not recall finding
my voice when my commander said he was sorry.

I'm going back home, to our home.

My home.

The words hold nothing but emptiness and suffering. My Osco, my
one and only, is now nothing more than his plate, and our bond nothing
more than a montage of past memories.

It is only when I am alone in my quarters aboard the transport that I
collapse onto the hammock, not processing if the door has closed
behind me - not even bothering to check - and cry. The tears slide down
my cheeks in a warm, steady stream.

I did not believe the news at first, not even after my plate assured
me it was true. It was only when I arrived here, when I saw the Union
seal upon the metal box that I knew that the very last piece of my Osco
was inside.

And yet, even though there is evidence that he is suspended - as real
as this box in my arms - I cannot bring myself to open it. I cannot bring

myself to hold his plate. I cannot bring myself to ask him about his last few standard minutes aboard the *Kaigaa*.

I faced the Secesh on Virgis but I cannot face my Osco.

I am nothing but a coward.

CHAPTER TWO

My Osco, Adahi Bashe, enlisted exactly one year, six months, three weeks, and twelve days ago, standard.

I had tried to convince him otherwise. Being a soldier myself, I had lived through it all - all of the terrible violence and blood.

How could I not disagree?

But he knew the Union needed naval officers and he had been a Spacer on a large freighter. He knew how to fly and how to live on a vessel. He knew he could be an asset, so he left, knowing that I would disagree.

We kept in contact through our oscos - the bond through our plate - when we could, when we were not busy with our other responsibilities. He often told me about his adventures above the planets and I told him of mine on the land. We were always careful not to give away our positions or strategies, as was protocol.

He had been transferred to the *Kaigaa* only a standard month ago.

I did not know that the Union was attempting to take Ter Chule.

I did not know that the *Kaigaa* would be under fire for the greater part of that attempt - that the ninety Confederate strikes upon the vessel caused such terrible damage that the Union navy had to abandon it - worthless scrap orbiting a worthless place.

I did not know that there hadn't been a Fixer anywhere on the Ironclads - that the closest allied Fixer was on Siana - and Adahi's body would shut down long before the Fixer arrived, his injuries too severe for even a Fixer to Fix.

All I knew was that his plate had survived.

Time has become arbitrary. I've ignored the messages sent by my few close friends and family. They would ask me about Adahi. They would ask if I have initiated the Merge.

Fact: It's been one local week since your return to Nova Penn.

Query: Initiate Merge?

One local week and I still haven't opened his box.

It sits on my lap, the sight of it more dear to me than eating or sleeping.

CHAPTER THREE

Before the war, Adahi had been a long-distance freighter working for a large company flying to places outside the system, most often to the Prokentrus.

He worked closely with my parents, who were merchants hired by the Nova Penn branch of the same company. By the time they had met Adahi, I had already enlisted. Though I visited often during breaks in my training, Adahi was always away on a delivery - till the day when I intended to visit them and unintentionally met Adahi instead.

My father had stepped out for a tic to check on some hired Freemen who were loading a few company ships. For whatever reason, Adahi had remained behind, his back turned to the door.

When I walked in, I only saw a man in my father's usual spot at the counter, so I stepped up behind him and wrapped my arms around him, grabbing his hands in a surprise greeting.

We both froze instantaneously. Though his hands were strong and intelligent and kind like my father's, I also felt an adventurous spirit in the heat of his palms and realized immediately that this man was certainly *not* my father. My father had never left Nova Penn before and had no desire to ever do so. *I leave the travel to the freighters,* he had often said.

I released the strange man and backed away, my cheeks reddening in embarrassment from my forwardness. Words - via lips or plate - were unnecessary. My hand upon his was the only communication we needed. That touch told me everything I ought to know about this man.

"I'm so sorry," I had said. "I thought you were my father."

His lips twitched upward in warmth and good humor. "You must be Santi. Olo's daughter."

He was at least ten standard years older than me - with his long, already greying hair hung in a thick braid over his shoulder and faint smile lines at his eyes. I noticed the flight suit, the fringed vest, and the work gloves in his pocket - all indications of his work as a Spacer, not a merchant. Even though I saw the forgiveness in his green eyes, I felt like a fool.

It was then that my father walked in.

"I see you've met Adahi," he said. It was all he had to say.

I didn't think about it back then, but I realize now that Adahi - with the welcome permission of my own mother and father - must have carefully planned all of his return trips to coincide with my visits, because every single time I dropped in to see my parents, he was there, eager to welcome me back.

At first, we talked about nothing of interest: the skies above Nova Penn, the weather on Nova Yan - a frequent destination of Adahi's.

A standard year later, we were discussing taboo subjects like politics and intimate subjects like our childhoods.

Two more standard years went by before we held hands again, our plates revealing a 94.6% compatibility score - high enough for us to form an oscos. I didn't care about the score. Adahi and I held genuine affection for one another.

Three standard years later, we had formed our oscos and were committed to each other.

Adahi continued to work as a freighter and I traveled some in the military, too, but we spoke everyday, sharing silly stories and jokes. I saw him every few standard months and as strange as it seemed, our long separations never hindered our bond. If anything, it brought us closer together.

I never saw him everyday, so I should not have felt as though part of me had been sliced away and lost without him.

But I did, anyway.

CHAPTER FOUR

Fact: It's been eighteen local days since your return to Nova Penn.

Query: Initiate Merge?

My head's been filled with nothing but an endless barrage of reminders:

[Initiate Merge?]

[Initiate Merge?]

[Initiate Merge?]

There's news from the front, too:

[United Systems expands territories into Onaska.]

[Union troops repelled from Sansellvue.]

[S. Gansen accidentally cuffed by own men.]

There's the advertisements:

[Drone service. The way it was meant to be.]

And there are the endless messages from family and friends, which I still haven't responded to: [Santina? It's Auntie...]

[Santi? It's Pella...]

[Sergeant? It's Nyrie...]

[Sarge? It's Hucks...]

I have not left my apartment. I have not eaten. I have not gone to the public bath. I have not spoken to anyone. I have not yet opened his box. I have not followed proper grieving protocol.

I have done nothing but count my inhalations for the last eighteen local days - 396,329 breaths that I no longer share with Adahi. Had he not been suspended, we would have had 252,288,501 more breaths together till his plate shut down on its own.

We could have had so much more time together.

I am awake well before dawn, staring out into the soft darkness and the quiet city, taking in the chilly air mingled with baked crackers and pine.

Adahi would often come back in the early morning. I almost expect to see him now, walking to the apartment, whistling a Spacer tune:

> *...And I'm homeward bound once more*
> *To where Tol shines like my Osca's eye*
> *Who longs for my return.*
> *To the land where she waits for me,*
> *To the land where liberty was born...*

I wait at the window, my head resting in my arms, watching. I hear the tune as clear as if Adahi were actually whistling it, but to my great disappointment, no one emerges from the shadows to greet me.

`Fact: His plate is infinite.`

How lonely my life has become, I realize, lifting my head and drawing my arms away from the sill and focusing on the box.

It still sits there, next to my bed, and I cannot stand the sight of it. I have been cheated out of those 252,288,501 missing breaths. I hold onto nothing but anger. I choose to ignore the brutal truth that Adahi isn't coming back from the war.

Tears prick my eyes. My apartment suddenly seems too small.

So under the grey morning haze, I pull on my cap and jacket and stand by the apartment door. It opens with a swish but I find myself unable to step through the doorway.

Go on, Santi, Adahi would say. *What are you afraid of?*

Closing my eyes and bracing my hands on either side of the door frame, I walk through with one foot and then the other. My hands drop to my sides and the door shuts behind me. I start at the feeling of unprotection.

One step at a time, he would say to me.

His gentle voice coaxes me down the steps and out the apartment. With my head down and my jacket wrapped tightly around my body, I slowly trudge to the cliffs, Adahi whispering softly in my ear, urging me on. It's like I'm back with the rest of my regiment, obeying the orders of my superior: *march, two, three, four, halt, turn, onward!*

The cliffs are only eight hundred and fifty paces from my apartment, but in the blue dawn they seem closer somehow, like I could reach out and touch them. Feeling the placement of one foot in front of the other and having a destination does me some good. For the first time in several standard weeks, I manage a small smile.

The cliffs are exactly like Adahi and I had left them: tall and imposing, but easily climbed if you knew how. I find the cracks in the cliff side and haul myself up mechanically: onward and upward, without pausing to rest.

The muscles of my arms strain as I finally pull myself onto the top ledge, gasping in air and then heaving the rest of my body up. I sit back, dangling my legs over the side, and wipe away the tears streaming down my dusty face with a dirty hand. I hadn't noticed I was crying till now.

Before the beginning of the war, Adahi and I often climbed the cliffs together. Now I climb them alone.

My hands are so empty without his.

I don't know how long I sit there in my misery, but eventually the tears stop and I notice the shape of a man standing at the edge of the cliff, about ten paces from me.

He's short - only a little taller than me - and dressed in a soft flaxen shirt and blue woolen trousers with brown leather shoes that shine in the early morning light. His jacket and hat are lying on the ground next to his feet. Tol is not yet completely above the horizon, so my plate adjusts my vision to take in his profile: short dark hair swept back and carefully styled, russet skin, the slim goatee along his cheek and chin, an almond-shaped hazel eye, long nose, delicate cheekbones but prominent jaw and chin. A handsome man, surely.

I don't know how long he's been here. He doesn't acknowledge me, doesn't even look at me. His face studies the morning light so intently it is as if I am not even there.

But it seems as though he is not here either, because I cannot sense him near me. It is as if he doesn't really exist, though my eyes don't lie.

Who is he?

I've never seen him here before.

`Fact: This is a big city. It is certain you`
`don't know everyone here.`

After the climb, I must be a frightful mess. I wipe as much dirt and dust from my face as I possibly can without the benefit of a mirror and glance at the man, who still stands there like a statue, as if I am invisible.

I could just ignore him as he ignores me, but polite curiosity gets the better of me. I stand up, straightening my clothing and hair and turn toward him, but before I can give him words of greeting, he says:

"Beautiful sunrise, isn't it?"

His voice is thoughtful, melodic, and wonderfully kind.

"I don't mean to intrude."

The man does not take his eyes off Tol. "You aren't intruding."

`Observation: He claims you are not intruding upon his space, but you are rude. You have not yet answered his question.`

"It is a beautiful morning."

His lips curl into a sympathetic smile. "And yet you are sad. I am sorry if *I* am intruding upon *you*."

I look into Tol, fighting back tears and embarrassment. So he *had* seen me. I cannot speak without crying, so I just look at the ground and shake my head.

The man bends down to grab the hat and coat at his feet. "I do apologize."

Tears fill my eyes. "Please, stay. You have every right to be here."

Out of the corner of my eye, I see the man turn his head to me. He scrutinizes me, a strange little smile on his face. I am not sure how to interpret it.

Then I look over at him fully and scramble away in shock, stopping myself from giving a yelp of surprise.

`Directive: Run. Run away. Now.`

His left temple is disfigured, a mangled mess of scars and bright scar tissue where his plate used to be. His left eye didn't escape the extraction unscathed: his eyelid is permanently half-closed, giving the left side of his face a sleepy look.

He was an extremely handsome man before he intentionally mutilated himself; before he became a Freeman.

To be clear, I have seen Freemen before. At busy times of the year, my parents often hired Freemen as general laborers. I'd see them loading and unloading ships at the docks. Even the Union military has enlisted Freemen, but they have their own regiments - separate from the Cyborn ones.

Before this moment, I had never actually met a Freeman, never actually spoken to one.

I act as nonchalant as possible and fail miserably. I've broken out in a cold sweat and my heart pounds against my ribs; even my hands are trembling. I hide them behind my back.

He isn't afraid to point this out. "Are you afraid of me?"

I cannot tell if he thinks my reaction is funny or not.

"Yes, sort of." The words are out of my mouth before I can stop myself. I clamp my mouth shut before I say anything else.

Idiot! I scold myself.

He smiles as if he is more amused by my statement than offended and turns back to gaze at the valley. From this angle, I can no longer see his ugly scar and he looks like a normal man.

"Why?" he presses.

I frown. *Why can't he leave this alone?*

Logic dictates that he deserves to know why I have such fear and hostility toward him, but the truth is, I don't know exactly why I am afraid of this man - who, if anything, has been nothing but respectful and kind.

`Speculation: Without a plate, you cannot anticipate his movements...`

This is true. I can't feel his breath or his heartbeat. I don't know what he's thinking.

`Speculation: ...as well as the stories you've heard about Freemen.`

None of those stories are very pleasant.

But neither of these reasons are good enough, so I shrug and pretend to admire the valley at sunrise, to avoid the intensity of his gaze.

Eventually, I give the most honest answer that I am able: "I don't know."

I expect the man to launch into some angry tirade about how I have nothing to fear because Freemen are not savages or animals, but he continues to stand there, watching the last of Tol emerge from the horizon.

"You do realize there's a path?" he asks, nodding at the boulders to his left. I peek over and realize that he is right.

"No," I say, smiling a little - the first in two local weeks. "I've come to this place for many standard years and have never seen it before."

"What, then," he says, "are eyes good for if you cannot see?" Then he bends down and scoops up his coat and hat.

The Freeman drops his hat on his head, touches his fingers to the brim and leaves, taking the path through the brush.

I stare after him, feeling utterly foolish.

CHAPTER FIVE

The next five local days are like any other. My plate dutifully lists all my reminders - including thirty-seven *Initiate Merge?* messages, the news, advertisements, personal connections. I think of almost nothing but Adahi, and - oddly enough, about the Freeman I met at the cliffs. He was nothing I had expected a Freeman to be. His tone, his words, even his advice - *"What, then, are eyes good for if you cannot see?"* - were kind, without an edge.

Truth is, over these few days, I pondered the exact meaning behind his words even more than I reflected on the many memories of my Osco. Did he mean it as a subtle slight - that he found my prejudice upsetting? Or did he mean it in the literal sense, that I should be doing something to change my position, so that I could see the path in front of me? Had he deliberately meant to unsettle me? Or were they just words, without a specific meaning behind them?

Today, I don't feel like replaying that incident another one-hundred-and-forty-three times. I need a distraction, something else to focus on, something besides the words of a Freeman and something besides my Osco's plate on my nightstand.

I decide that the Freeman must have meant that I literally needed to find another path - that I shouldn't be inside feeling sorry for myself. It is the least embarrassing of all the possible explanations I had formed.

So I am determined not to stay inside, not today.

I pull on my officer's jacket and kepi and leave, shuffling down the stairs one at a time till I'm half-way down and pause, leaning against the wall and staring at my feet, feeling the tug to turn around and go back upstairs, back to the familiar depression.

I stand there for another fifteen tics before I force myself down the rest of the steps, past the courtyard, and into the street without looking back.

I will go to a park, I decide. *The square. There are benches. I can sit and watch people.*

Relieved to have a plan, I set off for the city's square. Having been away at war, I had not been recently.

The city square is only a few blocks away, but I am so preoccupied with getting there that by the time I reach the park and plop down on the closest empty bench, I find myself winded. The few people milling about the park focus on their own activities and I am grateful no one noticed me arriving breathless and sweaty.

There's a mother and small child sitting on a nearby blanket, playing with some toys; a man wandering through the gardens, sniffing the flowers here and there; and a couple walking down the path, holding hands and laughing. I clench my hands, my cheeks burning furiously.

This was a terrible idea.

I prepare to retreat back to my lonely apartment, when I notice another man - a Freeman - across the cobblestone walkways and patios, hunched over his knees, concentrating on something on the ground. At first, I believe him to have a mental issue as a result of his extraction but then, I take another look and my mouth falls open.

Fact: It's him.

It is the same man from the other day, from the cliffs, I'm sure of it. I recognize his drooping left eye and handsome face. I'm certain he hasn't seen me - not yet, at least - because he's so wrapped up in staring at the ground.

I should just leave, shouldn't I? I grip the edge of the stone bench and tap my fingers against it. *Or should I go over there and...what? Say something? Talk to him?*

As I wrestle over this decision, I look over my shoulder. He's glancing up at me with a half-smile playing at his lips. There is a gleam in his eyes that I cannot place and my heart races with uncertainty.

He doesn't...surely he doesn't...but he...but does he know? Does he recognize me? I turn away from him, sitting bolt upright and then frown. I'm being foolish again.

I've been in the thick of battle for two standard years. I fought the Secesh on Virgis. Why shouldn't I be able to talk to a damned Freeman, for All That's Good?

I glare at him again, but the Freeman has once again focused on his feet. I take a deep breath. Then I stand up, fists clenched and determined to prove that if I'm not afraid of the Secesh, I'm damn well not afraid of a Freeman, either.

He doesn't look up as I approach; in fact, he seems content to ignore me. I'm about to hail him in welcome when I gaze down at the focus of his attention.

There's a piece of scrap fabric in his lap with several images of a nimblemouse. The Freeman clutches some kind of a small stick in his right hand that leaves behind marks as he rubs it against the fabric. His fingertips are completely black.

At the sight of such a realistic image, I forget to be tough and drop onto the bench next to him. "That's an incredible likeness."

"Do you think so?" The Freeman sits back and half-smiles, studying his image with a critical eye. From his right side, I can only see his profile and this puts me at ease because his extraction scar terrifies me - though this time I will have the proper courtesy not to say so. "The paws are much too big."

I watch the nimblemouse as it darts under and around the leaves of the flowers in the nearby bed. It's not easy to capture all the details as it moves so quickly from one place to another, but he's right - the paws are slightly larger in his image.

"It's still a good likeness," I insist.

The Freeman shrugs, then sets the black stick upon the bench and wipes his dirty fingers with the images of the nimblemouse. He wraps the stick into the fabric and puts it into his jacket pocket. I expect him to get up, to leave, but instead, he leans over his lap, his hands clasped together at his knees, his expression thoughtful.

"You've ruined the image."

"Does it matter?" The Freeman laughs pleasantly, his eyes following a couple on their walk. "After all, your plate recorded a perfect image of the nimblemouse in your memory, including the proper size of its paws. Compared to that exquisite detail, my image is a rather poor substitute, is it not?"

I lean against the stone bench and study the couple sitting nearby. They are smiling at each other and enjoying some private joke. My chest tightens in jealousy and tears prick my eyes.

He must notice my discomfort and pain because he rises from the bench. "I've been here for too long."

It's an indirect invitation to walk with him - at least, I think it is. I had intended to come to the park so that I wouldn't be thinking about this Freeman, but he's here, less than an arm's length away. As uncomfortable as the thought of walking alongside a Freeman is, I cannot stay here, angry at the couple who still share an oscos. I stand and step around him, my hands in my pockets and eyes focused on the cobblestones. Without saying anything, he steps beside me - taking care to turn the scarred side of his face away from me - and leaves the park.

He remains a good arm's length away, always keeping a step in front or behind me, as if we are not actually walking together.

Query: Destination?

Nowhere in particular.

"It's a beautiful day," he murmurs.

It truly is. Tol is out and there isn't a cloud in the sky. Although it's been overly cool for summer, there isn't a breeze today. I didn't need my jacket after all but I don't bother taking it off. It holds an odd sort of protection for me.

I sigh. "And yet I am sad."

"I apologize for my boldness when we last met," the Freeman says, all hints of humor gone. "Sometimes I forget my place."

"Actually," I say, stealing a glance at him, "the strange thing is...the only thing that got me out of my apartment today were your words."

His eyebrows lift in an unspoken question and his mouth twitches up in humor before he composes himself. Despite my sour attitude, I smile a little too as we continue to walk through the streets in silence.

"My Osco was suspended. In the war."

"I understand. Your hands are empty without his."

"Yes." I pause on the cobblestone walkway and keep my eyes fixed upon the ground. I don't know why I am surprised that this phrase is familiar to him - after all, he used to have a plate. Certainly, he would know.

The Freeman nods at my clothing. "Was he also an infantry officer?"

"No. He was a naval officer." The sudden scrutiny causes me to straighten my hat and pick a piece of lint from my jacket. I would have failed line-up in my sorry state. "Aboard the *Kaigaa*."

"Then he was part of the group that attacked Ter Chule several standard weeks ago?"

I bring my gaze up to his face, his right eye surveying me. It's a lovely shade of brown, deep and rich, like the earth of the Virgis soil. "You've been following the war?"

Something catches his eye across the street and he looks away. "Of course. Does that surprise you?"

"Yes." I hadn't anticipated a Freemen to be interested in what was going on out on Chule, Virgis, or Auracania. "I guess maybe I thought you'd be too far removed from what was going on to even know about current events."

He smiles, but does not look at me. "This war is not just a fight between men and women of differing opinions, you know."

"Of course not!" I exclaim indignantly. "This war is about getting those damn Secesh back in line."

"Has it never occurred to you that I might care about the outcome of this war *because* I am a Freeman?"

"This is *not* a war about your rights."

"Isn't it?" He regards me coolly. "This is a war about the legality of extractions. The winner decides what happens to people like me."

"This is a war about rebellion!" I huff. "Those damned Secesh had no right leaving the Union in the first place!"

The Freeman is about to reply when his gaze suddenly drops to the ground. He draws his arms and legs closer to his body, stepping another good arm's length from me in the process.

I am about to ask him what's wrong when I realize that there's another man standing right next to me, dander up and ready to whisk me away from a dangerous situation.

"Is this Freeman *bothering* you?"

The Freeman does not look directly at either us, but keeps his gaze firmly planted upon the cobblestones.

"I heard you cry out," the man insists, as if he is somehow compelling me to agree with him. "This *Freeman*, is he bothering you?"

Speculation: Say the word and you will never have to deal with the Freeman again.

Bewildered, I blink and stare at the strange man, numb to what my plate has advised me to do.

But...he has done nothing wrong.

In raising my voice, this Freeman had become a target. The man's prejudice reminds me of my own bias just a few standard days ago and I am angry - at myself, at this strange man - but also ashamed by my part in the ridiculousness of the situation.

"No," I insist. "He's a...he's...he's my Osco's manservant."

"His...manservant?" The man glares at me, his eyebrows raised doubtfully, then at the Freeman, then back to me. I stare at him, exactly as if I am being examined by a head officer, but meeting his eye, challenging him to accuse me of lying.

"Yes. We're buying my Osco a...a...gift. For his birthday."

The man frowns at me, skepticism radiating from his plate. Then his attention focuses on the Freeman and he moves in less than half a pace away. He lingers over the Freeman, his eyes dark and fists balled, hoping he will break in fear.

To his credit, the Freeman keeps his head bowed, his body as still as a statue. I can hardly hear him breathing.

The stranger backs away with a courteous tip of his hat at me. "Soldier."

He disappears down the street and around the corner. It is as if the exchange never occurred.

Once he's gone, the Freeman lifts his chin and I catch a flash of anger and defiance in his right eye. I'm uncertain of what he might do next till he takes a deep breath and slowly opens his hands at his sides.

He glances at me with a small smile on his lips. "Manservant?"

"It was the only thing I could think of. I'm terrible at false words."

"Maybe not as bad as you thought."

His self-control confuses me. Weren't all Freemen supposed to be lawless wild animals? Isn't that why they weren't allowed to interact with Cyborn?

It is obvious I don't know anything about Freemen.

I frown after the stranger. "I didn't mean to call attention to you...or to us."

The Freeman frowns and departs in the opposite direction. I follow him, keeping back a pace or two and at an arm's length distance as he had done.

The Freeman offers me a sidelong glance. "These sorts of interactions always make me hungry. What about you?"

I shake my head but - for no logical reason - I don't want to leave the Freeman just yet. He's a real curiosity to me - never having met one before - and I find myself wanting to know more about him. "Would you like company?"

He slows his pace and inches closer. "You would watch me eat?"

I don't know what to say - of course I have no interest in watching him eat!

Observation: He is asking your permission to do something and masking it under a layer of humor.

Exactly as Adahi would have done.

I respond as though I am conversing with Adahi. "Unless you chew with your mouth open."

The Freeman chuckles.

He directs me to a sad-looking kiosk a few streets away. The grizzled-looking Freeman behind the counter greets him with a big smile, but his smile falters when he notices me.

"The usual, Meelo." The Freeman does not acknowledge Meelo's hesitation.

"Sure thing, Nauru." Keeping an eye on me, Meelo assembles chopped items onto a disc which resembles a large, flat cracker. This cracker, however, isn't anything like the standard-issue bland and hard-to-eat Union nourishment crackers. Soldiers in my regiment often joked "one a day keeps the Fixer away" before dunking them into coffee or liquor to soften them up before choking them down.

The cracker Meelo prepares for Nauru is soft and pliable and smells fresh and alive - a tempting curiosity compared to what I am used to!

`Fact: Those crackers are a poor substitute. You'd need to eat four in order to obtain 75% of your daily nutrients. Even then, you'd still be missing valuable components in your diet.`

Both government-issue crackers and commercial crackers contain a Cyborn's daily nutrients, carefully proportioned to maintain full functionality. Commercial crackers, however, have a better texture. Soldiers will often beg family members to send them commercial crackers when the novelty of the standard-issue crackers has worn off.

The only soldiers who never complain about the Union nourishment discs are soldiers who can't afford the government crackers, let alone the various commercial crackers on the market. While it's true Cyborn only need one of these crackers everyday, the commercial crackers are often five or ten times the cost of the government crackers. Cyborn who can't afford pre-packaged crackers grow their own nourishment in garden plots like Freemen do. I saw more than my fair share of Cyborn civilians with gardens on Virgis and Auracania.

I wasn't going to eat it.

`Directive: As you will not.`

Meelo holds out the bundle and hands it to the Freeman - Nauru. Nauru hands him a few faithslips and nods at an empty bench nearby.

This time I choose to sit on his left. I need to prove to myself that I am better than the stranger because I am not afraid of a Freeman.

For twenty-three tics we sit on the bench together, watching people pass by, the silence broken only by Nauru's happy munching. I recall what he said about the war and wondering if I had been naive to insist that the intended conclusion was to bring the Union back together. After all, this war meant a significant, unquantifiable amount more to this Freeman, to Nauru. Whatever happened in the end, it mattered to him.

"Do you really believe that the war is about Freemen's rights?"

Nauru chews his last bite before he swallows and glances at me. "Do you really believe it is not?" He takes a clean handkerchief from his pocket and wipes his hands.

"I'm uncertain. When I enlisted, I thought it would be magnificent to be one of the brave soldiers bringing the Union back together. It never occurred to me there were any other reasons to fight the Secesh..." I'm at a loss as to explain, so I don't bother to finish. I let my ignorance end in awkward silence.

The Freeman sits forward, resting his elbows on his knees. "It is my understanding that most soldiers fight to preserve the Union but that some fight for us, too. There are not many Abolitionists in the military, but they stand behind the essential creed of the United System: that *all* men are created free."

"May I ask why you became a Freeman?"

"You may," the Freeman says with another small smile and a shrug. He doesn't say anything after that.

Query: Do you see his smile?
Observation: He is teasing you again.

"*Why* did you decide to become a Freeman?"

He watches the passing hoppers. I am not certain he wants to indulge me and my silly questions.

"I moved to Nova Penn from Nova Yan. I was young and idealistic and perhaps a bit stupid, but when I discovered the Abolitionist cause, it spoke to me in a way that nothing else ever had."

"Is that why you extracted your plate?"

"No, not at first. I returned home and tried to convince my family they should extract their plates, too, but they would not have it." He offers up a reflective smile. "It was my sister and, to a lesser extent, my brother who really convinced me that I should follow the path I believed to be right."

"So what did you do?"

"I came back to Nova Penn and found someone to extract my plate. The recovery was painful but I healed and my face scarred over." Nauru takes a deep breath and sighs. "It took a long time to become accustomed to not having a plate, but I survived it and have never regretted it."

"And the man on the street?"

"What about him?"

"You don't regret becoming a Freeman and yet you have to deal with the likes of him."

The Freeman half-smiles again, but it looks less friendly and open than the one a few standard minutes ago. "I've dealt with worse. You should see the scars on my shoulders and back."

I gawk at him, horrified by his transparency.

"You anticipate the suspicious stares. You get used to saying the right things all the time and maneuvering around plate-faces who see you as second-class citizens. And even when they don't treat you differently, you still wonder what their true motivations are." His words spill out in a rush as though he's been clinging onto them for far too long and needs a release.

Upon realizing that he is speaking to one of these "plate-faces," Nauru bites his tongue, guarded.

"I'm sorry." My voice quakes with something I can't quite pinpoint: fear? Sadness? Pity?

He shakes his head. "It's been ten standard years and I still don't know my place. I am speaking to you as if I still have a plate or if you have none. As if we are equals." His voice is gentle again, as though he has swallowed his bitter tone.

Fact: This Freeman expects too much.

But shouldn't he have what I have? Doesn't he deserve the freedom to be treated fairly and kindly? I question my plate.

Correction: Freemen have made their choice. They cannot blame Cyborn for their poor decisions. They must blame only themselves.

Though I find my plate's point alluring, I do not agree.

"It's not right. It's not right for you to be so guarded all the time and it certainly isn't right that you are treated so terribly." I hope that he doesn't interpret this as empty talk.

Nauru faces me, his sleepy left eye and scarred temple prominently in view. "Do you really believe that?"

I consider his even temper and humor. I consider his reaction to the stranger on the street and mine at the cliffs. "Yes. I do."

"Does this mean you are no longer afraid of me?" he teases, deliberately looking behind him so that all I can see is his scar.

I pause. At the cliffs, I was afraid of him. At the park, I wanted to prove I wasn't afraid of him. On the street, I protected him with false words. Now, here we are speaking together as if we were friends. It didn't matter that I had a plate and he did not. The scar left by his extraction is a normal piece of him, just as my plate is a part of me.

"No. No, I'm not. Nauru."

At the mention of his name, he leans toward me, a broad smile spreading across his face. "I am at a disadvantage. You know my name, but I don't know yours."

"Santina, but I prefer Santi."

CHAPTER SIX

I spend most of the night thinking about the Freeman, Nauru. Yesterday, we had drifted about town in such pleasant conversation that I did not recall the pain of missing Adahi. His agreeable manner and playful teasing shaped Nauru into a normal man.

`Fact: Without a plate, Nauru is not a normal man.`

At dawn, I watch the sky brighten in grave anticipation.

That little part of me that so enjoyed his company would like to see him again.

`Speculation: He may not wish to see you again.`

I frown at the truth of this statement and sigh, resting my head against the window frame.

I could go back to the park.

`Speculation: If he is at the park, then he will be there to create images of nimblemice, not for you to obsessively query.`

"Oh, shut up," I grumble, screwing up my face in disgust and retreating into my apartment.

I pull on my shoes and jacket, deciding that I will definitely go to the park later to find Nauru. I am not sure what hours he keeps or if he is working today, but he'll venture out at some time during the day, surely.

For now, I plan to climb the cliffs.

They seem closer today, I muse on my way, keeping my focus on the outcropping at the top. Adahi had named it Santi's Spot, but I just called it The Top because I couldn't come up with anything better.

On the occasions that he and I were both home, Adahi and I spent hours at the cliffs, climbing the steep sides to Santi's Spot and then sitting there until nightfall, just holding each other. Adahi would tell me sky stories and I would tell him dirty jokes that I picked up from my fellow soldiers. His hearty, throaty laugh echoed across the canyon and always spooked any nearby critters, causing them to scamper away. He always promised that he'd save the best ones for his crew. I don't know if he ever did.

Tears prick my eyes as I touch the cliff face, slowly feeling the rock for the familiar cracks which I use to hoist myself up. My movements are mechanical, memorized from years at the cliffs. I reach The Top and am about to lift myself up when I catch sight of a neatly dressed, dark-haired man standing less than a pace away. He stares down at me with an amused, but warm, expression on his face. I inhale sharply from surprise and grasp the outcropping even tighter, the muscles in my arms tensing.

Nauru.

"You do recall I mentioned a path?" He sits down and lets his feet dangle off the edge. He makes no move to assist me, but I see his shoulders stiffen - ready to grab at me if he needs to, though my grip will not fail me.

I haul myself up and settle next to him, keeping a careful arm's length away. "Yes, but - "

"But?"

"I didn't expect to see you again."

When he cocks his head at my statement, I flush and complete my thought. "Here, I mean. I didn't expect to see you again here. At the cliffs. Today."

"I come here quite frequently. I like quiet mornings." Nauru picks up a pebble and tosses it away. "Since this is our second chance meeting here, I can only assume that you do as well."

"Yes. My Osco, Adahi, and I used to come here all the time." I pat the ground between us and swallow away the prickle in my throat. "He called this Santi's Spot."

Neither of us say anything for a few tics. I am relieved to have a moment to compose myself.

"What did you and your Osco like to do up here?"

The question is so unexpected that my voice catches in my throat. I sift through flashes of thousands of memories.

"He and I would race each other up the cliff. Sometimes we'd sit here all day without saying anything. He would hold my hand and sing softly in my ear. We'd wait till dark and he'd tell me stories about his adventures, but I liked his sky stories the best." I let the tears slide down my cheeks as I recall his clear, rich voice in the still evening. I don't bother to wipe them away.

"Sky stories?"

I sniff and draw in my legs, crossing my arms over my knees so that I've formed my body into a protective little shell. "Nomadic tales. His grandmother taught him their songs and told him their stories when he was little. I could have gotten lost in everything they both knew."

"He chose not to stay with his tribe?"

"Adahi was restless, which is why spacing suited him so well. His grandmother used to blame it on him being a Sky Baby - born high above the planets, on a ship in the middle of nowhere. She always said that I was the first and only thing that cured him." I smile, shaking my head. "I don't think it was anything I did as much as my occupation. I travel a lot as a soldier. Adahi wasn't expected to follow me, nor I him."

"You were a good match."

"Yes." I wipe away my tears. "We were."

Nauru stares out at the valley. I catch a flash of sympathy in his upturned lips. He picks up another rock and weighs it in his hand before dropping it into the abyss.

I watch the rock disappear. "What about you? Do you have an..." - I struggle to find the right word - "...Osca?"

Nauru's lips twist into an awkward smile and he places his hands on his knees. "No, but it's...different for Freemen."

"How so?" I do not know how to interpret his facial expression or the tone of his voice, so I mimic his position and peer at him through my eyelashes.

"You knew that you and Adahi were compatible the moment you touched his hand." Nauru looks me square in the face and gives me an unreadable half-smile. "If I touch someone's hand, I don't know whether or not they will fulfill all of my needs."

I don't understand anything he just said, but I nod, pretending that I do. Nauru's discerning eye, however, is unfooled.

"For me, a relationship is built purely on a guess," he clarifies, sitting up straight and clearing his throat. "I don't know if someone will be compatible with me even if I spend a significant amount of time with them, or hold them in my arms, or..." He trails off uncomfortably.

"So far I've guessed wrong."

`Fact: This makes no sense.`

My mind reels as I attempt to put the pieces together in a way I am

THE LAST FULL MEASURE OF DEVOTION

able to comprehend. "How do you guess right?"

Nauru shrugs. "It's not unlike finding an Osco, actually. You meet a person. You talk to them. You get to know them. The difference is that *you* know in an instant whether or not they will be a good match for you. Their temperment, their personality, their thoughts, everything about them - it all speaks to you in a way that allows you to determine how compatible the two of you would be.

"But that's not how it works for a Freeman, for me. I haven't found that person yet."

Observation: He is avoiding your question.

My brow furrows. I intend to continue this conversation because I need to make sense of this. "But how do you guess right?"

Nauru shrugs again. "You don't. Not completely."

"But," I persist, "*how do you guess right?*"

Nauru pauses for a few tics, considering how much to indulge me. Then he holds out a hand to me and lifts his eyebrows expectantly. I balk at his extended arm but he doesn't lower it.

"If I was a Cyborn and you took my hand, what would happen?"

"Everything about you would be explained. You would be known to me and I to you."

"Exactly. You would have the potential to gauge everything about me and compare it to your own person." Nauru withdraws his hand and gazes out at Tol. "But I have to rely on my own intuition, my own knowledge about the other person, and how connected I feel to them, all without the convenience of a plate. Sometimes I am right. Sometimes I am not."

I am beginning to understand.

Speculation: "Guessing" is nothing more than flawed interpretation.

"What happens when you are wrong?"

"The bond between two people becomes broken and you guess again. A Freeman may have to form many different bonds with many other Freemen before they finally guess right. Or at least right enough to remain bonded."

The disgust on my face is obvious because Nauru laughs.

He fumbles with another rock he's picked up. "It isn't a perfect system. There's only the hope that eventually you'll choose someone who accepts you as you are." Nauru hurls the rock away, not out of anger or resentment, but as a distraction from his thoughts.

Is he ever frustrated by his failure of guessing wrong?

He looks at Tol again and sighs.

"I'm afraid I must leave now, Santi. I have to work." He rises and I scramble up next to him.

"Will you be here tomorrow morning?"

"Unfortunately, no. I'll be working long before Tol rises." A slow, cautious smile creeps across Nauru's face. "But I will be at the park tonight for a little while. You're welcome to join me there."

I have hundreds of more questions for Nauru - if he'll allow it. "I'd be happy to."

"Well, then, Santi, I look forward to our meeting tonight."

His head tilts in a casual nod and he leaves through the path to our left, the one that I have yet to take.

I plop myself down, dangling my legs over the edge and sigh. Though I don't mind waiting here all day for Nauru to finish his shift, it's lonely up here without Adahi's company. My plate recalls some of Adahi's detailed sky stories intermixed with Nauru's explanations of flawed interpretations, but mostly, I wonder how it is that someone like Nauru has not yet guessed right.

***

At sundown, I climb down the cliffs and walk to the park, half expecting Nauru to be absent so that he'd avoid all of the new, uncomfortable questions I've formulated at the cliffs. As I near the park, however, I see Nauru seated at one end of his stone bench, watching the people walking by. His eye twinkles in recognition as he notices my approach.

"I'm ready for round two of the interrogation," he teases before I say anything.

I sit at the other end of the stone bench. "We can talk about something else, if you'd rather."

He shrugs and stretches out his legs, leaning against the back of the bench. "Ask me anything. I won't answer if I find the question too personal."

"That's fair." I scrutinize his face in the dusk, studying the scars on his temple. I don't want Nauru to believe I only see him as a curiosity, so I choose one question, the one I most want answered: "How is it that you have not yet guessed right?"

His lips turn upward in a wistful smile. For a tic, I believe he isn't going to answer - that he will change the subject or simply won't say.

"I have bonded with many different women, but none of them were compatible enough for an unbreakable bond. That's all."

He says it so simply, so matter-a-factly that I find the truth to be disappointing.

Nauru clears his throat. "May I ask you something?"

"Of course. It is only fair."

"Why did you become a soldier?"

I consider my answer. "I didn't have to be. My parents owned a shipping business at the docks. I could have taken it over when they retired."

"But you didn't want to?"

"My mother was a soldier. Most of her ancestors were soldiers. I recalled their stories of battle and I wanted to be like them, brave and strong and heroic. I excelled at all of the standard military tests. The docks wasn't the place for me." I hide a grin. "Plus, I knew I'd make the uniform look good."

Nauru's sudden laugh tears through the night but no one is close enough to hear him.

Speculation: Good thing. Sitting alone in the park with a Freeman at night will only invite trouble.

My smile fades. "I always wanted to be someone that the system could rely on during war. I wanted to be a person who would make things right."

I feel his watchful gaze settling on my plate glinting in the moonlight. "I wanted to join the Union army."

"Why don't you? The Union needs all the help it can get."

Nauru scoffs in indignation. "If I wanted to do nothing but manual labor for less pay, I would work at the docks."

"What do you mean?"

"Freeman brigades don't fight. They work. They do all the jobs that plate-faces won't do, just like we do here. And for less!"

I frown. Never had I contemplated the Freeman's position as a soldier before. Weren't they positioned in the thick of battle against the Secesh, like me? Was it so terrible that they were not?

"But that shouldn't matter. Anything toward the purpose of reunion is important."

"Santi, my disagreement is not about patriotism or sacrifice - it's the principle that my work is somehow worth less than yours, that I am somehow worth less than a plate-face." I can sense the exasperation in his voice as he sighs. "You don't understand."

"I don't. But I'm trying to."

"And that is why I chose to be here tonight. With you."

CHAPTER SEVEN

I awaken this morning to thoughts of Nauru, excited to see him again at the city park after his morning shift at work.

Mid-afternoon, he had promised last night before we parted. *I will be here.*

I grin and whistle a cheery battle tune, picking up dirty clothes and bits of cracker wrappers and depositing them onto a chair. *When did this place get so filthy?*

As I turn to grab another wrapper, I catch sight of myself in a nearby mirror. My jaw drops in horror at the state of my rumpled clothing, dirty face, and uncombed hair pulled back into a messy bun. Since my leave, I had not visited a public bath and it shows.

I shake my head in irritation as my fingers begin to unpin the bun and claw through my hair. A few stray pins clatter to the floor. I set them with the others on a nearby end table.

Fact: Not only has most of the city seen you in this state, but so has Nauru.

I smack my forehead in disbelief and groan.

What in All That Is Good am I thinking leaving the apartment like this?

Observation: You haven't been.

Query: Initiate Merge?

"Not now," I grumble, quickly braiding my hair and pulling on my jacket and kepi. I rifle through my rucksack, locating a clean shirt and undergarments. I dig out a clean pair of denim pants in my closet and stuff everything into my haversack.

It's only a few blocks to the public bath but the realization of my sorry appearance has made me self-conscious. If he was coming with me, Adahi would have teasingly suggested that I must camp less and

35

fight more.

At least then you'd have the honor of being covered in Secesh blood, he'd say, laughing.

It's too early at the public bath for the families and obnoxious youth. The professionals have already showered or bathed and left for work. I scoop up a couple fluffy towels and a bar of soap at the entry and remove my shoes before stepping inside.

It's quiet, deserted. Like the cliffs. Steam rises invitingly from the large, heated bathing pool in the center of the large room but I carry my things to the shower area since it will be far easier to wash my long hair there. I pick a stall and strip down, tossing my dirty clothes under the bench just outside. The faucet hisses on, pelting me with hot water. I stand there for a few tics, letting the water roll off my face and down the curves of the my body before grabbing the soap and scrubbing my hair vigorously.

It's not as bad as I expected - the water at my feet is mostly clear, not an ashy grey or muddy brown like the washing water we used to scrub off the blood and dirt after a battle - if we were able to find it. There were times we had to travel standard days or weeks before we found enough clean water to simply wash our faces.

The shower shuts off automatically. *It's never long enough,* I sigh inwardly. I reach for a towel to wipe my face and wrap my hair in, then grab the other one and quickly dry myself off. I dress and - thankfully - find a comb at the bottom of my sack. I pull it though my damp hair several times before carefully parting and braiding it, then twist the plait at the back of my neck.

I examine my reflection in the mirror and smile approvingly.

Now for my apartment.

I gather my things and walk back home.

The mess isn't much more than piles of dirty clothes, cracker wrappers, and gear but it still takes me the rest of the morning and a good portion of the afternoon to set things right. I locate Adahi's box under some dirty laundry on my cot and set it on the windowsill, pledging to Merge at my first available moment. I strip and remake my bed and even fluff the pillows. The piles of wrappers are easily recycled, the laundry is dropped into the chute, and all of my gear is unpacked and stowed in the closet.

I could actually have company now, I think. *Though I don't know who I'd invite over.*

Fact: You are going to be late.

I peer out the window. Tol's well past its midday peak. My plate's right. If I don't get to the park soon, I'll miss the opportunity to speak to Nauru today.

I hurry but I needn't have worried.

Nauru is there at his bench, dressed in a sunny yellow shirt, dark trousers, and navy vest with swirls and loops embroidered around the collar in gold thread. He holds a scrap of fabric in one hand and a black stick in the other and stares at the ground, fervent concentration on his face.

I take my place at the opposite end of the bench. "Hail, Nauru."

Bit by bit, the black stick marks the fabric with two squashed ovals and four short lines. "Hail, Santi."

"What image are you creating today?" I ask, craning my neck to peer at the black scribbles on the cream-colored fabric.

"The nimblemouse is back, but he is being rather uncooperative." Nauru shakes his head as something rustles in the leaves at his feet.

"He does not want his image taken today."

"He should be more grateful. I've hung up more than one of his images on the walls of my apartment."

"Is that what you do with all of your images?" I imagine the walls of his apartment plastered ceiling to floor with fabric scraps marked in black. The idea of putting up images to view on a wall intrigues me.

Nauru shrugs good-naturedly. "Most of them. Sometimes I give them away as gifts."

I wonder if Nauru and I will ever become such good friends that he would bestow such a lovely gift upon me. Secretly, I decide that if he ever does, I will hang it on the wall above my cot.

I shift so that I am facing him. "Why do you make these images? They seem to mean a lot to you."

"After my extraction, I became so frustrated by how easily I forgot details that I could have so easily recalled with a plate. What was that passing stranger's eye color? What of the texture of their hair? What of the shape of their mouth? What of freckles or dimples? How else was I supposed to record these memories but by hand?"

Fact: You can't.

He doesn't expect an answer but I agree with my plate. "You can't."

"No." Nauru removes the fabric and unfolds it. "But this way I could come close."

"What other images do you create?"

"Animals and flowers mostly. Whatever I can find around here."

"People?"

"Staring invites trouble. Besides, most people are too self-conscious to pose." He begins to tuck the fabric back into his pocket but I hold out a hand to stop him and scoot a closer.

"You're welcome to keep creating your image. I don't mind."

"Later." Nauru returns the scrap of fabric to his pocket. "I'd rather ask you a serious question, if I may."

"Go ahead."

He casually nods to one of the park visitors across the cobblestone courtyard. He's an older man admiring some flowers in the vicinity of three young mothers who are laughing and talking together while playing with their children.

"Do you suppose that man over there is a Confederate spy?"

Shocked, I glance from Nauru to the man and then back to Nauru.

`Observation: He's teasing you. His sly smile gives it away.`

Determined to keep the story going, I nod my head to a group of children. "Personally, I'm more worried about the child with the stacking blocks."

"Those aren't blocks!" Nauru whispers in mock alarm, leaning in to meet me in the middle of the bench. "They're a code breaker!"

"And what about that little boy over there?" I motion to a child trying to build a sand castle *just so*, but the sand isn't wet enough. The walls crumble every time he inverts the pail. I expect him to burst into tears at any moment, but he patiently and dutifully continues his attempts over and over again.

Nauru tilts his head in careful consideration. "A Fixer, definitely."

I could see that, with his exacting personality.

"In all my time with the army, I've never met a Fixer."

"My mother's sister is a Fixer. I believe she has voluntarily relocated to Virgis to assist Union and Confederate troops who have been injured in battle."

"The Secesh, too?"

"A Fixer is morally obligated to Fix anyone, not just those in the right." Nauru glances at me. "And a good Fixer will comply."

I shake my head. "Traitors don't deserve mercy."

"Mercy is what they get." Nauru's expression is unreadable. I am not sure if he agrees with me or not.

He points to another child. "What about her?"

I regard an argumentative little girl who had managed to convince her parents to stay for another five local minutes.

"A lawyer."

An instant smile spreads over Nauru's face and he chuckles softly.

"What is it?"

"I was once a lawyer."

I recall Nauru's dark trousers and white shirt - the uniform of a working man and not a professional. "What happened?"

"I became a Freeman, and unable to practice law."

"How come?"

"*I must rely on my own memory and not my plate. My logic may be unsound. I may make terrible mistakes in my argument.*" His voice is indifferent, but I catch the bitter disappointment in his eye. "Would you like to hear the hundreds of other reasons?"

"I'm sorry."

`Correction: You have nothing to apologize for. You did not make the rules.`

Though this is true, I frown. If there is one thing I have learned during my time with Nauru, it is that he is highly perceptive and precise, even without a plate. He could still be a lawyer, given the chance.

"What do you do now?"

He gives me a rueful smile and leans down, resting his elbows upon his knees and clasping his hands together. "A thoroughly unstimulating occupation."

I hope he will tell me more, but he moves on to formulating a new story about a young couple who has just passed us, hand in hand.

CHAPTER EIGHT

Another local week passes. Nauru and I steal time together around his schedule but it's never enough. I always have more questions that beg answers. I relish in our silly games. Today he does not have to work. We plan to spend the entire day at the cliffs.

I hope he meets me in his yellow shirt with the navy vest and gold stitching.

`Fact: He will meet you in whatever he decides to wear.`

`Query: Initiate Merge?`

"I'll get to it," I promise aloud, shoving some crackers into my jacket pocket, in case I need nourishment. I pick up my kepi, then put it back down. The weather's been unseasonably warm. I have no need for my jacket either, but I do not feel whole without it. I tug it on - I can always take it off.

Yesterday, I promised Nauru that I would meet him at the bottom of the trail. He's already waiting for me when I arrive. My cheeks flush with pleasure when I notice his choice of clothing: the neatly pressed yellow shirt paired with the navy vest.

My heart skips once at his warm smile.

"Hail, Santi."

"Hail, Nauru. What's that?" I point to the large bag hoisted over his shoulder.

"I can't spend a day at the cliffs without a few supplies."

I reach out to lift the flap and take a peek. "What's in there?"

Nauru turns away and the bag goes with him. "You'll see."

When we get to The Top, Nauru unpacks a large, colorful cloth from his sack and spreads it on the ground. It's made of bits of different fabrics stitched together in a patterned design. I've never seen anything like it and kneel down to better examine it.

"This is beautiful."

"I made it," Nauru replies offhandedly, but I catch the hint of pride in his voice as he removes two beat-up tin cups and a large bottle from his pack.

"You *made* this?" I stare at him in wide-eyed fascination and then back to the blanket. I trace the top stitching with my finger. This must have taken him several standard weeks or even months to complete. He shrugs but he is pleased by my reaction.

Nauru lies down on his back, using his elbows to prop up his upper body. He kicks off his shoes and nods at the empty spot next to him. "Have a seat."

I also remove my shoes and place them neatly next to the blanket so as to not get it dirty. Then I sit down, hugging my knees to my chest and wrapping my arms around my shins. I rest my chin on my knees and tilt my face toward Nauru. He's watching me, wearing a friendly smile.

I return his grin. "If you weren't here, what would you be doing today?"

Nauru looks out at the city in thought. "I would probably be home."

"Making blankets?"

He laughs. "Maybe."

"Who taught you how to do this?" I follow the ordered lines of white stitching with a finger. I stop when the trail travels too close to Nauru's arm and then pull away, bringing my hand back to my knee. Nauru doesn't move, doesn't acknowledge that I was less than a hand's width away.

"I taught myself after I became a Freeman. It kept my hands and my mind busy."

"It must have taken a long time."

"It did." Nauru sits up and offers me his familiar grin. "But with the healing and the adjustment period I had time to spare."

"Did your family know about your extraction? Or did they find out later?"

When Nauru takes a deep breath I believe he is going to change the subject. This must be a topic that he doesn't want to discuss.

"They did, actually. My parents came from well-known families in the Inner Planets. So, while they were not incredibly pleased by my decision, they did not argue."

"Why not?"

He stacks a few rocks in between us, his next words careful but decisive. "As hard as it is to believe, they had always given me and my siblings a large amount of independence. Our decisions - good or bad - were our own. I think it helped that we were born and raised on Nova Yan. There were far fewer expectations for us there than on Virgis."

"And your siblings? What did they think?"

"My brother thought I was a fool. He could not believe I would willingly give up my prestige for my principles. My sister, however, was supportive - even more than my parents. I rarely speak to either one of them now."

"That's too bad."

Nauru's fingers brush against the top rock as he attempts to place another pebble. The whole pile topples, spilling onto the blanket.

"It is the nature of becoming a Freeman."

As much as he has accepted his place, I detect the frustration over his struggle and feel a rush of pity for Nauru and all the things he can no longer do.

Nauru begins to stack the rocks again and this time I help. One by one, our little tower doubles in height. Nauru gingerly places the smallest pebble on top and this time, it stays. He nods to himself, satisfaction on his face.

Nauru reclines on his side in such a way that he does not disturb the rock tower. He props up his head with a hand. "Where did you grow up?"

"Here, on Nova Penn. Right in this very city."

"Do you have any siblings?"

I lean back and stretch out my legs. The rock tower wobbles but doesn't fall down. "No, but I do have a cousin - Pella. We were practically sisters growing up."

Nauru's eyes sparkle. "Did you ever get into trouble?"

"Never! Pella always tried to get me to pull a few pranks but I was too terrified of my aunt. She could take on the Grand Army of Virgis by herself."

"A formidable woman?"

"That's putting it mildly."

"Was your mother the same way?"

"My mother was quiet and incredibly kind. She had this calming presence about her. And she was so easy to talk to."

"I imagine her to be a lot like you."

Nauru's unexpected words fill me with warmth and I blush. "I liked to think so."

"Liked? Did something happen to her?"

My finger traces one of the stitched paths to the rock pile. "My parents retired and planned to move to Prokentrus. They sold their business to a family friend and packed everything onto a large passenger ship and left."

I pause, lowering my entire palm to the blanket and glancing away. It's been a while since I've recalled these memories.

"Santi? I understand if you don't - "

"No, it's okay," I interrupt, fiddling with the top rock on the pile. "On the way, the transport hit a storm. The entire ship was wrecked. Nothing salvaged."

"Nothing?"

"Nothing at all."

Nauru does not respond but his supportive gaze says it all. I don't have to explain that the loss of the ship and everything aboard meant that I was unable to Merge with my parents. All of their memories - as well as the memories of our ancestors - had been lost. Only my own insufficient recollections survive.

"But the worst part isn't that they've been suspended or that all of those hundreds of thousands of memories have disappeared. It's that there was no finality, nothing to tell me it's time to move on. I believe that they're here or on Prokentrus somewhere. It's only when I try to contact them that I receive the static."

"I'm sorry, Santi. That is a terrible burden to live with."

But it is not my parents I am thinking of. I recall Adahi, my one and only, my Osco. If I do not Merge with him, then there is nothing to prove that he has been suspended. He is on a delivery. He is in a Union naval vessel in the Inner Planets. He is anywhere but in the metal box at home on my windowsill.

Directive: Accept the finality.

Query: Initiate Merge?

I'll get to it.

Fact: You are running out of time.

"There's not much I can do about it," I tell Nauru, pushing my plate's demand away.

"I know, but it helps to have a sympathetic ear." He picks up the bottle and fills the tin cups to the brim. I accept the cup closest to me and Nauru lifts his.

"To friendship," he says.

"To friendship." I sip the contents. It's smooth and subtle and filling, quite unlike the burn-your-throat stuff I usually drink at field camp with my crew in the evenings. "This is amazing."

"I'm glad you appreciate it. I was afraid army life had dulled your senses."

"Not yet, anyway."

As he begins to describe how he came about this bottle, I take another sip of my drink and gaze at him fondly. Nauru, my constant companion for these local weeks, has no idea how much I've come to rely on him.

He has changed me in a way that I cannot wholly describe. When I see the left side of his face, I no longer notice his scarred temple and sleepy eye, but a man I have come to deeply respect. I spend my days waiting in longing for him to appear and my evenings dissecting every detail of our conversations, eager to see him again the next day.

I have memorized the articulations in his voice, knowing when he holds his breath for just a moment too long he has carefully deconstructed my most recent thought and detailed every single flaw in my argument, complete with evidence of my error. A husky whisper means that he is about to tease me. When he produces a low grunt in his throat, I know he agrees with my logic, but refuses to say it out loud.

I have come to accurately interpret his body language, knowing when a stranger approaches by the tense clasping of his hands or by his downcast stare or by his sudden change in speech, which becomes cool, closed-off, and distant - even though I know him to be philosophical, passionate, and intelligent. I know by the length of his eye contact and the narrowing distance between us that he is beginning to trust me - that I am more than just another plate-face. And I know by his glowing smile and the twinkle in his eye that he isn't merely happy to see me but that he *needs* to see me, as I need to see him.

Nauru is so much more than just another Freeman.

I have come to know him to be no different from me, a plate-face.

CHAPTER NINE

Today, Nauru wants me to meet him at the city park at midday. He needs to ask me something, something important. No matter how hard I tried to get it out of him yesterday, Nauru wouldn't say.

He's already waiting for me at our bench but without his usual black stick and canvas cloth in hand. Today, he watches the park visitors. When he finally spots me, he rises, smoothing out my second favorite of his vests - the green one with the embroidery about the collar.

"What is it?" I demand, too eager for his news to be polite.

"No good day? No greeting? No salutation?" he teases.

"Hail, Nauru. It's *so* nice to see you again."

Nauru breaks into a slow smile and slides next to me, his body close enough that I catch the scent of soap on his skin. "I have been invited to a party and I would like you to accompany me."

"A Freeman party?"

His right eye twinkles. "Of course. Tomorrow night."

"I...I don't think that's such a good idea."

"Why ever not?"

I hesitate. I had come to know Nauru and he knew me, but a group of Freemen? His invitation was utterly -

Observation: Preposterous.

"I...I shouldn't even be in the Freeman Quarter."

Nauru leans against the bench, arms spread out along the stone top, an invitation to argue with him. "But you are invited."

"Even if I am invited, I don't think I am welcome there."

He waves a hand dismissively, his counterargument prepared and ready. "Nonsense, Santi. I *asked* if you could come."

"What did they say?"

Nauru folds his hands in his lap and glances down at his hands. "To be honest, they didn't want you to come."

"Then why - "

"I insisted you were a model citizen, a Union soldier fighting for us. I convinced them you weren't going to cause trouble so there wouldn't be anything for them to worry about."

I sit forward, resting my elbows on my knees and wringing my fingers together. Even though I have gotten to know Nauru on a personal level, I don't call myself an Abolitionist.

"I'm not a freedom-fighter. The Freeman's fight is not my fight."

"They don't need to know that."

"I won't deceive your friends."

"Please, Santi. Consider it. It would be good for you to see how we live and good for the others to see that there are Cyborn like you who are willing to make an effort to know us."

Cyborn like you. Nauru has never described me in that way before. I have always been just like the rest of them, the rest of the plate-faces.

Our eyes meet and an uneasy expression settles on Nauru's face. His nervousness is endearing; I am accustomed to his self-assurance. "The party wouldn't be the same without you. And...well, I'd like you to be there with me."

"I see why you became a lawyer."

Nauru's mouth twist into a grin. "I don't need an answer right now."

I could not give an answer if I tried. My tongue feels attached to the roof of my mouth and I have no words to describe my discomfort and doubt. Nauru is unable to understand my hesitation - how can he? We do not share a connection beyond the words we exchange.

"Santi? Are you okay?'

Directive: You cannot go.

Statement: It is your only logical course of action.

It is a logical course of action, but not my only one.

Nauru's invitation is an important step in the progression of our friendship. I will not make a decision till I've examined all of my options, including the ones my plate refuses to give me.

I know he wants me to attend the party. While I am intrigued, I do not share his excitement. I stare at the ground, reluctant to meet his eye. "I have no more words. Not right now."

"I have caught you off guard."

Fact: An understatement, to say the least.

Before I can blunder through another explanation or excuse, he changes the subject, rambling on about all the preparations he has helped with over the last few local weeks. I appreciate Nauru's distraction - my mind's a muddled mess of jumbled thoughts and questions - so my plate collects his words to recall later, once I've considered my options.

If I entered the Freeman Quarter now, what would happen? Would someone approach me? Or would they give me my space? Would they look upon me with welcome, with scorn, or with fear?

Speculation: Fear. Cyborn do not go into the Freeman Quarter unless they want to cause trouble.

Would they welcome me if I was with another Freeman, with Nauru? Would they accept me? Or would I be looked upon with suspicion?

Speculation: Suspicion. Even if Nauru were a Freeman of great importance, the others would not trust you.

What was Nauru's role in the Freeman Quarter, anyway?

Nauru had not been forthcoming about his place in the Freeman community and I am ashamed to admit I had never asked. Having been an intelligent, well-spoken lawyer in his former life, I am certain he is well-respected among his group of Freeman friends.

Speculation: Considering his strong opinions about plate extractions and the war, it is possible he is an Abolitionist as well.

My plate is correct. Nauru spoke of being moved by the anti-plate message, which suggests that he is at least sympathetic to, if not a direct part of, the Abolitionist movement on Nova Penn. There is no reason for a plate-face like me to befriend a Freeman like Nauru unless I *am* an Abolitionist and fighting for their cause, as Nauru had convinced them.

Therefore, I am certain that other Freemen would look favorably upon me in Nauru's company.

The potential deception still troubles me. I fight this war to preserve the Union. I fight to avenge Adahi. I fight to protect this planet and my home. I fight for Nauru but I do not fight for every Freeman in the system.

I am not an Abolitionist. I know nothing about what it means to be one.

Nauru extracted his plate because he believed plate technology was enslavement. What of the other Freemen? Were there other reasons for extraction besides Abolitionism? Was is possible that the intention behind an extraction could be as varied as Cyborn themselves?

Query: And what of Cyborn Abolitionists? How do they justify their own conflicting actions?

It's painful to admit that there's still so much I don't know about Nauru's life.

Fact: More research is in order.

Yes, I resolve. *I need appropriate answers to questions these Freemen might ask about my place in Abolitionism.*

It barely registers that Nauru is trying to get my attention. His distant words ring hollow in my ears. My plate catches them and processes them for me.

Statement: "I will wait for you at this bench, mid-evening tomorrow. If you aren't here, I'll go alone. I hope to see you tomorrow, Santi."

I nod, enough to indicate he was heard.

Observation: It is a wonder that Freemen and Cyborn are able to communicate at all.

CHAPTER TEN

My research extends through the night and well into the next local day.

The Abolitionist movement, I discover, has been around longer than I realized. My own planet of Nova Penn was one of the first Outer Planets to grant basic rights of Freemen, guaranteeing that any Freeman who found his or her way here would be protected. I now understand why Nauru chose to come here rather than stay on Nova Yan. It was the promise of freedom.

I recall the stranger who approached Nauru and me in the street.

There must be times that he regrets his decision.

`Observation: Perception is vastly different from reality.`

Agreed. Perceptions are vastly different from reality.

I had expected the Abolitionist movement to be made of Freemen populations throughout the Outer Planets. I had also expected these populations to be engaged in varying degrees of activism, from pressuring politicians to reshaping the law and participating in rallies and protests.

I had not, however, anticipated the number of Cyborn who gladly worked alongside these Freemen, these Cyborn who also called themselves Abolitionists.

Despite this partnership, even Cyborn Abolitionists could not come to a consensus regarding their Freeman counterparts. Abolitionist circles throughout the Outer Planets generally agreed that anyone could choose to extract their plate, but most disagreed about what happened next.

Should Freemen be sent to another planetary system, one that was already established for them by the United Systems?

The thought of Nauru moving outside the system saddens me.

Should Freemen continue to live in the United System with rights and citizenship, but separate from Cyborn?

I would like Nauru to someday be my neighbor.

Should Freemen have full and equal rights, protected under the law to the extent that Cyborn are?

This is fair. I accept that Nauru is like me, but do I accept all other Freemen as equals?

Fact: This assumes that Cyborn and Freemen are inherently equal.

Query: How can they be equals when these Cyborn believe in freedom from the plate but still have their own?

I cannot answer my plate's question, just as I am no closer to making a final decision about the party.

Directive: If you cannot make a decision, then you cannot go.

I stare out my window, at the direction of the park. The air is cool and the sky grey. Soon it will be dusk.

What do I do?

Directive: If you cannot make a decision, then you cannot go.

I am able to make a decision, I retort. *I just need more time.*

Fact: You have exactly fourteen local minutes.

Fourteen local minutes. That isn't enough.

Can I accept all Freemen as equals?

From our many conversations, Nauru has expressed that he wants to be able to work and live in security. He wants to be able to walk down the street without arousing suspicion. He wants Cyborn to see that he is not dangerous.

I know he is not dangerous, but the rest of the system does not see him that way. Without the full support of the Cyborn - Abolitionists or no - obtaining full citizenship, equal rights, and the ability to vote will be impossible for Freemen. My plate recalls quotation after quotation in which Cyborn opponents question the very validity of the movement.

[Abolitionism threatens our very existence.]

[This movement is dangerous and illogical.]

[How can we give equal rights to those who can no longer function the way All That Is Good wished us to?]

[Freemen have no use, nothing beyond the flesh

of their bodies.]

Therefore, what of the other Freemen? Can I accept them as equals?

I do not know the answer to this question. I had never examined the system - never questioned it - before now. I had no reason to. I had not given any thought to the plight of the Freeman till I met Nauru.

Nauru has permanently altered my beliefs about Freemen by proving himself entirely unlike what I knew Freemen to be. He is a good friend and I am grateful for that. I do not need to be an Abolitionist to see him differently. I only have to share part of my life with him.

But what of the other Freemen? Am I willing to share that part of my life with them, too?

Showing up to the party means taking another step closer to actively supporting the Abolitionist cause, a step closer to believing that all Freemen - not just Nauru - are equal to me. It proves that I am willing to break down the invisible barriers that keep us apart.

This could be good for you, to see how we live, and good for them, to see that there are Cyborn like you who support us, Nauru had said.

But do I have to believe in their cause?

I believe in the Union so strongly that I am willing to return from this war in a small dark box decorated with the star and crescent, like Adahi did. Nauru left Nova Yan and started a whole new life without looking back because he believed so deeply in the Abolitionist cause.

Fact: Though you do not share each other's beliefs, they give each of you a purpose. They define you. They drive you.

Query: Do you believe that Nauru is doing what is right for him?

"Yes."

Fact: Therefore, although you do not agree with Nauru, you can still respect his beliefs.

As I could with all Freemen.

Regardless of beliefs, of causes, of purpose, of drive, no other decision exists.

I will go.

Cripes! I realize, planning the few standard minutes I have left to get ready.

Fact: One local minute to fix your hair. Three local minutes to dress. Five local minutes to the park. Any longer and Nauru will be gone by the time you get there.

I pull my brush through my long hair twice - enough to untangle it - then braid and knot it into a bun at the nape of my neck. I check my work in the mirror and frown. It wouldn't pass a military inspection, but it'll have to do. I don't have time to smooth down all my stray hairs.

Peering into my closet, I decide upon a simple sleeveless black dress, one I rarely wear because it isn't military issue. I throw off my flaxen nightshirt and put on the dress. Even with the endless marches and moldy crackers, it still fits.

Slippers. I need my black slippers, I think, frantically digging through the floor of my closet, tossing aside a pair of Adahi's old boots and several pairs of my own worn-out shoes. They're in the back, well-hidden under a pile of clothes and more shoes. I pull them on and wiggle my toes, soaking up the satiny feeling.

My Union jacket sits on my sofa and I shrug it on, fastening the top three buttons. Since the war, it's become such a staple of my wardrobe that I feel naked without it.

I take another peek at myself and shake my head. My hair's a mess and my dress is wrinkled. At least my shoes are on the right feet and all three of my jacket buttons are in the right holes.

Nauru will laugh when he sees me - of this I am certain - and ask me if I dressed in the dark.

There's just enough time to run down the stairs and to the park. With only a few tics to spare, I arrive to find Nauru sitting on the bench. He smiles broadly and stands as soon as he sees me.

Nauru's dark hair has been washed and combed. He's wearing a navy vest and coat, both well-cut and tailored. The vest is adorned with tiny white buttons and is a lovely contrast to his white shirt and light-colored trousers. In his left hand, he holds a pink flower with ninety-six petals.

He offers me the flower. "I'm glad you're here."

"Thank you...?" I don't take it. I'm not sure what to do with it.

Nauru smiles again and reaches around the back of my head, bringing his arms and chest close, close enough that I can smell the starch used to press his white shirt and his bath soap, reminding me that I didn't bathe. I hope I don't smell as sweaty as I think I do.

Observation: You are clean enough.

He pins the flower into my hair and tilts his head to admire his work. He scans my face, his eyes lingering on mine and I find myself holding my breath. Then Nauru reluctantly pulls his hands away and clasps them together at the small of his back.

"Sometimes Freemen women wear flowers in their hair. I thought tonight you should look as lovely as they do."

Lovely?

I shake my head, embarrassed because of my wrinkled dress and knotted hair and my tattered old Union jacket. I certainly don't feel lovely.

He cocks his head and smiles at me, his scars shining in the park lights. "It probably doesn't make much sense to you. I'm sorry if I'm confusing you, Santi."

My words tumble out in a jumble of nonsense. "No, no, it does, I didn't have time to get dressed - "

At this, Nauru's eyebrows shoot up and his mouth twitches in humor.

" - I mean, not in the careful way you have. I'm a mess compared to you."

He laughs. "I didn't notice."

"Liar."

Nauru steps closer and leans in, his face only a touch away from mine. "You'll always be lovely, with or without time to get ready."

I take a deep breath to steady my heart which thuds wildly against my chest. I find myself staring into his good eye and becoming lost in the depths of greens and browns.

Nauru nods toward the street. "Shall we go?"

I tilt my flushed face and hide my shaking hands. "Yes."

Nauru leads me out of the park and directs me down a main street. We walk side by side, so close our hands almost touch. Neither of us say anything for a long while.

He gives me a sidelong glance. "I'm glad you decided to come."

"I knew how important this was to you. I didn't want to disappoint you."

"I assume your research helped sway your decision?"

"I learned things I did not know. My research helped me understand but I came tonight to be with you."

Nauru falls silent, in tandem with the emptiness of the night. Although he's right next to me, his pace matching mine, he is hundreds of paces away, our familiarity missing somewhere in the darkness. I attempt to get it back. "Who's the party for?"

"Lem, a close friend of mine. I've known him since I became a Freeman."

"What is he celebrating?"

Nauru glances at me, his extraction scar hidden in the shadows. "He is to be joined together with Udarah. This is a celebration of their bond, their love."

"Oh."

Had I recalled this information, I am certain that I would not be here now. I will already be treated like an invader for being in a place I do not belong, but I am also a fool for neglecting to review what Nauru said yesterday during my musings. We continue on in silence.

Eventually, we turn a corner and music fills the air with wild abandon. I strain to identify the distinct tune from each instrument, but there's no order to the music, no pattern or beat, nothing that I can grasp onto and follow, not till we enter the brightly-lit quarter where a crowd of Freemen slap their hands together, clapping out a beat, one that I finally recognize as a popular dancing song.

Whispers of our arrival flow through the crowd. One by one, the musicians stop playing. They lower their instruments and stare at us. Then the noise in the Freeman Quarter disappears entirely as the Freemen stop dancing and clapping and singing. They reach for each other's hands.

We face each other in an uncomfortable showdown - me against a group of fifty-four Freemen. I study their faces, their panicked eyes, their expressive extraction scars. There's a man whose scars have left him perpetually playful holding a woman with droopy scars like Nauru. A brother and sister - each with angry hatched lines down their temples - clutch to the hands of their mother whose scars reflect timidity. The scars of three young men demand an answer to my presence here. Only one young woman in red stands, arms crossed, her chin out defiantly, as if to assure me that she can't - or won't - be intimidated.

They ignore Nauru. They wait for me to to say something - anything! - but my voice has abandoned me.

Nauru still has his. "This is Santi. She is Osca to Captain Adahi Bashe, a naval officer who fought valiantly aboard the *USS Kaigaa*. She is a sergeant in the 56th Nova Penn Brigade and fights for us. Consider her an honored sister and friend to all Freemen."

For a few tics, no one responds. But then, as if on cue, as if it was planned, the Freemen begin to hum. The musicians pick up their instruments and with the pomp and solemnity of any military band, they play the opening notes of *The March for Freedom*. It's a song I recognize from camp - though admittedly never sang. I wonder if this song had meaning to those soldiers singing it, or just to Nauru and everyone else here. All of the Freemen, old and young - even the young woman in red sitting on the steps - also sing, their voices imperfect but loud and clear:

> *Our Union's forever - so we'll fight and defend -*
> *Against Secesh traitors and all unworthy men.*
> *And we'll continue ever onward till the bitter end,*
> *Forever marching on toward freedom!*
> *They'll never really know what we gave -*
> *So many of the Union's loyal, true, and brave,*
> *Who battle on so no one shall be a slave,*
> *Forever marching on toward freedom!*

Tears prick my eyes and I blink hurriedly to hold them back. I glance at Nauru. His gaze is focused on the Union flag hanging on a post atop one of buildings. His voice is the loudest and I know that though he may never admit it openly, he had something to do with this.

When the song ends, there are three tics of silence, then the musicians play another song, a song I don't recognize. Children begin to pull away from their parents. Some look at me curiously, but most chase each other through the crowd, weaving in and out of the small groups of Freemen talking to each other. A few couples take hands and dance in the empty streets while others take plates and nourishment from nearby tables.

Nauru leads me to four Freemen engaged in conversation near the drinks. He shakes their hands one by one and asks of their families, their work. They respond politely, laughing and teasing each other, but all the while, their eyes are on me. It is awkward to be scrutinized so, but I am encouraged by Nauru standing at my side. Because he does not question my being here, neither do they.

Finally, during a lull in the conversation, Nauru introduces me.

"This is Gailen."

A broad man lifts his cup.

"Kitani."

The woman tilts her head to me, her eyes downcast.

"Caigh."

Another man wearing a grey homespun suit tips his chin.

"And this is Sim."

The third man with rough hands drums his fingers against the bottom of his plate.

They do not reach for my hand as they would another Freeman.

Their smiles are faint and there is no laughter. Even though they no longer have plates, an unspoken dialogue passes between them as they look to each other for something more to say to me.

I puff myself up, trying my best to appear confident and unafraid in my uniform jacket, instead of humbled and small since I am on their terms now. "It's a pleasure to meet all of you."

Sim clears his throat. "We are sorry to hear of your Osco. Your hands must be empty without his."

I falter at the mention of Adahi. Till now, I had not thought much of my Osco, though I had yet to initiate Merge with his plate so that I could finally move on. All of that time had been spent with Nauru.

"It's been easier with Nauru's friendship."

At the mention of his name, all eyes flit to Nauru. He doesn't offer anything to the others besides a pleasant half-smile.

"What does his friendship mean to you, Cyborn?"

I turn to face the sharp voice behind me. It's the surly woman, the one in the red dress. Her hands rest on her hips. Her lips press together into a thin line. Her brow furrows. Her good eye flashes angrily. Her other eye is nothing but a glittering bead trapped between folds of scarred skin.

"Anma," warns Nauru. "She isn't here to make trouble."

The woman steps closer into my space, hoping to make me uncomfortable. "Neither am I."

Her approach does, in fact, make me uncomfortable, but I stand my ground, refusing to let her see my discomfort.

Sensing trouble, Caigh hands Gailen his drink and grabs Anma's hand, tugging her into the crowd. "C'mon. Let's dance."

Although she follows him willingly, she continues to glare at me as they cross the street, to the far side of the group. The others quickly make excuses and leave for nourishment, to drink, to dance, to mingle.

Fact: This situation contains the truth of your reality. It is what Nauru said before - that not everyone wants you here.

I watch Nauru, who is frowning at the woman dancing with Caigh. I offer him a small, reassuring smile. He sighs.

"I'm sorry, Santi. I had hoped to avoid any unpleasantness tonight."

"I'm sure she's not the only one."

"She is not," he concedes. "But she was the most vocal about it."

I am about to say more, to ask why she hates Cyborn so, when two more people approach Nauru. Both are dressed elegantly, in well-fitted, colorful clothing and radiate happiness. This must be the couple we are here to celebrate.

Nauru clasps the man's hand, then embraces the woman. "Congratulations."

Udarah giggles and pulls away, then faces me. It's clear she's fighting the urge to take my hands or embrace me and I am appreciative of her self-control. "You must be the lovely Santi."

Lem nudges Nauru in the side. "You're the only subject Nauru speaks of these days!"

"Am I?" I look at Nauru, who's *blushing*.

Lem laughs. "It's always *Santi this* and *Santi that*."

Udarah pokes Lem in the shoulder. "Lem! His business is his own. He's just kidding."

The embarrassment and annoyance on Nauru's face tells me otherwise.

"Perhaps Udarah should know what you actually thought of her mother's gift," Nauru counters mischievously.

Lem's eyes roam to Udarah, who raises an eyebrow questioningly. "Well put, Nauru."

Udarah brushes aside Nauru and Lem's banter and focuses on me. "We all thank you, Santi."

I am taken aback. "For what?" My words are barely loud enough to be heard over the music.

"For fighting, of course."

"I'm honored." After the song and the mostly warm welcome, how could I not be?

"And your Osco. He made the ultimate sacrifice."

It is the second mention of Adahi tonight - and in less than ten local minutes!

"He was very brave. As are all who serve." I force a tight smile but the guilt hangs there, a reminder that the time needed to follow proper protocol is running out.

Udarah's smile is sympathetic, motherly.

Nauru watches the dancers and taps his foot to the music, clearly uninterested in getting involved in conversation about the war - though on any normal day, he would happily indulge anyone in such discussion.

Lem takes his cue by clasping Udarah's hand and raising it to his lips. "Perhaps a dance, my love?"

Udarah giggles again and gives me a carefree wave as they step into the street, melding into the rest of the dancers.

I face Nauru, unable to contain my curiosity. "What have you been saying to your friends?"

"Nothing." He will not admit it, but his voice indicates he knows exactly what I'm talking about.

"Lem thinks you hold some kind of high opinion of me."

Nauru inches closer, his body almost touching mine. His warmth is suddenly unbearably hot in the chilly air. He bends his lips to my ear. "Will you dance with me, Santi?"

I study the Freemen dancing - well, *moving*. There's no clear beat to the music but that doesn't seem to bother them. They sway back and forth, hands linked, moving to the music without any formal dance steps, but there's nothing I can really follow in an organized way. I'm not sure I would be uncoordinated enough to dance in that odd fluidity as they do.

My gaze falls upon Lem and Udarah, hands together, laughing. I can't take my eyes off them.

Will Nauru expect me to dance hand-to-hand with him like the Freemen do?

The thought horrifies and intrigues me. Nauru was a Freeman and unreadable to my plate. If I took his hands, what would they say to me?

Nauru studies me curiously.

Fact: You are here because of Nauru.
Query: Remember?

My blood pulses in my ears and cheeks. "Okay."

To my immense relief, Nauru doesn't take my hand. He nods his head toward the street where the other Freemen have gathered and then directs me toward the edge of the group where it is less crowded, less likely that anyone will bump into us.

He leans in and counts out a beat for me. I'm not sure how he is able to find something in this musical mess, but I appreciate it. Then Nauru steps toward me and I step back and we turn about in a tight, rigid triangle to his steady counts of *one-two-three*, *one-two-three*.

"Cyborn dancing must not be very interesting for you now," I say, after our fifth triangle, nodding to the other Freemen.

He tilts his head. "What makes you say that?"

"It's not as lively as Freeman dancing," I point out. "And there's no touching."

He pauses for a few tics. His next words will point out some flaw in my logic. "You assume I like to dance like a Freeman."

"Don't you?"

"Yes, I do. Very much." The corners of his mouth twitch upward. "But sometimes it isn't about the dancing. It's *who* you're dancing with. Are you happy to be here?"

"Yes."

"Then that's enough for me."

I do not entirely understand his meaning so as I ponder his words, I catch sight of Anma. As she meets my gaze, her eye hardens territorially and her mouth sets into a stiff frown.

CHAPTER ELEVEN

It's dawn, two local days later and I am still humming the merry music at the Freemen party. Without effort, I am able to recall the obnoxiously loud singing, the one-two-three dancing, the numerous introductions, the over-seasoned nourishment and powerful drinks, the ever-flowing kind words for Lem and Udarah in one toast after another, the scent of flowers in the air.

Nauru is working today but he promised to meet me at the park once his shift has ended. My plate insists I do something before mid-afternoon but I feel unmotivated without him.

I lie back in bed, resting one hand on top of the other and settling them both under my ribcage. I listen to my body, feeling my belly lift up and down with my breath while my pulse beats a consistent rhythm that I feel in my wrists, then my thumbs, and the insides of my ankles. My stacked hands are comfortingly warm and soft and heavy on my body - exactly how I envision Nauru's to be if he ever dared to touch my hand.

Did Nauru have a lawyer's hands once? Soft? I muse. *His hands will be rough and calloused now. And strong - his hands and arms would be strong from laboring.*

A secret, selfish part of me wishes that Nauru was still Cyborn because then I would take his hands without question. I would know him completely and share with him all I had to give.

If Nauru and I had an oscos, his hands would tell me why his eyes are always laughing.

Fact: It is impossible for you and Nauru to share an oscos.

Merely hypothetical, I remind gently. I am not cross at my plate for pointing out the obvious, not right now.

60

Fact: Your Osco, your one and only, was Adahi. It is not proper for you to share a second oscos with another.

I realize this, too.

I have to constantly remind myself that knowing Nauru as I knew my Osco doesn't matter. As hard as it is to maintain such an unusual friendship, I am mostly content with our connection as it is.

Observation: This is a deception you tell yourself. The brutal truth of the matter is that you are afraid it will end if you want more than he can give.

Shut up, I throw back, tired of my plate's logic.

Speculation: If anything goes wrong, you have only yourself to blame.

I ignore my plate, instead recalling the conversation I shared with Nauru as he walked me home last night.

[Nauru: Would you care to meet me tomorrow afternoon at the cliffs?]

[Me: It will be too muggy tomorrow for a hike. What about the park? It's shady and there's always a nice breeze.]

[Nauru: True, but we always go to the park. Let's go to the bridge to skip rocks instead.]

[Me: Of course you want to go to the bridge - you're a much better skipper than I am...]

I expect my morning to be filled with the repetition of our silly exchange and the count of my own lazy breaths; however, eleven local minutes later, I am caught off guard to hear my aunt's voice slice through my mind.

[*Santina? It's Auntie.*]

Auntie.

Ever since I was placed on leave six standard weeks ago, I had brushed aside her attempts to reach me. Auntie doggedly kept at it, repeatedly hounding me to contact her. She is my closest family but too overbearing to visit regularly.

[*Santina?*]

Fact: You cannot ignore her forever.

I sigh. So much for a quiet morning.

[*Hi, Auntie. How are you?*]

[*It's about time you responded. How are you doing?*]

[*Fine. I'm fine.*]

[*Well, you certainly sound fine.*]

[*It's been hard, but things are -*]

[*Pella is visiting me and would like to see you. Can you meet today? She's leaving tomorrow.*]

I roll my eyes and hastily push away my impatience so Auntie won't notice. Of course Pella's leaving tomorrow. Auntie prefers to schedule family events on the last leg of a visitor's trip because anyone invited can't say no. It's rude but no one dares to offend Auntie.

[*Yes. I have some time this morning.*]

[*The city park is lovely this time of year. We'll meet you there in twenty-five local minutes.*]

And then she's gone, the pleasantries over and done with.

I sit up and stretch, gazing out the window.

Fact: Today will be pleasant, with no breeze and plenty of sun.

Just one turn around the park, I hope. I am not excited to be obligated into joining my aunt and cousin when I'd rather be home, though I admit it will be nice to see them.

I braid my hair and dress without hurry, then set off for the park. Nauru's bench is free and I plop onto it, watching the only other person at the park with a careful eye in case something amusing happens that I can relay to Nauru later - but nothing does.

Exactly twenty-five local minutes later, my aunt and cousin arrive, arguing over...dresses?

My aunt looks as she always does: stern and unfriendly. Her dark hair is pulled back into a tight bun, which does not help soften her features, but she smiles warmly at me once she sees me.

"Hello, Auntie." I clasp her hand and she returns my touch with a tight squeeze. Her hands are softer and lighter than I recall.

Pella grabs my other hand in both of hers. "Oh, Santi. I'm so happy to see you! I was hoping you'd be here on such short notice." She passes a meaningful glare at her mother before turning back to me. Pella's the only person in the family who is able to challenge Auntie without sending her into a rage.

Auntie ignores Pella's jab. She simply plows on to reveal the reason I'm here.

"Pella is *finally* forming an oscos," Auntie explains, a hint of exasperation in her tone. Since we have already exchanged pleasantries, she is completely without care that my own Osco was suspended two standard months ago.

Delighted to be the center of attention, Pella flushes.

"Congratulations," I say. "When?"

Auntie shakes her head. "Next summer. I can't imagine a worse time - and outside no less! How uncomfortable it will be for you and Lexin in your dress clothes. Spring. You should be marrying in the spring."

Pella and I exchange glances.

[*How long has she been going on about that?*] I ask Pella, who shrugs.

Pella rolls her eyes. [*Ever since she found out. Apparently, spring is prettier than summer, too.*]

I fight back the urge to laugh. Auntie has always had a strong personality. But so has Pella. No one ever needs to guess what they want because everyone already knows. My own mother wasn't nearly so domineering.

Neither Adahi nor I wanted this much fuss for our oscos. It seemed a bother to plan such a big event that we wouldn't have much fun at. [*And what of your plans?*]

[*Oh, Santi, it's ridiculous. We have nearly a whole cycle to plan but I don't think that's going to be enough time.*]

[*Won't it? What's left to do?*] I try hard to be sympathetic to Pella's complaints but it is a problem of her own making.

Auntie answers for her. "Pella needs help choosing a dress."

I cannot imagine a worse way to fill empty time.

"Surely, Auntie, you can't mean for me to - "

"Of course, Santi. Who better to help than someone who has gone through this before?"

Entrapment!

I want to remind her that I didn't wear a dress to my own oscos - I wore my uniform instead - but I bite my tongue. Any excuse I come up with will be countered with four more. It's impossible to say no to Auntie, so I nod.

Pella's face lights up with elation. As she and Auntie direct me into a clothier's across the street, I resolve to choose the dress both of them like the best. Straddling the line will increase my chances of leaving in less than a local hour. Of this I am certain.

Directive: Don't bet on it.

Auntie steps to the viewing wall. Pella begins to browse a nearby rack. I inch over to the window, wistfully looking out into the freedom of the street before stepping further into the room and glancing around.

Though it's too cramped in here to be a showcase room, it's well-lit and tidy. Four mirrors hang on the wall opposite the entrance but could be rearranged around a carpeted platform in a blink of an eye. Seeing nothing of interest on the store's single rack, Pella has joined Auntie at the viewing wall, where her plate changes the search to reflect her own style and color preferences. They argue over Pella's favorites.

A dark, lush curtain in the far corner separates this room from the back.

So clients don't have to see the Freemen who work here. I am surprised by the slight bitterness that creeps into my thoughts.

Fact: This is the way of things.

This is the way we choose *to live. This isn't the way things* have *to be.*

Not able to contain my curiosity, I peek through the crack between the curtain and wall. I spy someone in rapt attention hidden in the shadow of his Cyborn supervisor. He wears a clean white shirt and dark pants. I cannot see his face, so I shuffle a few paces in one direction and then another in an attempt to recognize him. Does he know Nauru? Is he someone I met at the party?

The Cyborn steps aside and I take in the Freeman's features: the dark hair, the drooping right eye, the extraction scars, the strong jaw and chin, the cautious smile -

Nauru.

I freeze in shock and anxious surprise.

Nauru never told me where he worked - much less explained what he did. The only piece of vague information I possess about Nauru's employment is that it is uninteresting. I am torn between curiosity - *what does Nauru do here?* - and discomfort - *what, exactly, will I see here?*

Fact: There is a reason he has not revealed this part of his life before now. What you observe here will not please you.

My plate's right: nothing good will result from this unintentional visit. I will see far more of Nauru's life than is proper. I cannot be here.

With my aunt and cousin occupied at the viewing wall, I edge toward the entry, taking care to avoid the line of sight the Cyborn and Nauru have from behind the curtain. Less than two paces from the door, the Cyborn man steps out from behind the curtain. Nauru follows dutifully behind, scanning the room. When his eyes lock with mine, there's a scant upward twitch of his lips and then it disappears.

This is the only hint of acknowledgement I receive from Nauru. Compared to the relaxed smile and warm greeting I usually get, this one is distant and hollow.

I would rather him look at me the way he does at the park.

Fact: To do so would only invite trouble.

Yes. I know.

I know this, yet I hate I cannot give Nauru a decent greeting. I hate that he has to pretend not to know me. And I hate I have to pretend I don't see him.

"Inda!" the Cyborn man coos at Auntie as he crosses the room and sweeps up one of her hands. "Back for another dress? So soon?"

Auntie allows the man one gentle squeeze then removes her hand from his grasp. "No, no, Hosoi. It's not for me. Pella, my daughter, is forming an oscos next summer. She'll need a dress for the ceremony."

"Ah!" Hosoi gushes, clapping his hands together and turning to Pella. "Congratulations!"

Pella beams.

Hosoi slides seamlessly into questions about the cut and fit of the dress, while Pella and Auntie speak over each other to answer. At Pella's suggestions, Auntie sighs in exasperation and grumbles about immodesty. Hosoi comes to Pella's rescue, insisting her choices are in fashion but that there's a way to incorporate Auntie's ideas as well.

All this time, Nauru remains a shadow at Hosoi's side, his face stiff and bored. I know he's actually absorbing the conversation with earnest - the concentration in his eye prove otherwise.

Speculation: Since Nauru is out here and not behind the curtain, he will be the one making Pella's dress.

So, he must pay attention to every single detail in order to get it exactly right.

Nauru has no plate to recall the conversation or measurements; he is unable to send images to Pella or Auntie or Hosoi. Despite lacking a plate, Nauru must be more than capable - he told me he has been working at the same job at the same place for three local years.

Hosoi directs Pella and Auntie to the dress rack. He explains that each of the dresses are made of different fabrics with a distinct drape or layer, depending on the style that Pella wants. Pella chooses three fabrics she likes. Auntie insists upon two more. Pella stomps her foot in protest. Auntie crosses her arms.

Resigned that I will not be able to leave in a local hour as I had hoped, I step toward the rack, pretending to have some interest in what's going on with the decision-making. In actuality, I edge closer to where Nauru stands motionless, waiting to be managed.

Without taking his eyes off Auntie and Pella, Nauru bends his head slightly toward mine. "I had no idea you were in need of a new dress."

"I'm here against my will. Save me."

"This must be...family?"

"My aunt and my cousin. They're dress shopping for Pella's oscos next rotation."

Nauru glances at me. "Your cousin should have come alone."

I bite my lip to keep from giggling. With clipped words and clenched teeth, Pella glares at her mother, ready to erupt. Auntie, however, ignores her and continues to engage Hosoi in a barrage of questions about sheen, quality, softness, and breathability of his fabrics - oh, and does he also have any of those new iridescent fabrics that change color?

To his credit, Hosoi notices Pella's frustration and suggests she accompany him to the platform where she can examine the fabrics more closely.

As if on cue, Nauru leaves, ducking behind the curtain.

Pella stomps to the platform and steps up, Auntie trailing behind with Hosoi.

Nauru returns obediently to his place next to the platform, holding a stack of brightly-colored bolts extending well past the top of his head.

I stand close enough to Pella, should she want my opinion on something, but also within earshot of Nauru, should he want to continue our conversation.

"This is my personal favorite." Hosoi lifts the first bolt of fabric off Nauru's pile and holds it out for Auntie and Pella to feel. Auntie quickly waves it away.

"It's much too thick for summer. Do you have anything in that color but lighter?"

"I want it draped," Pella insists, hands on hips and a pout on her lips. "I like it."

"Of course." Hosoi unwinds a length. "It's a very forgiving fabric. Excellent for formal dresses."

He sets it on her shoulder and across her body, clipping it in place. Pella moves about while Auntie scrutinizes her, face scrunched and lips pursed.

I join Nauru behind the bolts of fabric he carries. "I'm beginning to see what you mean. This *is* a thoroughly unstimulating occupation."

Nauru glances at me and half-smiles and I know he's glad I'm here. "You thought I would lie?"

"No, but I wonder how you don't drop from complete boredom."

"I hold onto a special image. It keeps me motivated."

"What is it?" The thought of Nauru having a special image that he recalls during the day intrigues me. What is so important for him to hold onto for eight to ten local hours at a time?

"You must know?" he asks off-handedly in order to tease me.

"Yes! Tell me!"

Shivers run down my spine when Nauru suddenly inclines his face to my ear, his breath warm on my skin. My heart thuds against my chest, its powerful rhythm echoing in my ears.

Why are my palms so sweaty? We've shared a closeness before, him and I.

"I think about you, Santi."

For two breaths, I forget to breathe.

Hosoi's irritated order cuts through the tension. "Nauru! Bolt!"

He turns to Auntie as he snatches the next bolt from Nauru's outstretched hand and begins to unwind the fabric. "Inda, my apologies for the poor service. This Freeman has worked for me for three local years and today he is completely useless."

"It is quite all right, Hosoi." Auntie lays a critical eye on Nauru striding back to his place beside me with hasty steps. His face is unreadable, his eye blank. He has returned to his earlier state - his distant, Freeman form which is invisible till he makes a mistake.

Auntie sniffs. "I find most Freemen are."

Hosoi drapes the new fabric around Pella but she shakes her head.

"Do you have anything less dull?" she demands.

And just like that, the conversation has shifted away from Nauru. I stare at him with an odd mixture of admiration and indignation.

How can Nauru do this all day? How can he stand here and listen to people insult him without betraying his own resentment?

Fact: He is a Freeman. This is his place.

The others may not see the quiet rage boiling in his brown eye, but I do.

Auntie surveys the bolts in Nauru's arms. "What about this one?" She points to a pale pink shimmery fabric.

"Ah!" Hosoi exclaims. "I think you'll be quite pleased with that one."

"Mother," whines Pella. "I hate pink!"

"We have a number of other colors available in that same fabric." Hosoi excuses Nauru with a snap of his fingers and I follow him with my eyes till he disappears behind the curtain.

Somewhere on those shelves in the back there is a fabric that Pella absolutely loves - I hope Nauru finds it so that we can leave him in peace.

`Observation: Pella wants your attention.`

I focus on my cousin. She stares at me, a curious realization dawning across her face.

[*You know that Freeman,*] she accuses me.

`Directive: Deny her claim.`

`Observation: It is your best course of action.`

For once, I agree with my plate. Telling Pella the truth is guaranteed to invite trouble. She'll ask too many questions and demand too many answers, loudly and openly. I cannot let it get that far - I am not ready to explain my relationship with Nauru.

[*No, no. Of course not,*] I insist, my eyes flitting away.

`Directive: Deflect her fixation elsewhere: on her preparations, on the fabric samples, on her resulting dress - anywhere but Nauru.`

[*I thought the first fabric looked stunning on you.*]

[*Stop it, Santi.*] Pella is not fooled by my attempted distraction. "You *do* know him, don't you?" she presses in a hushed, excited tone. She knows Auntie will hear but she doesn't care - this is the best news she's heard all day.

Auntie takes the bait and breaks away from her polite conversation with Hosoi. "Know who? What are you two going on about now?"

[*Don't, Pella -*] I beg, at the same time stammering out: "Nothing, Auntie."

Pella draws her mouth into a deep frown and then opens it wide.

`Speculation: She is going to tell.`

"I thought the first fabric best for Pella's figure. What about you, Auntie?" I cut in, silencing Pella in one quick sweep. She glares at me in response.

"No, it won't do at all." Auntie waves her hand and sniffs. "It's much too heavy for a formal dress. Pella will need something lighter for the summer."

"I've seen some beautiful wraps made of that exact fabric. It can be used another way, just not for the dress."

Auntie considers the idea while Pella begins to speak, but I interrupt her again.

"What do you think, Auntie?"

"Yes. It could work. The wrap would need to be highly decorated. Is your staff is able to handle such a detailed order, Hosoi?"

"Absolutely, Inda. "

```
Directive: Keep Auntie distracted on Pella's
oscos.
Speculation: She won't have the opportunity to
-
```

"Santi knows that Freeman!" Pella blurts out, pointing to the curtain in the corner of the room, the curtain that is hiding Nauru.

It is the same curtain I wish I could hide behind, too.

I hold in my breath as everyone processes what Pella has just said. The room - so vibrant and carefree just twelve tics ago - is burdened by this new revelation. Hosoi senses an unraveling scandal, Pella's satisfaction is hollow, and Auntie's disdain weighs deep in my heart.

Auntie is the first to speak, using the same stern and unforgiving voice she did whenever Pella and I got into trouble as children.

[*Santi, do you know that Freeman?*]

```
Directive: Deny Pella's claim.
```

I can't lie to Auntie - she knows me too well. She will know I am being deceptive before the words come out of my mouth. What good will that do me?

```
Observation: Both of them suspect that you are
on familiar terms with Nauru.
```

Yes.

```
Speculation: Since you cannot lie, then
explain yourself. They will see the logic in your
friendship.
```

Despite that what my plate says makes sense, I am uncertain Auntie will see reason; she did not approve of Nauru only fifteen local minutes ago. Why would she approve of Nauru now?

```
Speculation: She will never approve of Nauru,
but she will see reason, given enough of it.
```

With few options that won't get me or Nauru into trouble, I decide to pursue reason as my plate suggested.

[*Yes. I know that Freeman - Nauru, his name is Nauru.*] The words flow surprisingly easy and I push on, buoyed by my efforts. [*We're friends - good friends - *]

Before I have a chance to spit out my next thought, Auntie interrupts me. "*Friends?* You are *friends* with a filthy *Freeman?*"

"Please. Auntie, listen - " I try to regain control of the conversation, but Auntie ignores me.

"Freemen are *not* men, Santi!" she scolds me, as if I am a child. Her cries of indignation are loud enough for Nauru - who is still behind the curtain - to hear. "If you have any sense at all, you'll stay away him."

I have never seen her so angry over something so trivial. If only she knew what I know about Nauru, about his kindness and compassion! Surely then she would see he is not a threat to me, to her, or to any other Cyborn.

"Nauru's been a great help to me - "

"I will not hear of this, Santina! I will not!" Auntie screams over me. "Freemen are dangerous!"

The weight of Auntie's disgust towards Nauru crushes my sense of purpose. I stand rooted to the spot, everything - my words, my mouth, my brain, my plate - is numb in disbelief. I cannot respond to her illogical statements with logic because I am the illogical one, the one in the wrong.

No amount of reason will sway Auntie.

Speculation: It is possible to convince Pella - her input has been minimal so far.

Pella's empty victory at uncovering my secret, our childhood bond - yes, it is possible.

[*Pella.*] I turn to my cousin in one last desperate attempt to defuse the situation. [*You don't know Nauru like I know him. He isn't the monster you believe him to be.*]

Pella's eyes dart from me, to Auntie, then back to me again as she struggles to make sense of where she stands.

"Santina." Auntie reaches for my hand and squeezes it tightly. Her concern washes over me like a sudden storm. "Freemen are not like us. What you are doing is risky and I don't want to see you hurt."

I am not certain if Nauru is able to hear her any longer, though I know he must be hanging onto every word he is able to make out.

[*Pella, if you only knew him,*] I appeal again. [*He is a good man.*]

Pella only turns her face toward the window. I'm furious with her: she brought this up and now she is reluctant to finish it.

"You can't trust him, Santi," Auntie insists. "Release him back into the company of the other Freemen where he belongs."

She speaks of Nauru as if he were nothing more than a nimblemouse or a catchtoad or some other animal plaything!

I yank my hand from hers.

[*Auntie, I - *]

Before I can process my next words, Nauru opens the curtain and steps out without the stack of bolts he was ordered to get. His good eye is fixed upon Auntie.

Fact: This is bad. Very, very bad.

No, no, Nauru. Go back, please go back behind the curtain, I plead with my eyes. He can't get involved - he mustn't get involved - but here he is, fists clenched and face drawn up in an expression of determination as he prepares for a face-off with Auntie.

Fact: She will not back down.

Neither will he.

Pella shrieks and stumbles off the platform, as far from Nauru as she can get.

"Go away," Auntie hisses. "This matter does not concern you."

"I disagree. You were discussing Freemen and I am a Freeman, am I not?" Nauru poses this question as though he is asking about the weather, but I detect the edge to his voice. It is the same one he always uses when we discuss Freemen's rights and his second-class status.

"Nauru," Hosoi warns, "you are making the customers uncomfortable."

But Nauru does not budge.

"Santina, tell this creature to go away. Immediately," Auntie demands of me. She does not stop staring at Nauru.

"But Madam, I feel it my duty to clear up some of your backward notions about Freemen. Where shall we begin?"

"Nauru - " I caution. He holds up a hand to silence me, his eyes still directed upon my aunt.

Fact: Neither will listen to reason.

Auntie almost knocks over Hosoi as she leaps at Nauru. "*Backward notions?* You will do no such thing. I do not need a lecture from *you.*"

"I don't know where you have gotten your information about Freemen, but it seems to me that you have been misinformed. I only wish to clarify some of your points which are so obviously wrong."

"You will *not* speak to me this way, you horrid abomination." Auntie seethes, her hand twitching at her side.

Fact: She is going to strike Nauru.

He will not strike her back - of this I am certain. That is the difference between the two.

Because of his extraction, Auntie believes Nauru is less than half a Cyborn, an unpredictable freak, unable to do more than stupid, menial jobs since he lacks a plate.

But Nauru - Nauru had given *me* - a *Cyborn* - a chance.

He didn't have to. It was against his better judgement to do so, but he did anyway.

She is the horrid abomination, not him.

I wedge myself between Nauru and Auntie, facing him.

I beg of him with my eyes and voice to understand that I do not agree with my aunt. I stand here because I can't let her abuse him. "Don't argue with her. Please."

But Nauru does not have a plate. He does not know of Auntie's intention. He does not know my true purpose in separating them. All he knows is that I am a poor deceiver - I have admitted it myself. Therefore, if I stand here in front of my aunt, protecting her from him, I must - in some small way - be siding with her.

Nauru steps away, bewildered. There's a deep hurt in his eye.

My aunt's triumphant smile taunts my back.

"Santi?" His voice is low and hard in order to mask the pain of my request.

Surely he will understand what I am asking of him. Surely, he will know without me saying it aloud. *"Please."*

Without another word, Nauru presses his lips together and leaves the shop. He does not look back.

Relieved, I slowly let out the breath I didn't realize I was holding in.

He's okay. Nauru's going to be okay.

Fact: He will not be arrested. He will not be thrown into detention. Physically, he will be fine.

Although...?

Observation: There was no acknowledgement in his eye to indicate he actually understood what you meant.

Images of my last interaction with Nauru flash through my mind: brow furrowed, fists balled up tight against his sides, the betrayal in his eye...

Fact: You have lost him.

I have to tell Nauru what happened here. He needs to - no, *deserves* to know of my true intentions, clumsy as they were. I scramble toward the door but my aunt grabs my wrist and yanks me back. I struggle to pull free but she clings to me, her fingernails digging into my skin.

"He's nothing, Santi," she reminds me. "Only a Freeman."

I wrench my hand free. "Not to me."

[*Santina.*]

I pause in the doorway, tilting my head to take one last look at her.

[*If you walk through that door, there are no second chances.*]

Speculation: If you leave now, she will never speak to you again.

If I don't leave now, I won't catch up to Nauru - then there will be no chance at all.

Without looking back, I pass through the doorway and onto the public walkway.

Resolved to locate Nauru, I check up and down the street. When I cannot find him, I scour the surrounding blocks and the park, the search area becoming larger and larger till I make the horrible realization that I'm too late.

Fact: Nauru is gone.

CHAPTER TWELVE

The next morning, I returned to the dress shop to apologize for everything - my aunt, my cousin, even my own actions that led to this misunderstanding. By now, Nauru certainly believed me to be no better than the other plate-faces he had to deal with.

Hosoi was not pleased to see me and even less pleased when I asked to speak to Nauru. He told me *the Freeman* had been fired. I begged him to give me Nauru's address or a piece of information with which to contact him, but Hosoi frowned and slammed the door in my face.

So, every morning for the last three mornings, I watched Tol rise at the cliffs, desperate for Nauru to appear. When he didn't show up, I then raced to the park, hoping to see him sitting at his bench, making images. To my great disappointment, he never came.

Today is the fourth day since my mistake at the dress shop.

I sit at Santi's Spot.

Tol rises.

Nauru does not come.

I drag my feet to the park.

I sit on Nauru's bench for five local hours.

Nauru does not come.

Leaning over to rest my elbows on my knees, I bury my face in my hands.

He is deliberately avoiding me.

`Speculation: Because he has not yet forgiven you.`

I had foolishly misjudged the situation by not clearly taking the position I wanted to. I did not face Auntie. I did not stand beside Nauru. I did not take his hand. I did not audibly defend him, only myself. I did not refute her terrible words in a way that he could hear.

Nauru's absence leaves an emptiness in my heart, one that I need to mend, but to do so, I need to find him.

The public dossier only contains links to other Cyborn; therefore, I will not find Nauru there.

I do not know exactly where Nauru lives, other than where Freemen are permitted to live within the city: the Freeman Quarter - which is where most live - and the docks. I do not know any other Freeman well enough who would help me locate him.

Fact: The only path to lead you back to Nauru is the one to the Freeman Quarter.

Going to the Freeman Quarter means facing the consequences.

Certainly by now, Nauru has told all of them every sordid detail of what happened. The Freemen there will no longer be as friendly as they were at the party - of that I am certain.

I will be chased out.

I remove my hands from my face and catch sight of a nimblemouse darting across my left foot.

"Should I go?"

It only stuffs seeds into its mouth.

I do not expect an answer from the nimblemouse and I am not given one, but it does remind me of Nauru. While there is no guarantee anyone in the Freeman Quarter will help me, it is worth a try. I rise from the bench, my plate recalling the directions to the location of the party.

At first, I cannot believe this is the same place. Without the dim lights in the darkness to mask the shabbiness of the buildings, they seem darker and older and more imposing than they did just a few local days ago. The streets are deserted except for five children chasing each other in some sort of game. When they see me, they bolt into a nearby alley. I am about to call after them when -

"You lost, plate-face?"

I recall this defiant voice challenging me, questioning why I am here. It belongs to the Freeman who glared at me across the cobblestone streets, the one whose appearance is forever cross because of the angry red lines of her extraction scars at her temple. I turn to face her.

"I need to speak to Nauru. Where I can find him?"

Anma, the sulky woman from the party, rests against a poorly-painted door frame set atop stone steps leading into a tired building. She appears confident and unafraid; in truth, she holds her folded arms too close against her chest to be relaxed. Anma lifts her chin and spits, but not in the way Spacers like Adahi spit because their mouth is gritty from all the dust. This woman spits because she is telling me she doesn't like me.

"If Nauru wanted to talk to you, he would."

I do not break eye contact. "Please, Anma. It's important."

"Why can't you get it?" Her features don't soften, even with mention of her name. "Nauru doesn't want to see you."

"I need to speak with him."

Anma approaches me with calculated slowness, making a great show of dropping down one step at a time. I brace myself for whatever abuse she's about to hurl at me, as she stands in front of me and spits again, her eyes never leaving mine.

"Get lost."

"I need to speak with him."

"He doesn't want to talk to you."

"You don't know that."

"I do." She smiles cruelly. "You should have seen his face when he came back. Angrier than I've ever seen him."

"It was a mistake. I was trying to protect him. Tell him that."

Anma moves past me, slamming her shoulder into mine. I leap back, away from her touch. She laughs at my discomfort.

"That's the way it is, isn't it? The plate-faces are always trying to protect us, always trying to shield us from all of the dangers out there because we don't know better."

"That is *not* what I meant!"

"Isn't it?" Her eyes flash. "You've got a lot to learn about Freemen, plate-face."

"I'll admit to that, Anma, but right now I am not your enemy. I just want to speak with Nauru."

"*All* of you Cyborn are our enemy," she counters furiously. "The sooner Nauru sees that, the better."

The mention of Nauru again gives me pause.

Observation: Look at her eye. She holds
affection for him, too.

I shut it out because I don't want to hear it. I don't want to hear about how she also dreams of Nauru at night, or that she replays their conversations over and over again in her head, or that she finds the smell of his shaving soap intoxicating. I don't want to hear about how she also can't stop thinking about his kind smile, or that she blushes when he teases her, or that she knows intimate details about his life as a Freeman - details I would never, ever be able to truly comprehend like she can, not unless I became a Freeman myself.

I am terrified of her answer, terrified of what it might reveal, but I must know.

"This isn't about me or the Cyborn at all, is it? You want to be with him, don't you?"

Anma glares at me. "What would you know about that?"

Observation: She did not deny it.

"I don't know anything about it, but I do know what happened to Nauru was wrong. He shouldn't have been mistreated by my aunt. Or me." I hope this admission will encourage her to bend. "Please, Anma. Will you tell Nauru I'm looking for him?"

Anma stomps up the stone steps and into her home. The door slams shut behind her.

Fact: Anma knows where Nauru lives.

Then I'll wait. She'll tell me eventually.

Query: How long?

As long as it takes.

I settle on the bottom step, put my hands in my jacket pockets, and wait.

As a soldier, 76.23% of my time is spent being patient.

Eighty-one percent of new recruits don't understand this and constantly complain of not seeing any action, but I don't mind the silence of the field so much. Once a battle starts, there is only chaos, so much going on, that if you try to differentiate it all, you lose focus.

Not all of the new recruits understand that either.

But I do.

I rest my elbows on my knees. My breath slows.

Only six local hours till Tol sets.

The children return to their game of chase.

The afternoon comes and goes.

Darkness falls.

Anma is still safely inside her apartment.

And still, I wait.

CHAPTER THIRTEEN

It is two local days later, and I am seated on the stone steps of Anma's apartment. Thanks to my plate, it's easy for me to forgo food and water and sleep. I am less certain Anma is as comfortable as I am, but she has not left her apartment since our last encounter and often glares at me through her window. We have reached a stalemate, neither one of us willing to break down.

In the meantime, I spend most of my days watching the Freemen children play in the street. At first, they were reluctant to interact with me, but today they are pleased to have an audience to show off for. One child begins to kick around a large yellow fruit he found on a nearby bush and shouts to me. "Watch how far I can kick!"

"I can kick it farther!" someone else brags.

Another voice chimes in. "No way! You couldn't kick it past the end of the street."

I nod and smile absently, my mind fixated on my next confrontation with Anma. I am impressed by her stubbornness.

Something bumps against my foot, breaking my thoughts. It's the fruit, now a sad-looking, bruised, brown ball of mush. I look up to see the Freeman children huddled together in a large group about ten paces away. They whisper to one another, each one egging on somebody else to go and collect their makeshift ball.

I pick it up - inwardly cringing at the squish beneath my fingers - and hold it out to them.

Finally, after more hushed whispers, a little girl with wide brown eyes and two large scars that criss-cross at her left temple breaks away from the group. She's no taller than my waist but marches toward me with such purpose. She pauses only a few paces away. I continue to hold out the fruit but she does not take it.

The girl smiles at me. "Would you like to play with us?"

I rise, a giant compared to her, and drop the fruit. Then I kick it to her. She breaks into a large smile, her left eye lost in the folds of her scars. She kicks it back to me and I return it, sending it sailing over her head, beyond the group of other children. They take off running to fetch it back.

No one explains the rules. No one has to. After watching them all morning, I find the game simple enough: kick the fruit to a target on opposite sides of the street without using your hands.

The older children appreciate the competition and chase me wildly as they attempt to steal the fruit away. The younger children enjoy the commotion and cheer affectionately whenever I make a goal.

As it grows darker and darker, the children disappear one by one, called in for supper or bedtime or a trip to the Freeman public bath. Eventually, only the sorry-looking fruit and I remain on the street.

I settle back at my perch on the stone steps, tired but strangely satisfied.

CHAPTER FOURTEEN

The next day, seven more children arrive on the steps of the apartment building where I am seated among a crowd of twenty-seven others. Two of the bigger boys are already tossing a brand-new fruit back and forth. No one bothers to ask me to join in; it is already assumed I will.

The two oldest children pick teams. I am chosen by a freckle-faced girl with a jagged scar running from her forehead to her chin. Her opponent, a scruffy-looking boy with a delicate pink facial scar, gets two extra players. The other children are soon divided into two groups - even the younger ones who are brave enough to dare to play with the big kids. The youngest children fill the steps of the apartment buildings.

Admittedly, eleven Freeman children are no competition for nine Freeman children and one adult Cyborn. Though I do try my best not to beat them soundly enough to make them cry, by the time the children dispersed for supper, my team had won, 137 to 12.

"We'll switch teams tomorrow," I promise as they leave. Most of the children, however, just wave, eager for tomorrow morning. A few of the older children dare to exchange some tough words with me and I return in kind.

That evening, I study the damaged fruit that had been busted open from a particularly hard kick in just the right spot. The gooey insides shine in the street light.

The games, the children, the fruit - they've all given me an idea.

`Fact: But delivery drones don't venture into the Freeman Quarter.`

I check the window to Anma's apartment. Her lights were turned off two local hours ago. If I go, even just for a local hour or two, it is possible that Anma will notice and leave. My chances of finding Nauru

would drop substantially.
    I rise, taking the steps down two at a time.
    It's a risk, but one I am willing to take.

CHAPTER FIFTEEN

Today, the younger children crowd around me on the steps, chattering together. A boy has wedged himself next to me. He kicks his legs while he asks me questions about the war. When he discovers I am in charge of an artillery unit, he aims at buildings across the street and pretends to blow them up. A girl unpins my hair without my permission and begins to run her fingers through the length of it, combing it out. I shiver from the unexpected touch of tiny, soft hands with dexterous fingers. She expertly twists my hair into a new braid and then pins it up again. Another little boy climbs into my lap and claps his hands, ready for the match. The older girl with freckled cheeks tosses a new fruit to the older boy with the delicate scar. She points at me in a playful challenge. I point back.

Am I still Cyborn to them? I muse. *Or have I morphed into something else entirely?*

Then the older girl tosses the fruit to me and nods her head, the signal to start the game.

I catch it but instead of throwing it back, I give it to the boy in my lap who squeals in delight. The younger children begin to whisper in confusion.

"Aren't we going to play?" asks the older girl. She is just as stunned as the others.

"Of course," I assure her, lifting the boy into the outstretched arms of his sister. "But I wonder…"

As I meander down the steps, I reach inside my jacket pocket to remove a mysterious object. The children crane their necks to see. Even the older children puzzle over what it is.

"…wouldn't you rather play with this today?" I remove a tiny, bright red, rubber ball and hurl it to the ground. It bounces once and explodes into a large ball, the perfect size for kicking back and forth. The freckle-faced girl catches it, her mouth wide open in surprise.

The children leap up and down, each clamoring for a turn to play with the ball. The older boy with the pink scar grabs it and hoists it up out of their reach. He orders everyone away while he tests the ball: squeezing it, bouncing it three times, then finally kicking it to the girl. She returns it and the boy gathers the ball into his arms. He glances at me, his face deadpan, but with obvious excitement in his eye.

"It'll do," he approves in his most bored voice. The children cheer as the ball is passed from one to another to be bounced and kicked, tested and tried.

A shout from somewhere in the crowd welcomes two approaching figures. The first is the little girl with wide eyes and the crossed scar, the same girl who invited me to join their kick-the-fruit game. The other is -

"Nauru," I whisper, my throat dry and prickly.

"Hail, Santi."

At the mention of my name, I want so much to take his hand, take *him* into my arms and draw him close, into my own space. But he has not yet reached for me, not yet approached me, so I grasp my clammy hands together behind my back, forcing myself to maintain that distance between us, though I do not want to.

The little girl tugs on his hand and smiles up at him. "Nauru isn't working today so I invited him to play, too."

"You're working again?"

"I work at the docks now."

"Oh."

It's all I am able to muster. Nauru says nothing more.

We stare at each other. My heart pounds against my chest. I am at a loss over what to do next.

Directive: Say something.

But fashioning words in front of all these people is a struggle, my voice and tongue too twisted and shy with the words I so want to tell him, with the words I need him to hear.

I'm so sorry, Nauru. I didn't mean for any of this to happen.

"Are we going to play?" whines the older boy, tossing the ball to Nauru.

Nauru catches it, his lips twitching upward in a momentary truce. "Let's see if I can even the odds."

***

Although Nauru's team loses, he manages to redeem them with only a 73 point loss.

"It's better than nothing," he assures his team as they grumble about their failure. Nauru retrieves my jacket from the steps and hands it to me. "Come on, Santi. I'll walk you home."

There's no malice in his voice, nothing that belies his feelings of seeing me again, and I am encouraged by this observation.

Fact: You are too hopeful.

As I slip it on, the children beg me to return tomorrow for a rematch. The little girl with the wide brown eyes tugs on the bottom of my jacket, urging me to bend down. When I give her my ear, she whispers loud enough for anyone standing three paces away to overhear: "Nauru is a good ball player, isn't he?"

"Yes, he is," I agree, peeking up at Nauru. His lopsided smile indicates he heard everything. The girl joins the rest of the children who are now bouncing the ball back and forth to each other in a large circle. My heart sinks at her pleasure in seeing us together again.

What will I do if this ends badly?

Directive: Don't draw conclusions before you have all the data.

"Come on, Santi," Nauru murmurs, leading me out of the Freeman Quarter.

Neither of us speak on the long walk back to my apartment. I use the unwelcome silence to rehearse what I am going to say when we finally stop, but nothing I plan is adequate enough.

I'm sorry, Nauru.

I didn't mean for any of this to happen.

I had to stop my aunt from striking you.

My hands are empty without yours.

Bowing my head so that Nauru cannot see me blinking back tears, I follow his feet till they stop outside the familiar gates of my apartment.

Directive: Be reasonable, rational, and –

Logical?

Affirmation: Yes.

Directive: State your claim and Nauru will understand.

This time, in this situation, my plate is wrong. While Nauru is highly sensible for a Freeman, now is not the time to spout intention and sense. Now is the time for apologizes and confessions. I will reveal my feelings in order to regain his friendship.

I concentrate on a crack in the cobblestone walk. "I'm so sorry, Nauru. I didn't mean for any of this to happen."

"But it did."

I turn my face to his and find his eye kind - sympathetic, even - but his face stern. "Yes, it did, but not in the way you think."

"Enlighten me."

"My aunt intended to strike you. Even though you wouldn't hit her back, you would have been punished anyway. I couldn't let you face the consequences of her actions. You needed to leave before the argument escalated to that. So I stepped in."

Nauru's eye softens at this revelation.

"But I couldn't share my intentions with you because we don't share an oscos and I didn't speak of my intentions aloud because my aunt wasn't listening. She would not see reason, but I knew you would."

He drops his gaze to the patch of grass growing in the cobblestone cracks.

"I misjudged my approach to the situation. I hurt you." I close the distance between us and catch his eye, basking in his presence under the moonlight. "That was never my intent."

Nauru turns toward the gate, grasping the metal rods with his hands and mulling over my words, my sincerity. What he says next comes as an unexpected surprise.

"I should not have spoken to your aunt in the manner I did."

"But she was *wrong*!"

"Indeed she was. But being a fellow Cyborn and her relation, I hoped that *you* would have. I stood behind that curtain waiting for you to speak up, to *tell* her she was being an idiot."

"I told her of our friendship, of your kindness. She would not listen."

"Perhaps you had in a way I couldn't know." Nauru releases the gate and reconsiders his argument. "Either way, it was unfair of me to expect you to communicate in a way that is contrary to how you would usually speak to your aunt."

We have reached a point of understanding, him and I, only I don't know what happens next.

"What do we do now?"

"Shall we think through our options logically?" He studies me expectantly and I catch sight of Nauru, my friend.

I nod.

"Option one: perhaps the best course of action is to part ways."

"Not at all," I disagree. "Parting is a mistake."

He lifts an eyebrow. "How so?"

"There is still so much I *want* to learn from Freemen, from you. If we leave each other now, there will be so many questions left unanswered, so many things to ponder."

"Couldn't you find another Freeman to feed your curiosity?"

"No."

"Why not? There are many of us here."

"Because I have already shared so much with you. Because I *trust* you."

At that, his lips twitch up in amusement. "Perhaps you would rather choose option two: we go back to the way things were before this nasty incident."

"Yes."

"But how will I know words won't fail you next time?" he murmurs.

"You will never truly know because we do not share an oscos."

"Then we are back at option one."

"Only if you believe I can't be trusted."

"Can I trust you?"

"You must trust me, otherwise you would not be here."

"And what of your aunt?"

"She no longer speaks to me."

"Why not?"

"Because I chose to follow you."

At my admission, Nauru steps even closer till we are less than half a pace apart.

I could reach out and touch his chest.

I tremble at the thought.

"You would no longer speak to your own family? For me?"

"Yes."

"Even though I am not fond of your aunt, I am sorry for my part in that."

"No, Nauru. There's no need. Your friendship means more to me than an oscos with her."

I see the glimmer of forgiveness in his eye. If I were a Freeman, he would have wrapped his arms around me.

"I've missed you, Santi."

CHAPTER SIXTEEN

Naturally, I was expected to return to the field eventually.

My orders came exactly twelve standard weeks after my Osco's plate had been delivered to me on Virgis. I had two standard days to report to my regiment, which was now on its way back to Nova Penn to stop General Edelli's troops from venturing any further into the Outer Planets. The damn Secesh had arrived only a standard day ago and had been plundering the countryside, looting and burning anything in their path - revenge for all of the mistreatment of their own planets by the Union. Citizens throughout the Outer Planets - not just Nova Penn - were terrified of Confederate troops capturing Union territory.

I had no excuse. I had not been placed on medical leave. I had not been discharged. According to regulations, I was no longer grieving.

It was time to go back.

I report to the nearest precinct. The commanding officer informs me that I will be marching out with a few other brigades under General Ardow. I will meet the rest of the 56th Nova Penn once they've arrived outside the community of Gerin-Bue. There, we had to put a stop to the encroaching Grand Army of Virgis.

"We won't allow Old 'Li any more ground on Nova Penn," the officer declares with defiant glee.

I go home, brimming with renewed patriotic cause and courage. For the rest of the day, I prepare for my departure. I polish my shoes. I pack my haversack. I check my gear. I think of Nauru. I think of the words I must say to him.

As excited as I am to return to the front, I am reluctant to leave Nauru's company and his gentle teasing over the *scratch-scratch-scratch* of the black stick against canvas as he produces delightful images with his fingers. I hesitate to leave the comfort of his handsome face with its drooping eye as he lectures me about the rights of Freemen using all of the verbal cues I have come to know and others I have yet to learn.

`Fact: Your bond of ten standard weeks will no longer exist.`

For an indeterminate amount of time, Nauru and I will share no contact with one another. The realization that we will be unable to communicate till I return saddens me.

`Query: And what if you are suspended?`

The uncertainty sends a chill down my spine.

Nauru will never know how much he's changed my life.

I did not know this Freeman - this dear, unexpected friend of mine - would lift me from my grief. How do I begin to repay his kindness?

`Directive: You must tell him before you leave.`
`Fact: He deserves to know of his worth to you.`

While it is true that he deserves to know, will I be brave enough to tell him?

My plate does not respond. It is just as uncertain of the answer as I am.

I conduct a final review of the contents of my packs, then I recheck my uniform. To my dismay, there's a missing button on one of the sleeves. I curse - if only I had found this a standard week ago! Now there's no time to send my jacket away for repairs. I can't wait till camp when one of the Freemen sutlers could mend it, either, because I wouldn't pass inspection without that stupid button. Sewing it on myself would ensure a tangled mess. As intelligent and logical as Cyborn are, they are not as capable of fine motor handiwork as Freemen.

`Fact: Nauru will make the repair if you ask it of him.`

After checking for an extra button on the inside of my sleeve and digging out a spool of navy thread and a needle, I shrug on my jacket and pocket the sewing items.

When I arrive at the trailhead, Nauru greets me with a friendly smile and a tender *Hail, Santi.* Since our second meeting, I've heard it daily; never before has it imparted such a deep gloom. How is it that two little words hold so much meaning?

Instead of welcoming him in kind, I choke out a reply and head up the trail. We hike in awkward silence. Nauru refrains from asking silly questions. He knows what is happening.

At the curve in the trail, I hesitate, ready to shatter the peace that follows dusk. Regardless of how it pains me, I can't keep my news from Nauru any longer. "I got my orders today."

Nauru stops by my side, his face unreadable in the darkness. "It comes as no surprise. With General Edelli's advance, I knew you'd be leaving sooner or later." His words are neutral but I hear the pause in his voice. "Then this is to be our last meeting - till you return, of course."

We reach Santi's Spot, the very place where we first met. The sky is hazy and pink. Tol is just setting. Nauru takes off his jacket and spreads it out upon the ground near the edge. We sit together, our feet dangling off the side. We point out emerging stars in the night sky and I tell him some of the Nomad stories that Adahi used to tell me. When I can't recall any more, I lean back, resting my weight on my hands.

Nauru leans back, too. Our shoulders and arms nearly touch. His hand grazes mine. It's warm, solid. My cheeks flush at the physical contact. He removes his hand. My knee brushes against his. I linger. His body stiffens. I pull back. He draws closer. He leans in. His hot breath tickles my ear. My cheeks flame.

Nauru points out another star. "Does that one have a story?"

I don't look at the bright blue star he points to. I study his face, memorizing the amber ring around his pupil, the five deep scars cut along his left temple, the sweep of his hair. "That star is part of Setta's Burden."

"Do you know the story?"

"No. Adahi never told me. He said it was too sad."

At the mention of Adahi's name, Nauru breaks eye contact, surprised at my Osco's name. I no longer speak to Nauru about my Osco.

He reaches for a pebble and rubs it between his fingers. "Are you afraid, Santi?"

The question catches me off guard. I do not know how to respond.

Fact: You were not afraid through the fatigue or the endless marches or the times you were cuffed.

The Union needed me and I was not afraid.

Fact: The campaigns in the Inner Planets. The ambushes. The Secesh.

The Union needed me and I was not afraid.

Query: Are you prepared to answer Nauru's question thusly?

No.

Query: Why not?

Because I am afraid. I am afraid of returning in a metal box with a Union symbol because...

Query: Because?

I am afraid of leaving Nauru.

Adahi had not been afraid to leave me. He had not been afraid because all of him, all of his family, his past, his stories, his memories, his images would remain in suspension through his plate. By Merging with him, I would be able to recall any part of him simply by touching his plate with my hands. Had I Merged with Adahi, there would be no risk of being forgotten, no reason to be afraid - the Merge absorbed everything on his plate into mine.

It is different for Nauru. Without a plate, it is not possible for him to retrieve information from another's plate. He has no means of suspension, no means to gather and process information in suspension, and no potential to Merge. Freemen call it the End - the fear of being forgotten, the fear of the unknown. For Freemen, the End is final.

I recall the stiffening of his body as I brushed my knee against his. I recall the pain in his eye at the mention of Adahi. I recall the distance between our bodies, our minds, our desires.

Observation: You cannot tell Nauru you are afraid because he doesn't feel the same way.

It is unfair to put him in that situation.

Putting on the bravest face I can muster, I grab a pebble and hurl it into the haze below. I hear the dull thud as it lands. "The Union needs me and I am not afraid."

Nauru hunches over, elbows resting on his knees, his face turned away so that all I can see are his scars. He drops another pebble into the dawn. "I commend you, Santi."

"I will recall you often."

He laughs, but it's too intentional, practiced. There's a wistfulness in it I cannot define. "As will I."

The grey dawn explodes into bold yellows and pinks and oranges. It is time for us to part. I have no more words to say, nothing more to explain, nothing except for the burning need to rest my head on his shoulder.

One touch. Only one.

But Nauru is too quick for me. He rises and waits for me to stand, too. He does not help me up.

We walk side-by-side to my apartment, each lost in our own thoughts. I am tired of the quiet and sick of the distance between us. I long for a way to fill this void besides *the sunrise was beautiful* or *it will be warm today.*

All too soon, Nauru and I stand outside my gate, unable to say anything more of importance. He shifts from one foot to the other. I brace myself for his last words, words that I will hold onto till I return because Cyborn do not say farewell. There is no need.

"Be safe, Santi."

Before he turns away, before he leaves me, before he retreats down the street and through the park, before he disappears into nothing, I grab his hand and savor its pleasant comfort, its warmth and weight, its calluses and sinew. I will never know Nauru's thoughts, but his touch is satisfying, as though our fingers were meant to be twined together.

"Farewell, Nauru."

I can't say anything more.

Nauru releases my hand and walks away. He does not look back.

My hands settle into my pockets and I finger the spool of thread.

Damn!

I neglected to ask Nauru to repair my jacket.

We were together for six local hours and you didn't remind me!

Fact: You were preoccupied.

I check the street, squinting to magnify Nauru's path, but he has already turned the corner and is well out of sight.

Now I have to deal with this myself.

My plate offers no hints or tips to help me with this project. Sighing, I drop the spool of thread into my pocket and drag myself up the stairs and back to my apartment, back to a soldier's life, back to the front.

Once inside my apartment, I take out the thread and needle. Instead of unwinding a length of navy thread and passing it through the eye of the needle, I tuck the items in my pack, my heart heavy. I can't bear to touch them. They remind me of Nauru.

Rap!

A sudden tap at the window breaks my concentration.

Rap!

From the window, I spot Nauru outside the gate. I open it and smile. "But I thought - ."

He lifts a hand to me in greeting. "Let me in."

I survey the empty streets before my plate opens the courtyard gate and unlocks the front door.

What is so important for Nauru to come back?

Query: Does it matter?

Observation: He's returned.
Directive: Ask him to sew on your missing button.

I snatch up the needle and thread from my pack. Clutching the items in my hand, I meet Nauru in the doorway of my apartment. His eye blazes with intention and unspoken words. My grip on the spool of thread tightens.

I hold out the thread and he accepts it with mild curiosity. Our fingers brush in the exchange.

One more touch. Just one more.

Nauru examines the spool. "A parting gift?"

I lift my arm, pointing out the missing button. "I need a little help. Do you happen to know a good seamster?"

"I might know of someone." He reaches into his pocket and holds out a tiny brass button with the emblem of the Union stamped onto it. "I even have a button right here."

I gasp in surprise and upon further examination, it is indeed mine. The button still contains a tuft of blue woolen fibers trapped in the remaining threads. "How did - where did you find this?"

Nauru motions for me to take off my jacket. "I found it at the cliffs after the dress incident."

I swallow the hopefulness deep down into the pit of my stomach. "And you've been carrying it around with you all this time?"

Rather than answer my question, Nauru settles onto a nearby chair. With practiced care and nimble fingers, he removes the damaged threads from the button, threads the needle, and fastens the button into place. It takes less than a local minute for Nauru to finish.

"Thank you."

He holds up my jacket, inviting me to put it on. "You're welcome."

I insert my arms through my sleeves and turn to face Nauru. Starting from the bottom, he fastens the buttons of my uniform. His fingers linger at the collar, smoothing it out. I force myself not to fidget as Nauru plucks away bits of lint from the front of my uniform.

Nauru brushes away the last fleck of lint from my shoulder and offers me a hint of a teasing smile. "You'll do."

"*I'll do?*"

He cocks his head. His smile broadens with affection. "You make a very handsome soldier, Santi. I'm so proud of you."

Blood rushes to my face and I find myself sweating under my uniform, but I act as though his words have no affect on me. Surely he didn't come back to make small talk.

"What are you doing here, Nauru?"

Nauru glances at the door. It's closed and locked. "I did not give you a proper farewell."

Before I can process his words, he gathers me into his arms as if I am another Freeman and presses my body against his. I inhale the soap smell of his skin and the borax on his clothes. I savor his stubble on my cheek and his excited, uneven breath.

I wrap my arms around his neck.

One more touch.

Negation: No. No. No.

Directive: You must leave.

Despite my plate's protest, I cannot disentangle myself from Nauru's embrace - I don't want to.

Fact: You are not a Freeman. This behavior is inappropriate.

I cling to him, holding him tighter.

I don't care.

Fact: You have not yet Merged with your Osco.

I allow a single tear to spill.

I'm sorry Adahi.

Fact: You will miss your train.

Nauru releases me, cups my face in his hands, and brushes his lips over mine. There is no more doubt. I know how he feels about me by the heat of his body, the touch of his embrace, his soft lips against mine. These sensations are permanently etched in my mind, forever captured by the memory of my skin.

I am no longer afraid.

Nauru suddenly breaks away, the physical connection between us disappearing when he drops his hands. "I'm sorry, Santi. I should not have done that."

"I want you to touch me." As if to offer proof, I grasp his hand with mine and am surprised to feel it tremble at my touch.

Nauru traces the line of my jaw with the fingers of his other hand, then tucks some stray locks of hair behind my ear. His gaze is pained, as though a great weight rests on his shoulders.

"What is it, Nauru?"

"I've grown rather fond of you."

I rub the top of his hand with my thumb and give him a light smile. "I'm fond of you, too."

"No, Santi, you don't understand." Nauru drops my hand and forces out an exhale. Behind his helpless stare lies immense torment and struggle. "I've grown so fond of you that...I think I'm falling in love with you."

I am not able to understand *love* beyond what little I know about it. I recall the hurt and anguish in Anma's eye outside her apartment. I recall Nauru tenderly speaking of *love* as we walked to the party in the Freeman Quarter. I recall the adoration in Lem and Udarah's eyes as they danced together in the dim lights. I recall my own sense of loss when Nauru refused to speak to me.

How does one word invoke pain and sorrow, hurt and anguish, yet also devotion and affection, tenderness and adoration? How will I understand a concept so contradictory?

`Fact: Love is complicated and illogical. It is not meant for Cyborn.`

Words alone will never reveal the full scope of love.

`Fact: It is because no words like that exist.`

Then how will I learn love? How will I know if I love Nauru?

`Fact: Measurable compatibility, not love, is meant for Cyborn.`

I don't know if Nauru and I are compatible.

`Fact: To know or not know. That is the Cyborn way.`

Upon the realization that I intend to remain speechless, Nauru gives me a rueful half-smile and shoves his hands in his pockets. "I should not have said anything, but before you left, I wanted you to know I finally guessed right."

Despite my plate's insistence that I will never know the complexities of love, I am determined to reach an understanding of some kind. "But why? Why me? Why am I your right guess?"

Confusion spreads across his face. "Santi, I...where do I even begin? I admire your bravery and dedication to the Union cause. I applaud your courage to fight for something greater than yourself..."

My cheeks flush at Nauru's words.

"...When you tease me, I bask in your easy smile. I delight in watching you play ball with the children in the Freeman Quarter. I regard your opinion more than most Freemen. I treasure our visits to the cliffs, our time at the park, and our friendship. Most of all, I appreciate your willingness to consider and respect my point of view even though I am a Freeman and undeserving of such courtesy."

My mind flails about for what to say next. None of the reasons he gives are calculable. I am at a loss as to how to accurately interpret his claims. "While I appreciate your kind words, Nauru, I cannot say with certainty that I love you, too."

He reaches out and takes my hand. "You're overthinking the situation. What matters is how you feel in here." He brings his other hand to my chest and touches my heart.

Fact: That is nowhere near the expanse of an oscos.

I recall my oscos with Adahi. I recall feeling his sadness or pain or affection from across the system. I recall experiencing the images he sent me and the memories I exchanged with him. I recall him so deeply and so vividly that I could have been him.

Without an oscos, I can't give Nauru my eyes or my thoughts or my memories. I can't give him everything I have to give. The bond Nauru and I share would be limited by what we said and what we did. "My feelings are not all I could potentially give you."

Nauru shrugs and brushes his lips against my hand. "Santi, if you are willing to share yourself with me however you are able, then I will be satisfied."

Am I satisfied with limitations, considering what I used to have?

Directive: Accept no limitations.

Our coupling will be flawed from the start.

Directive: Accept no other oscos.

I close the gap between us, drawing my arms around him and nuzzling my face into his neck. "If you'll have me, Nauru, then I am willing."

Nauru joins his lips to mine. My fingers grip his collar. I tug him closer, but it isn't enough. He tears his fingers through my hair. Pins fall to the floor and my hair cascades down my back. His lips press against mine in a fierce and certain truth: there is no more space between us.

He slides his fingers through the length of my soft, dark strands. "I've wanted to run my fingers through your hair for some time now."

I unhook the fastenings of his vest with fumbling fingers and slip it off his chest. It falls onto the floor in a messy pile behind him. "Stop talking."

Nauru's lips slide down my face and brush the nape of my neck as his fingers reach for the fastenings of my uniform. He unclasps the eight buttons of my jacket and wrenches it off my shoulders. He drops it onto the floor behind me and then focuses on undoing the fastenings of my itchy flannel shirt. This lands in the pile, too.

My hands lift his neatly tucked-in shirt from his trousers in several jerky, uneven movements and flounder through its many hooks. Once the last hook is unfastened, I slip the sleeves down his arms and drop it onto his vest. The thin flaxen undershirt he wears underneath it all is also unceremoniously ripped off and tossed somewhere.

`Observation: You missed the pile.`

Nauru fervently brings his lips back to mine, pausing only once to yank my thermals over my chest. He lowers me down onto my cot, his fingers entangled in my hair, his lips grazing against my chin and journeying a trail along my collarbone and right shoulder, then down to my breast. His fingers gently twist one nipple and his tongue glides to the other, his mouth swallowing up the other nipple and rolling it around playfully. Then his teeth close lightly around it and I gasp, my body shivering. The room seems outrageously hot and I am suddenly too cold.

As he suckles my breast, his hands reach for mine, pulling them over my head and securing them with one warm hand. The other wanders to my other breast and massages it. Feeling emboldened by the growing warmth in my lower belly, my lips brush against his wrist and forearm, not once or twice but four times. His body stiffens and he brings his lips back to mine, releasing the grip from my hands. This time his tongue ventures in, probing around my teeth and the inside of my lips, sliding next to my tongue, inviting it into his mouth, but I am too timid to try anything so shocking right now, so I just press my lips firmly to his.

Nauru understands this.

He lowers his mouth to my ear and twists his fingers in my hair. His soft brown eyes shine and his lips curl upward in an almost shy smile. "What can I do? Tell me what to do."

`Fact: He needs to hurry or you will miss your train.`

"Take off my pants. I'm running out of time."

Nauru unfastens my trousers with practiced fingers, sliding them down my legs and then dropping them to the floor. I reach out to unhook the fastenings at his waist and with our lips still entwined, he shakes himself free of his last two garments. He lowers down on top of me, our bodies lining up perfectly - the tip of his member hesitating at my slit.

He strokes my hair. "I love you, Santi."

"My hands are empty without yours." They are the words closest to his own.

Nauru slides inside of me. We move together, in tandem. His thrusts are rhythmic, methodical. I record the pressure of his weight and heat on top of my body, capturing those sensations to recall when I am away on the march, pitching camp, in the thick of battle. My hands grasp his back tighter and tighter as he quickens his pace, his movements becoming faster and faster, his breath becoming harried and ragged.

[Attention on the platforms: this is the first boarding call for Union transport to Gerin-Bue. All officers proceed to the departure platform immediately.]

I ignore it. There are always three boarding calls. I still have time. I dig my fingers into Nauru's back, trying to hold onto this moment forever.

Just as no words for love exist, nothing lasts forever. Nauru groans, giving one final thrust and falling on top of me. I close my eyes and inhale the scent of his shaving soap. My fingers trace a circular pattern upon his back and arms. Our chests rise and fall together as our breath merges.

Nauru rises to his elbows. "I'm sorry, Santi. That was...not my best."

"Then I expect more from you next time."

Nauru laughs. "It will be done, my Cyborn Mistress." He glances out the window and stands up, pulling me with him and joining our lips one last time. "I will await that day in great anticipation, but now, we are both very late."

We separate flannel shirts from flaxen undershirts, wool trousers from embroidered vests and dress. Nauru braids my hair with expert fingers and pins it in a bun at the nape of my neck. I pull on my jacket and -

[Attention on the platforms: this is the second boarding call for Union transport to Gerin Bue. All soldiers proceed to the departure platform immediately.]

I hoist on my pack. "Second call. Where's my kepi?"

Nauru upturns pillow after pillow on the cot, finally finding it hidden underneath the sheets. He plops it onto my head. "Ready?"

"Let's go."

I cut through the city park, dodging people walking along the cobblestone paths, leaping over benches, whipping around corners and hoping there isn't anyone on the other side. Nauru follows as close behind is he is able - I'm so much faster than he is. He looks as though he is chasing me.

The last call sounds at twenty paces.

[Attention on the platforms: this is the third and final boarding call for Union transport to Gerin-Bue. All soldiers proceed to the departure platform immediately.]

Ears pounding and heart racing, I sprint through the station and onto the platform where the last three soldiers step inside the transport. With a leap, I spring inside as the door slides shut behind me. I catch my breath, turning to see Nauru outside the transport, a sad smile on his lips and his hand pressed against the door's tiny window.

I uncurl my fingers and lay my hand on his, centering fingers and palm.

The engine rumbles. The pistons and gears shift. The transport screeches to life.

In a single tic, my dear Nauru is gone, leaving behind a sweaty imprint of his hand on the other side of the glass.

CHAPTER SEVENTEEN

[*Welcome back, troops.*]

Throughout the crowded tram soldiers cheer at Commanding Officer Ardow's greeting while I stare at my hand touching the outline of Nauru's hand on the window pane.

[*We'll be marching to Gerin-Bue from The Green to drive out the Secesh and running most of the way. So enjoy your peace now. Hope you left your heavy stuff at home.*]

Titters of laugher echo throughout the tram.

[*The Secesh hold Gerin-Bue, but not for long! Got some federal reinforcements coming in from the east and the south lines. Should be here later today or tomorrow.*]

More cheers and shouts.

[*Edelli's been enjoying the Nova Penn countryside but we're coming to give him some trouble!*]

Shouts of approval fill the tram. I lower my hand.

It's only two local hours to The Green, the closest transport station outside Gerin-Bue. From there it will be another two hours to march all the way to Gerin-Bue - if we keep up a good pace. True, it's mostly fields, but there are plenty of hills, too.

I take a quick glance around. It's as though every available soldier on Nova Penn is here, swapping bloody stories and joking about all those times they whipped the Secesh - leaving out all the good number of times they ran in defeat. A few soldiers in the front of the tram begin to sing one of my favorite marching songs, replacing the lyrics with their own rowdy words:

We're gonna capture Old 'Li with our Union soldiers true!
And frighten old Virgis till she trembles through and through!
We'll cuff them all for traitors and build the Union anew!
And we'll keep marching on!
The rest of the tram joins in with the chorus:
Never, never will they stop us!
Never, never will they stop us!
Never, never will they stop us!
We'll just keep marching on!

I remain in the entry and stare out the window, the words blurring with the passing fields.

I needed my companions, needed to belong to something special, something bigger than myself, but now, instead of focusing on what's to come, what's to meet us in Gerin-Bue, I find I am unable to stop thinking about Nauru and what I've left behind.

The absurdity of it all! I rarely thought of my Osco when I was out soldiering, yet I cannot stop thinking of a Freeman!

How complex my life has become by inviting Nauru into it.

The farther I travel to my destination, the more I see him. He's among the groups of Freemen and their children who stop and wave at the tram. He's in the crowd of my fellow soldiers, waiting to disembark. He's in the mass of civilians who have gathered at The Green's station, shouting and cheering. He isn't here - I know this - yet he is everywhere.

Since arriving late, I had jumped aboard the first open tram. As a result, I had been mixed in with the Third Corps, even though I was assigned to the Fifth.

The soldiers from the first seven trams disembark: two hundred and fifty-three members of the First, Second, and Third Corps - and me. They file together in neat rows, waiting for their cue to march north, a field of deep blue kepis and uniforms, ready for action and glory. The signal is given and the First Corps begins marching out, then the Second, and the Third. I watch them from the platform, my heart bursting with pride.

What would Nauru say of this?

Ever ernest for news of the front, Nauru would want to talk strategy. He would ask about our defenses against Edelli, about Edelli's numbers, about the number of Secesh artillery units, about Union reinforcements, about where Edelli's been hiding for the last local week. I smile at his imaginary barrage of questions.

I could not send him an image, but Nauru would also be interested in the scene before me. In as many details and exacting words as I was able, I would describe the lines of blue, the crowds, and the excited cheers. I would tell him, too, of the anxious enthusiasm on the tram ride, Edelli's song, and the fields full of waving Freemen. He would admire us, all of these men and women working together toward a single purpose and common goal.

Then, as if to prove his appreciation for my commitment to duty and system, he would lean in. His lips would graze mine. He would wrap his arms tightly around me...

[Sargent Santina (Bashe) Metizon, proceed to the Fifth Corps.]

The color creeps up my neck and into my cheeks as I fall out of line and toward the Fifth Corps, my temporary regiment till I reach Gerin-Bue. As I pass the soldiers next to me, I ignore their embarrassed glances in my direction. They believe I've been exchanging affectionate words with my osco, not daydreaming about a Freeman.

The members of the Fifth Corp barely acknowledge me as I take my place with the rest of them at the far side of the platform, so I study the nearby civilian activity instead.

Every single person in The Green - Cyborn and Freeman alike - must be lined up to see us off, though I notice with a painful realization they do not stand side-by-side. Cyborn are to my left, Freemen on my right.

The old Santi, the Santi-before-Nauru, would not have seen it, even though the entire scene was so obviously laid out before her.

Fact: You would not have cared.

I stand on the end of a line of five, closest to the Freemen civilians. Children run from soldier to soldier, pressing handmade hard candies into their hands as tokens of appreciation, but only a few soldiers gladly accept the treats. Other Freemen clutch scraps of fabric with the Union seal embroidered on them. They wave them merrily as the Fourth Corps prepares to leave the platform, celebrating us, the soldiers who will - by All That Is Good - send those rebels off our planet and back to Virgis. I count seven members of the Fourth Corps who nod or tip their hats at the Freemen civilians lining the walls. This small gesture pleases me greatly and I promise to recall this observation when I return home to Nauru.

The last row of soldiers from the Fourth Corps leave the station. Now it's my turn to march with the Fifth.

We move past face after smiling face. My hand is jerked open by a Freeman girl no taller than my waist. She deposits a candy into my hand

and races away before I am able to thank her. The candy sits there, heavy and inviting, but I slip it into my pocket, resolving to eat it later, when the moment is not so sweet.

As we slow at the corner, waiting for the Fourth Corps to march on, I pick out a voice weathered with age and seeped in experience. "Be careful out there, okay?"

I turn toward the voice, matching it with an elderly Freeman whose wrinkled, scarred face is etched with honest concern. I am so touched by his words and his worry that I reach out and firmly take one of his worn hands, shaking it once. The Freeman is surprised by my reaction - and rightly so, given all of the other possibilities - but his eyes shine with gratitude that I have met him half-way. He returns the shake, his grip warm and hard.

"Thank you," I say in a low whisper, as if the two of us share some sort of secret. "You be careful, too."

The man releases my hand and nods.

Then there is nothing left to do but march.

***

Throughout the various regiment channels, it's obvious there is general confusion about how exactly the Secesh made it to Nova Penn. Everyone has their own theory and as I listen to the chatter, most of it seems completely illogical or nonsensical, though I don't have a better idea.

[...I'm telling you, if we had a blockade around Nova Penn, this never would have happened!]

[That's stupid! There ain't enough war ships for that!]

[Besides, they still could have gotten in. The whole Inner Planets are blockaded and there are still plenty of Secesh that get in and out!]

[Ever hear of Captain Sal?]

[Yeah, yeah, alright, but you can't deny that Old 'Li would have had a harder time of it!...]

[...bet those Secesh did something to the flyways!]

[Dummy! You can't do something to the flyways.]

[Then how do you think they got here?]

[Well, I dunno...]

[...know what I think? I think they flew in on hidden ships.]

[There ain't no way they could have come here on hidden ships. There's no such thing.]

[Maybe they invented some. The whole planet could be surrounded and we'd never know!]

[Dang! We sure could use some tech like that!...]

[...had something to do with the hills and valleys, I just know it!]

[That don't make sense.]

[You can't just fly in without anyone seeing you!]

[Sure you can! You drop in from a certain angle and no one can see you. My uncle's a freighter and he does it all the time. I was in his ship when he did it!]

[Doesn't he get into trouble with the law?]

[Never has before...]

[...and then they looped around Mereri's Land and dropped down here.]

[That makes sense.]

[But if that's true, how come nobody on Mereri's Land told us they were coming?]

[Aw, they're all a bunch of Secesh sympathizers over there. Bet they cheered on Old 'Li as he was flying overhead!...]

After some time, I stop listening. As amusing as these theories are, they clearly provide no real, factual information as to how the Secesh were able to land on Nova Penn.

I don't know how General Edelli did it, but like everyone else here, I'd sure like to.

The best possibility I am able to cobble together from all of this madness is this:

About a standard month ago, General Edelli had somehow slipped out of Virgis with a force of over 50,000 Confederate soldiers and engaged Union transports over the course of several standard weeks. Our generals were on alert and knew he was no longer on Virgis, but could not be certain of his exact position, only that he seemed to be on his way to invade the Outer Planets.

After an analysis of the flyways and planetary locations, it was determined that General Edelli was, in fact, headed to Nova Penn. Somehow, he must have known which flyways were busier than others and that we don't have any Union troops patrolling our skies - all of our Ironclads are either blockading the Inner Planets or trying to track down the notorious pirate Captain Sal.

He was able to navigate through the hills and the valleys - just like that soldier's uncle and, on occasion, even my Adahi - till he found a suitable place to hide his transports. From there, he could easily march his men throughout the countryside, taking whatever he wanted in supplies or tech.

By the time Union officials realized he was on Nova Penn, he had been able to cause enough trouble to create confusion on a massive scale, not only on Nova Penn, but within the rest of the Outer Planets as well. Would Nova Yan be next? What about Vemron? Were there any planets safe from his grasp?

Unfortunately, no one, not even the Union generals who had tried to track Edelli, knew exactly how many soldiers he possessed. There had been sightings all across the Nova Penn countryside, but nothing to indicate exact numbers. More than 50,000 Confederate troops was simply an estimate based on our best intel.

Within the next few local hours, General Edelli and his Secesh rebels, wherever they were now - would be confronting our 50,000 Union troops and our thousands of incoming reinforcements in Gerin-Bue.

Fact: It is a certainty that you will be outnumbered again.

But we aren't going without a fight.

I had encountered Edelli's Grand Army of Virgis before, a good many standard months ago. It had been an attempt at offensive strategy and ended in another Union failure.

The large transports we arrived in were unable to cross the rings around Virgis and while we waited for the smaller, more maneuverable transports to be deployed, Edelli was able to call in reinforcements and set up a perimeter of artillery units. We dodged rock and slinger fire, finally landing safely in Fick's-Bue. We easily took the city, but could not take the area around it or drive Edelli away. For five standard days we fought hard to push through, but with all of his reinforcements he had already successfully dug in his heels. We were on our own - the Union had no one else to spare - and so many good men and women had already been suspended.

What other choice did we have but to leave?

Once again, Edelli had managed to send us on the run.
But not this time.
This time, he would be the one to flee.

CHAPTER EIGHTEEN

I had been to Gerin-Bue four times as a child. Each time, my parents and I took a tram to get there and spent the day wandering the city. Each time, it had been an adventure and the few times that my parents didn't take their work with them. The city itself was the largest in the area, full of gleaming stone buildings, perfectly uniformed cobblestone streets, brightly-colored flowers, and towering statues of revolutionary heroes.

As a child, I didn't particularly notice the hills and cliffs surrounding Gerin-Bue but - having marched through them - I do now. The Secesh transports are hidden somewhere in those hills, as is the rest of Edelli's army, waiting to strike.

According to Union intel, the Secesh had been in Gerin-Bue for at least a local day. Up till that point, the rebs had shown up outside the city in small groups and the local militia - not really knowing how many of them there actually were - tried to scare them away with some angry cuff fire in the air. When the Secesh finally marched into the city, they identified the militia members and secured them in the basement of city hall. They are still there.

Even with the Confederates, life in Gerin-Bue has remained mostly peaceful. We received word that the Secesh had already carried off most of the residents' supplies and harassed some of the Freemen. Three unlucky civilians had been assaulted when they refused to obey the curfew.

I hope to All That Is Good the civilians remain indoors when we arrive. The Union soldiers are itching for a fight and the Secesh aren't going to back down if they can help it. It wouldn't be right if the residents got caught in the crossfire.

Here's hoping, too, that those Secesh meet us directly in the streets of Gerin-Bue instead of hiding out in houses, like cowards.

For the first local hour of the march, the Union chatter is nothing more than good-natured banter between soldiers. As we approach our destination, however, Union chatter picks up, much of it about the confrontation between our troops already in Gerin-Bue and the enemy:

[...we're approaching from the west and south...]

[...any Secesh?...]

[...where are the rest of them?...]

[...important that we protect the tram lines around the city in case we need more supplies...]

[...take aim! Don't lose sight of them!...]

[...I hear cuff fire to the west! What's your position?...]

[...we've been spotted!...]

[...damnit, beat them back!...]

[...hold your ground!...]

[...we must charge!...]

[...charge!...]

[...charge!...]

[...charge!...]

Fifth Corps would be meeting with General Enol's troops to the northwest of Gerin-Bue and reinforcing the lines there, with the ultimate goal to hold the area and keep the Secesh from advancing. It wasn't an elegant plan, but it would do while the rest of the Union army was slowly converging into Gerin-Bue from other areas of Nova Penn, Mereri's Land, and Virgis.

With so many troops coming, we'd be able to send the Secesh running, but if we failed, would there be enough time for us to beat a hasty retreat to the nearby hills?

How lucky do you feel today? Adahi always asked me during our daily talks.

Lucky enough, I would say. The ritual had become a private ironic joke between the two of us. Cyborn do not credit luck as having an effect on the outcome of events.

Today, I am lucky. I confront the Secesh head-on, on my planet, on my terms.

***

It is the smoke I see first, great billowing dark grey clouds from Gerin-Bue. My heart sinks.

The city has been attacked!

Observation: Not a word of this has been spoken by your fellow soldiers.

My plate is right: after studying the bleak scene, I realize all of the smoke is from the artillery crossfire of the troops located at the nearby ridge and valley. As we fan out into the countryside and around the city into the smoke and the shrieks of artillery fire, I secure my cuff at my wrist and remind the others around me to do the same.

Through the haze, I am able to make out the faint colors of a Confederate flag waving from the top of the ridge surrounding Gerin-Bue. Another waves from the far end of the hill. Tears prick my eyes - from the smoke or the sight, I do not know - and I vow to personally take down every single rebel flag I see, given the opportunity.

Lucky enough.

Adahi's words ring in my ears as I hold my ground with the other members of the Fifth Corps. The wind shifts, masking the Secesh in haze and smoke. Except for the flickers of light from the artillery encounter on the hills, I cannot see them, even with my plate's adjustments. The Union artillerists return fire and at the general's command, Union soldiers from the Fourth Corps march across the field to engage the Secesh.

[...General Enol is heading to Ivy Hill...]
[...the enemy is upon you!...]
[...double-quick, soldiers!...]
[...set up the artillery!...]
[...approach Gerin-Bue with caution...]
[Fifth corps!]

Our moment has come.

[Move out!]

At the superior's signal, our lines are sent forward and up the ridge, our commanders urging us forward. The soldiers on either side of me shout above the noise of the shot and wave their cuffs in the air. We are ready and willing to meet the Secesh.

We duck and cover to avoid cuff blasts and the shrapnel that explodes above our heads like fireworks. It bombards us with scrap metal and energy shot instead of sparkling lights and patterns. We've marched close enough to the hill that our position is risky and the Secesh know it.

Lucky enough.

We traverse over rocks and abandoned packs as though nothing can stop us, but falter as we step over the bodies of our fallen brothers and sisters in blue. They scream at us through their mangled plates, begging us to carry their messages home.

[Tell my sister...]

[Tell my father...]

[Please, tell someone...]

We choke from the acrid smoke, growing ever thicker as we approach the hill, and watch the skies, ever alert for the screams of the artillery units and the hail of fire and metal.

Halfway across the field lies a broken stone fence - temporary safety from the cuff fire. I hunker there with five other soldiers, pausing only to fire at the distant Secesh line through a break in the smoke. The soldier next to me rises too early, heedless of the sudden wailing above us and the screeching around us.

[Incoming!]

I flatten my body against the stacked stones, shielding myself with my pack. Hot metal pours from the sky, crushing anything and everything in its path. The soldier beside me crumples from the impact. The odor of singed hair and burnt flesh fills the air. He screams in agony at his legs, splintered and broken. His clothing burns to ashes. His flesh melts from his plate. Gritting my teeth, I ignore his howls of pain, trying unsuccessfully to shut out his cries from my memory.

The residual energy from the shot causes his body to shock and spasm, then he's quiet and still. There's nothing I am able to do for him now, even if I wanted to.

I signal to the others.

[Let's go! We're almost there!]

We leap over the fence and rush to the ridge together in a tightly-packed line. Other soldiers fall into line with us. There's nothing on the other side of the barrier; nothing but more blue-jacketed bodies with mangled plates and splintered limbs; nothing but the pleading, eerie whispers of the newly suspended. I wipe my brow and keep going.

I concentrate on identifying the artillery fire above me and avoiding the soldiers below me. The shots and shells hide behind the haze. The bodies lie so close together I could walk across them without touching the ground -

[Watch out!]

I nearly trip on one of my suspended sisters.

An onslaught of metal shards drench us with crackles of hot energy and sprays of dirt and mud. Our line disappears as we take cover. Some of us don't get back up.

I squint through the grey haze at what's left of us.

Our line's decreased by 27%. We've only gained seven quick paces. My best calculations indicate there's about sixty-three to go.

Fact: At this rate, very few of you will actually meet the Secesh at their position at the ridge.

And the ridge is so far away...

I inhale and close my eyes, crouching down as the whistles of another round of energy fire soar overhead. They hit the ground one after the other - *boom, boom, boom* - creating craters in the field.

Directive: Move!

Observation: You only have a few tics before the next charges are loaded and calibrated.

I hoist myself up and signal to the rest to keep moving ahead. Footsteps pound next me as we gain ground - seven paces, ten paces, twelve paces. The next round of shot screams above us.

[Find cover!]

I flatten myself to the ground, into the stinging dust and sweet-smelling grass, till the sky is quiet again.

[Move!]

The haze here is denser and stinks strongly of ozone, but still we run - covering five paces, nine paces, eleven - and passing dozens upon dozens of other soldiers on the ground. Some are Confederates, but most are Union, their faces frozen in silent screams, their plates wailing for mercy.

My heart pounds from the race to gain ground, my ears deafened from the shrill blare of the blurry blue streak overhead. I drop and cover my head, pushing away the muffled voices of six more immobilized by the last shot.

Grimacing, I haul myself up, desperate to reach the ridge that's so close, but so impossibly far away. I don't recognize the soldiers next to me anymore - I have left those brothers behind me, somewhere in the field.

I glimpse reflections of silver cuffs through the smoke and dust, the weapons of the Secesh soldiers lined up at the bottom of the hill and waiting for us. We're finally within reach, less than thirty paces away.

We stop to adjust our cuffs, hoping to get the first shot. One of the rebs spots us. He shouts a warning to the others and they join his call, emitting a humming vibration that pricks through our plates and tingles down our spines. The air fills with that cursed Rebel's Call ringing loud and clear above the squeal of slinger blasts.

I lift my cuff, take aim at the Secesh in front of me, and fire.

All along the bottom of the ridge we give it to them in an angry hailstorm of cuff shot. My target crouches down at the last tic to steady his return shot. I hit his arm high, at the shoulder. His cuff discharges into the dirt.

He snarls a few choice curses, lifting his furious, watery eyes to mine. He raises his cuff. The return shot grazes the collar of my uniform, a finger's-length away from my head.

Lucky enough.

I blink away the thick dust from my eyes. The Secesh is no longer there. He's been cloaked by the smoke. I fire at the same spot. The discharge disappears. I'm not sure if I've actually cuffed anyone.

Our shots spent, we duck down behind anything we can find - large rocks, partial stone walls, wounded soldiers - waiting for our cuffs to re-energize. The Secesh return fire. One blast hits the soldier next to me. He sinks down. I catch flickers of his final message to his family on Nova Yan:

[...I have engaged the enemy, and to go like this, with such courage and bravery!...]

The rest of us, the final 53%, lift our cuffs. We aim at reb shadows through the thick clouds. We fire again.

I hide my face from the sudden shrieks above, the artillery unit's signature. By now, our position next to their infantry lines have been determined. Their artillery has been recalibrated. They are ready to release their worst. They are ready for us to relinquish our hold. They are ready for us to retreat.

Resolved to stay, I crouch into a more comfortable position on the ground. Rebel fire flashes around me. The straps of my pack weigh heavily on my shoulders. My plate forces the pain from my mind. The soldier behind me drops from the return cuff fire - or shrapnel from the last artillery shot, I don't know which. We huddle together: tired, miserable, frightened, our bravado spent.

Lucky enough.

Collectively, our energy is running low. Our cuffs are too heavy from the weight of our charges. I shake off the doubt, the fear, the hesitation. I raise my arm, aim for whatever seems most solid through the smoke. I fire.

I persevere on an endless loop. My cuff recharges. I fire again.

Adahi's words, Nauru's smile - they fuel me.

Lucky enough.

Recharge.

Fire.

Recharge.

Fire.

Lucky enough.

But luck, like cuff fire, eventually runs out.

Whatever courage, whatever bravery, whatever fortune the Union had possessed at the beginning of this engagement, we quickly lose it upon the realization that General Enols had been cuffed. The message flies throughout the ranks like wildfire.

`[Enols has fallen!]`

Soldiers grow uneasy, glance at each other, uncertain.

`[...what do we do...?]`

`[...now what..?]`

`[...should we run...?]`

With Enols down, who is now leading our brothers and sisters on the ridge?

A few of us maintain our drive, our commitment.

`[...keep fighting...]`

`[...damnit, keep going...!]`

Fire.

Recharge.

Fire.

I will not run.

But the Rebel's Call from the top of the hill only gets louder, more persistent. A shiver vibrates through my plate and down my spine. It's in the earth, felt through my thin brogans, impossible to ignore.

"They're coming!" Someone releases a panicked scream. "The rebs are coming!"

The newer recruits fade away into the haze, their terrified faces wide-eyed and ashen. Our numbers have declined by 73% - the only ones who remain at the front are the officers and career military, like me.

Cowards! I dig in my heels.

Fire.

Recharge.

Fire.

But the absence is too keenly felt, my plate too aware of the numbers rapidly dwindling, of the feet pounding in the direction of Gerin-Bue.

"Cowards!" I choke out through angry tears.

Fire.

Recharge.

Fire.

Artillery shots scream overhead, enraged by our stamina, our grit. The explosions rend the air, severing the breath from my lungs. I gasp, sucking in the thick air, cough, take aim.

Fire.

Recharge.

I am about to fire again when hundreds of rebs emerge from the wall of dust, swearing and yelling like fools, a wild madness in their eyes. They throw themselves upon us, swinging their cuffs wildly, pushing us back - even those of us who vowed to stand still.

I dodge a quick swing at my left only to almost be unbalanced by another on my right. Still more of them pour down the hill, joining their fellow soldiers in cuffing the rest of us who dared to stay behind.

    [...retreat!...]
    [...retreat!...]
    [...RETREAT!...]

I am swept up in a mad dash toward Gerin-Bue and away from the shrapnel, the suffocating odor of ozone, the rebs, my own cowardice - but I won't stop running, not with the city so close.

My heart pummels against my chest. I push myself onward, gulping down the smoky air and struggling not to cough or slow down. Their footsteps, their cuff fire, their savage screams are right behind me, easily able to keep up with my pace. I reach the city, pausing only to study my surroundings.

    [No time!]
    [Move!]

An artillery blast tears away chunks of a stone building above me. I duck and cover as debris bombards my pack. I don't see the remaining members of the Fifth Corps anywhere in the confusion, but I hear their frenzied voices in my plate:

    [...get to the hills..!]
    [...protect the hills...now...!]
    [...which way are the hills?...]

[...everybody to the south, to the hills, to safety!...]

I stand shakily, stumbling over the fallen stones and concrete. My plate directs me through the maze of city streets that I recall from my childhood.

Focus on getting there, on the arrival. Hucks will be there with Nyrie and the others. And our artillery, thank All That Is Good.

I turn a corner and come in contact with a small group of young soldiers. One of them lifts his cuff anxiously, ready to fire, but quickly lowers it when he notices our identical uniforms. The group looks from one to the other, seemingly calm, but their eyes lie. It's a wonder they made it this far.

Directive: The right. Take the junction at the right.

I motion for the soldiers to follow. They gladly allow me to take the lead.

Another right and a left and I am able to see the hills - those beautiful, looming ginger-colored hills - through the clearing haze. The soldiers run toward them, giving whoops of happiness.

Hucks stands at the top of the west hill next to a row of artillery units with a smile so wide I can't help but grin back. It's been several standard months since I've seen my crew. Despite the strong Secesh advance and the awkward Union retreat through Gerin-Bue, I feel as though I won.

He waves at me from the rock pillar he leans against. I lift an arm in reply.

It's a steep climb to the top. Hucks cheers when I drop my pack at his feet.

"Look who's back!" he calls to the others. "Hail, Sarge!"

The others - Nyrie, Ceska, Dai, and Bokay - gather around us, imparting welcome, excited words of reunion. I shake each of their hands in turn, their touch a pleasant reminder of our bonds, of what we've been through these several standard years together.

I look around in amazement. Pari, our cannon; the limbers; the caissons; even our tents are put together - everything is as it should be. "You're already set up."

"Yeah," Hucks says proudly, stroking Pari with affection. "They wanted us to be prepared - just in case those Secesh decided to follow you all up the hill." He squints at the city and laughs, his eyes shining like the Freeman children receiving their red ball. "Who's got the high ground now?"

Nyrie ignores Hucks and his excitement. "Orders, Sergeant?"

I turn back. Union troops are still fleeing the city and trickling up the hills. Tol is starting to creep toward the horizon. By the time the Secesh move their artillery units to a better position, it'll be too late for them to attack.

"We won't hear from them till morning," I say, nodding at Nyrie. "I'll take the first watch. The rest of you can get stacks of charges ready for tomorrow, then turn in."

Nyrie herds the others to the caissons and limbers. "You heard the Sergeant."

Glancing around for superior officers and spotting none, I lower myself to the ground, tossing my kepi onto my pack. I unstrap my cuff and shrug out of my jacket and bask in the cool evening air.

Except for an occasional distant cuff blast or a greeting as another one of us makes it to the top of the hill, the city's quiet now, as are the nearby fields. We've retreated to a good spot - high ground, sitting between two major roads.

It's going to be difficult for the rebs to uproot us now, I reflect with some satisfaction, leaning against the rock pillar and watching Tol disappear.

I draw in my knees and hug them tightly, sighing. Though I am back with my crew, back where I belong, Nauru's absence is acutely felt tonight. I would like nothing more than to be the recipient of his gentle teasing, or the object of his affectionate words whispered playfully into my ear, or the target of his profound observations of today's events.

What is Nauru doing tonight? Has he decided to take an extra shift? Is he drinking with Lem and Udarah? Is he at the park trying to track down the nimblemous? Is he playing ball with the children in the Freeman Quarter? Or is he at the cliffs, letting his legs dangle from the side and wishing I was there next to him?

Is he thinking about me, like I am thinking about him?

I shiver at the recollection of his warm lips upon mine, of our bodies pressed together and turn my blushing face into the shadows, away from my crew.

Nauru could be doing anything. There is no way for me to know what he has actually chosen to do tonight. I must simply...guess.

`Fact: Cyborn do not guess. Cyborn know or do not know. There are no assumptions.`

My plate's right, of course. Cyborn do not guess.

So I settle in, recalling the warmth of Nauru's body next to mine as we identified each of the eight stars of Setta's Burden above us. I brace myself for a long, sleepless night.

CHAPTER NINETEEN

It's a hot and sticky midday. We're restless. Although plates are, for the most part, able to adjust for the heat, there's not much that can be done about the impatience. We have yet to see much of the Secesh, besides a few scouts and some small, buzzy rebel drones that are quickly shot down by our artillery units.

Reinforcements arrived during the night and stationed themselves along our position just south of Gerin-Bue all the way to The Big Slope, almost a thousand paces away. Only a few of these groups had much spare ammo, so some of our reserves were shuffled down the line - quietly, of course. Nyrie grumbled loudly about it till I reminded him that if the line fell five hundred paces away, it would be the end of us, too.

General's orders this morning were to hold this position at all costs. We spent our time firing test shots toward the Secesh lines and aligning the trajectory. When they finally approach the hills - and they would, sooner or later - we would be ready.

But with the artillery units set and ready since mid-morning, there's not much more to do. Nyrie and I stand at the rock pillar, observing the restless rebels from the only spot of shade on the entire hill. Hucks leans against Pari, flicking little pebbles away with his foot and watching them tumble down the hill one by one. Dai and Ceska neatly restack the charges while Bokay grounds and resets the pull with the threader.

There's a little tap at my heel and I glance back at Hucks. He gives me a goofy smile and kicks another rock at my foot. I return the rock without looking at it.

Nyrie squints at the rebel line. "Are they on the move?"

My plate compares their current position with their previous one.

They've approached the hill, but only by a few paces. "What do the drones say?"

"They've moved up." Nyrie glares at Hucks, who has accidentally kicked a pebble at his foot. Hucks averts his eyes, pretending to buff Pari with his sleeve.

Sudden rumbles and shrieks a distance away send our attention to the skies, waiting for the hail of shrapnel and energy, but it doesn't come. The shots fall short; the rebels are too far a field and we're too high for their artillery to have any impact.

Hucks whoops. "Shall we give it back to them, Sarge?"

The others nod their agreement but I shake my head. "Unless they're coming full force up the hill, don't bother wasting our ammo."

The commotion doesn't last long. With that pathetic display, the rebs hunker down, almost as if they realize that they shouldn't be wasting their ammo, either.

***

It's late afternoon when we hear from the Secesh again.

This time, instead of those few half-hearted attempts of mid-day, they begin to bombard our position with artillery shot, the shrieks of slinger fire warning us of impending attack. They've aimed their artillery units higher and higher to meet their targets, but the shrapnel rains onto the bare, rocky hill, too low to reach us.

Then their artillery units stop firing but it's too soon to catch breath: a line of rebs come charging at the hill, climbing furiously up the sides, howling and shrieking that damn yell of theirs! Several of the soldiers along our line cover their plates and ears to keep from getting disoriented.

Nyrie examines the rebels' strenuous climb. [*Keep it together, everyone! They're just trying to scare us!*]

[*They ain't looking so good, huh, Sarge?*] asks Hucks.

[*I made that climb yesterday - don't know why they can't seem to hack it!*] I give him a sideways glance and grin. [*Thread her up!*]

My crew flies into action, readying Pari's first shot of the day.

Ten of our artillery crews have already discharged shots. The smoke hides our position from the enemy, but also obscures my vision. I hear our drones zipping overhead in search of the rebel line.

[*Ready!*] Hucks signals from his position.

[*Fire!*]

The shot discharges, leaving behind the powerful stench of ozone and a trail of dark smoke. The charge explodes above Hucks's estimate of the rebel line. Hot metal beats upon the Secesh. Their screams penetrate the thick air, though it is uncertain exactly how many Secesh we hit.

[*Thread!*] I shout again.

Nyrie grounds the charged build-up while Dai and Ceska shuffle another charge to the slider. A drone has spotted a group of ten Secesh fifty-three paces to our right. I forward the coordinates to Hucks, who begins to make adjustments to the trajectory. Hucks is the youngest and newest recruit in our regiment and a damn good gunner.

[*Ready!*] he calls. The others step back to avoid the recoil.

[*Fire!*]

The canister flies from the slinger. It shrieks a fair warning to the oncoming Secesh. Still, they come, their vague shouts alerting each other of the danger from above. Cuff blasts soon follow. A drone falls into an unrecognizable scrap heap just seventeen paces to my left. The rebs howl in victory.

The other drones calculate a new flight plan, modifying their path so that the entire hill can still be observed at some point. The cuff fire persists. Another drone crashes to the rocky ground. The rebels holler as our drones readjust their flight paths once again.

[*Thread!*]

With more ground for the drones to cover and the thick smoke from the slingers, determining the exact location of the rebel line proves difficult. Their long line has splintered into smaller groups of ten or twelve, making it far easier for them to find cover as our shots are blindly released into dusk.

[*Ready!*] calls Hucks again.

[*Fire!*]

Slinger fire blares throughout the top of the hill. Shrapnel from an errant shot hits another drone, sending the shattered pieces raining down upon the Secesh who happen to be below.

I know what they're going through.

[*Thread!*]

I dove behind rocks and walls to dodge the pounding of metal and energy from overhead. I nearly retched at the smell of ozone. I exchanged cuff fire with the rebs. I know full well what the Secesh are going through tonight, but this does not make me any more sympathetic to their predicament.

[*Ready!*]

[*Fire!*]

Those three words - *thread, ready, fire* - are repeated in an endless series of automatic loops, on and on till I can no longer recall without help from my plate exactly how many times we've fired on the rebs. Even Pari's distinct call has become indistinguishable from any of the other artillery units on this hill.

[*Thread!*]

I hear their yell before I see the five looming figures approaching my position, cuffs raised and ready to fire.

[*Secesh!*] I scream, ducking down behind the edge of Pari. I raise my cuff at the intruders and begin to fire. Dai and Ceska dive behind the other side. Nyrie and Bokay insert the next cell into the slider without dropping it, their movements both frantic and careful. Hucks stubbornly continues the adjustments even though the cell hasn't been loaded.

[They've breached the hill!]

The rebs readily return my fire as the message is passed down our line. An errant shot strikes the caisson behind Pari. It hisses and sizzles violently, sending sparks flying outward. Dai's uniform catches on fire and she shrieks in surprise, straying into the darkness to keep the flame away from the shot. I hear her pounding her arm and side with her opposite hand to extinguish it. Ceska lowers her cuff, too, and trails after Dai to help her smother the flames. Bokay and Nyrie quit firing to extinguish the caisson, but the box continues to belch out black smoke.

A staticy odor fills my nostrils. It's not ozone, but just as distinct.

Fact: The slider.

My arms sag with alarmed realization.

Pari isn't grounded!

Secesh pour in around us. The entire hill erupts in a rapid exchange of cuff fire. I join in, but my attention is fixed upon the location of the threader. I can't find it in all of this madness. I dodge rebel fire as I continue my wild search, eying the ground for anything the same size and shape.

[*Nyrie! Where's the damn threader? The heat's making Pari unstable!*]

There's no answer from Nyrie who now juggles both the smoking caisson and returning cuff fire with two groups of advancing Secesh. Bokay now ignores the caisson completely. His focus is concentrated on attacking the rebels.

I duck behind Pari, listening to her squeal and screech as the slider gets hotter and hotter, and mentally tick off the members of my team.

Nyrie and Bokay are at the caisson.

Dai and Ceska are in the line, thirty paces away.

[*Hucks?*]

Fact: It's too late to ground Pari.

[*Where are you, Hucks?*]

Directive: Abandon this artillery unit.

I dash seven paces away, squinting into the shadows and smoke and turmoil, twisting and turning to evade the rebel shots around me. I'm without cover, an easy target.

[*Hucks!*]

Then I turn to find Hucks struggling with a Secesh. The reb swipes at his back with a clawed cuff. Hucks manages to elbow the reb in the plate but another one materializes out of the haze and darkness and cuffs Hucks across the face. Hucks steadies himself and retaliates, swinging at the reb.

Directive: Abandon Hucks as well.

I can't - I can't leave Hucks behind!

Ducking to avoid Confederate fire, I tear back toward Pari. [*Hucks! Get out of there!*]

Hucks ignores me. Using his clawed cuff in place of the threader, he yanks the line to the clip. He's nearly there - a hand's width away - when a third rebel cuffs him in the arm. Hucks yelps and draws his hand back. As Hucks cradles his arm, the second Secesh raises his cuff, takes aim, and -

I charge at the reb, slamming him in the back. We crash onto the ground. The Secesh kicks out at me and I roll to the side to avoid his strike.

Arm shaking, Hucks reaches for the line again.

Pari shrieks and explodes into shrapnel, catapulting the cartridge into the air.

Hucks and the two rebels are ripped apart from the blast.

I am blown back from the force of the impact.

***

Fact: His eyes widened.

[*Hucks?*]

I saw his brown eyes widen before he was wrenched apart.

My eyes blink open, but only one can see. The other, the right, is shrouded in darkness.

My right ear, too, is ringing. Even with support from my plate, I can't get it to stop.

My mouth tastes sharp, metallic.

How long was I pressed against the cold ground, choked by the mud and wet grass?

`Directive: Get up.`

There's a weight on top of me, struggling, moving, crushing me down. Not shrapnel, not part of Pari - it's warm, alive.

I can't.

The rebel's hand digs savagely into my plate, the other rises above his head, ready to strike. Muscles in my neck strain from the struggle.

I can't breathe.

I swing out and up with my left hand, striking his face. The weight's gone, he's off me. I limp out and away, out and away, straining to distance myself from him. I can't get away fast enough. Half my body is unresponsive, paralyzed, burning from the radiant heat of the explosion.

Wavering, the Secesh picks himself up and hovers over me. He's been injured, too, but he's nowhere near the disastrous state I'm in. The reb grabs my collar and strikes my face. His thorned cuff is shiny in the moonlight, wet with my blood. I cough out blood and mud. He shakes me; the world spins.

Again and again, he pummels me, again and again. I pull my right shoulder to block - it won't move - then my left. I kick out with my left leg and strike something solid. The Secesh buckles, his knee joint twisted, contorted. I roll to my right.

Get away, I must get away.

My left arm brushes against something long and cylindrical next to me.

The threader.

The reb reaches for me again but I grip the rubber end tightly, so tightly, and swing up, thrusting the hooked end into his gut, and yanking it across his belly hard, hard enough to rip out his insides. Eyes widening, he grips his belly, his grey uniform darkening with blood, his blood.

Gasping, he collapses to the ground.

My shaking hand drops the threader and my lungs labor to choke in the smoky air. I release a sob into the ground. There's satisfaction in the deep vibrations, the impacts of the shrapnel, the ongoing shrieks of slinger fire because, despite the chaos, we haven't run yet.

Updates flood my plate:

```
[Breaks in the center line!]
[Hold them off!]
[Stay put, troops!]
[Reinforcements are coming!]
[Flank 'em! Flank those damn rebels!]
```

I struggle to sit up, to stand, keeping my left arm propped under me, my useless right tucked against my chest.

I will not go down without a fight.

Edelli will run.

Without direction, without focus, without awareness of anything else around me, I use the threader to hoist myself to standing. With my senses gone and nothing to indicate which way to go, I inhale careless, ragged breaths and search for some way to find my bearings.

Clinging to the threader, I take several desperate hobbles to my left.

My left is where I feel the vibrations of the artillery units' recoil. My left is where there will be caissons and limbers and stored energy shots. Left is where I will send the Secesh scattering.

Step, hobble, step, hobble, breathe, step, hobble, step, hobble, breathe...

My eyes, my ears - they detect nothing in the impossible blackness, the hazy air, the merciless screams - but my left foot is still active, alive. This pattern, and only this pattern, inches me across slippery ground, back to the slingers, back to salvation.

```
Fact: Four people. You need four people to
load a slinger.
```

I don't have a crew. I don't have a plan. I have nothing but the threader and my own determination. I stumble to the closest abandoned caisson and slinger.

Edelli will run.

Drawing a fresh shot from the caisson, I tuck it into my jacket, into the space between my right side and my waist. My left hand grips the threader. The nearest slinger is ten paces away.

Step, hobble, step, hobble, breathe...

Head spinning, eyes watering, I swallow hard.

Don't puke. Don't puke. Don't puke...

With the slinger within reach, I rest the right side of my body against it and force myself down the length of the slider. Gasping and panting, I reach the loader and extract the shot from my jacket with fumbling fingers. I don't know if this unit's been grounded and I can't waste time to check - our line's been broken and battered and the next round of Secesh are emerging from the hillside.

The shot fits into the slider without difficulty. The slinger hums to life.

Thank All That Is Good.

Clasping the threader and leaning against the slinger, I stumble to the back of the unit. The right side of my body spasms from the pain, but I push on shakily, centering my breath and counting my uneven steps. Nyrie's words echo through my head: *Keep it together!*

Finally - finally! - I stagger to the back of the unit and lift the threader with my left hand. The sheer weight of it gives me pause - I've never had to raise it one-handed before - and steer the threader against the slider, in an attempt to catch the hook.

Miss!

I unleash a grunt through clenched my teeth and savagely try again.

Miss!

Hot, angry tears stream down my cheeks. In sheer desperation, I navigate the pole again, roaring my own rebellious, frustrated howl.

Miss!

The right side of my body aches, so ready to sink onto the bloody ground, ready to embrace rest and darkness and - if it shall be - suspension.

But my left arm, my left leg will fight - *I* will fight - till I am nothing more than bruised and battered flesh attached to a trampled plate.

With nothing more to lose, I grasp the threader, yank it back hard, fast, and catch the hook. I secure the cable into place, exhaling gratefully.

But my struggle isn't over, not yet. With failing steps, I limp to the gunner's position - *Hucks's* position. My plate computes some quick calculations. I adjust the slider and jerk the switch.

The slinger fires into the night.

Without time to step aside, the recoil pushes me back, my breath knocked out of me, my right side trapping me to the slick ground. I gasp for air and lower my throbbing head.

I don't know if my shot hit anyone. The shouts and wails of the broken all sound the same.

Tears sting my eyes, tickle my nose, slide freely down my face.

The world blurs around me.

Tears are all I have left.

Through the haze and smoke hang the eight bright stars of Setta's Burden.

I laugh - what else can I do? - choking on tears and blood and bile.

I wish I could tell him, one last time: *The Union needed me. And I was not afraid.*

I am not afraid, Nauru.

I recall the warmth of his fingers...

Deafening cuff fire.

...his teasing smile...

The odor of iron and damp earth.

...my knee brushing against his...

My head droops to the right.

...his soft lips locked onto mine...

I am able to see the night sky with my left eye.

Till suddenly - I can't.

CHAPTER TWENTY

When I awaken, I expect to suffer the thunderous vibrations of slinger fire, to hear the screams of soldiers, to smell blood and smoking metal and ozone, to see out of only one eye.

But as I open my eyes and absorb my surroundings - the stone ceiling above me, the cot under me - relief washes over me. My vision has been fully restored in my right eye. Whatever happened in the field was only temporary. I savor the peace for a few tics, slowly wiggling my fingers and toes. Everything's there, except for an unsettling numbness in my right limb. Temporary, surely.

When will I go back to the hill?

`Fact: You won't.`

Ignoring my plate, I tip my head to the right, then the left, taking in the soft whispers and quiet moans. Most of the other soldiers are sleeping. Those who are awake speak to each other in hushed voices, their eyes darting about in miserable glances. I count fifty-three soldiers in all - fifty-four, including myself.

A young woman wearing clean white robes and gloves sits at the foot of my cot. Her dark hair is neatly combed and tied at the nape of her neck. She isn't any older than fifteen.

When she sees me awake, she stands. I note her perfect posture and cool eyes and unsmiling lips...

A Fixer!

When I get back, I can tell Nauru I've met a Fixer!

"How do you feel, Santina?" she asks in a voice aloof and steady, a voice much too old for this child to have.

She is not what I expected. I stare back at her, not knowing what to say.

"Are you aware of any pain in your extremities?"

"I feel...fine, actually. Quite good." I sit up and struggle for words. How does one properly thank a Fixer? A simple *thank you* isn't sufficient for someone who's repaired your battered body.

Correction: Do not thank the Fixer yet.

What do you mean?

Directive: See for yourself.

My eyes dart around the room, lingering upon soldier after soldier - he has a missing hand, she has a missing leg, he has a bandage wrapped carefully around half of his face.

Chills slide down my spine as I turn to my right arm, the arm I cannot feel.

It's gone, sliced off between my shoulder and elbow.

I no longer have a right arm.

This can't be real.

Fact: This is real. This is your new reality.

Panic rises in my chest. I fumble out of the cot and crash unsteadily to the floor. "No, no, *no!*"

The Fixer's gaze is dispassionate, intimidating. She makes no effort to restrain me. "Santina. With all you have experienced, with all you have seen, surely you comprehend that amputation was an eventual possibility for you as well?"

I blink away hot tears before they are able to slide down my cheeks. "Given the situation, *my* only possibility was suspension."

"You suffered significant burns to the right side of your body and trauma to your vision and aural capacities. These injuries were uncomplicated to Fix; however, most of your right arm had been severed during the explosion of the artillery unit." The Fixer eyes me without expression. "With a fully functioning plate and bodily capabilities at 83.76%, suspension was not an option for you."

I can't believe what I am hearing. The tears spill from my eyes, wetting my face. I want to wipe them away because I am embarrassed to cry in front of this child, but I can't bring myself to acknowledge what's left of my right arm. "But there were no other options left."

Fact: Your brokenness does not drive your need for suspension.

Please, don't.

Fact: Your failure to follow proper protocol drives your need for suspension.

I had chosen to ignore the Merge. I had chosen to take 1,244,160 breaths without closure. I had chosen to find affection in the arms of a Freeman instead of following proper protocol. And now, the consequences of my actions have finally caught up with me. I have failed my osco. Without two hands to form a connection between myself and Adahi's plate, I am unable to complete the Merge, as is proper protocol, the only way.

The Fixer offers me a hint of a smile. "Had you already resigned yourself to the same fate as your osco, you would not have fought so valiantly at the top of the hill. You would have simply accepted your position without a second thought of *other commitments*."

I lean against the wall and look away, avoiding the Fixer's unblinking gaze.

She knows about Nauru.

What else does she know about me?

Does she also know of my guilt over Adahi?

And my sadness over Hucks?

And my worry over Dai, Bokay, Ceska, and Nyrie?

And my hate of the Secesh?

And my anger at her?

`Fact: She is a Fixer. She knows everything about you.`

Mending broken plates and bodies is what a Fixer is trained to do. With a single touch of their hand, any ailment leaving you broken or somehow disconnected - a psychotic break, a physical wound, an internal injury - can be treated by a Fixer. They gain unrestricted access to your body and mind, to your images and secrets so that you'll emerge from the process as you once were: whole and unbroken. Try as you will, nothing is hidden from a Fixer.

I have no words to respond to her subtle reference to Nauru. There is nothing I am able to say that she doesn't know already.

The Fixer feigns ignorance and smoothly transitions to her final thought. "Santina, your actions prevented twenty-one Confederate soldiers from advancing upon the hill. You saved Union soldiers from your osco's fate. Suspending you would have been an undeserving conclusion to such an act of bravery."

She tilts her head. I follow her gaze with my eyes. Across the room, two soldiers are packing hundreds of metal boxes into a large crate. Each is stamped with the Union symbol.

Hucks.

`Fact: His plate is in one of those boxes,`

awaiting transport home.

I scrutinize the metal boxes in silence, my throat prickly, my chest ready to burst. I can't Merge with Adahi. I can't face Nauru with a horrid stump for an arm. The Fixer can't claim that my life - my reality - will be the way it was before Gerin-Bue.

She had no right to decide the outcome for me.

"Go away, Fixer." I don't care if I am being rude.

"Very well." The Fixer rises from her seat. "Should you change your mind, Santina, I would be most happy to accommodate you."

Without a further glance at me, she leaves, tending to another soldier in the row of cots.

If I had a right hand, I'd knock that smug look off her face.

Fact: You'd be dishonorably discharged before you were able to draw another breath.

I stare at the soldiers shuffling from the boxes to the crates, trying to ignore the watchful eyes of the other maimed soldiers around me. The floor is hard and uncomfortable, but I choose not to get up and call more attention to myself. I choose to wallow in my misery.

One of these soldiers slinks over and crouches down next to my cot, trying to catch my eye. "Hey. You okay?"

His slight country-boy accent reminds me of Hucks, but instead of meeting his eye, I remain fixed on the hundreds of boxes, my eyes pricking with tears.

The soldier hunkers down beside me. "It ain't that bad, really, Sarge."

I turn my head to face him. I don't recall his voice, his face, his eyes, his sorry half-smile. He is not familiar to me.

But he called me Sarge. Am I familiar to him?

The soldier shoves the kepi from his head with the remainder of his arm. It's exactly like mine, nothing but a useless stump. The kepi falls into a heap next to him. He picks it up and crumples it under his fingers. "You helped me out of Gerin-Bue. Remember?"

I recall the bright red hair and the frightened blue eyes but I refuse to acknowledge him.

He isn't fooled. He stretches out his legs and gets comfortable. "We did it, Sarge. The Secesh are gone. On their way back to Virgis."

Instantly, I'm drawn in, even though I don't want company. "What happened?"

"Two days of fighting and they couldn't break our line on the hill. They finally packed up and left last night. In a hurry, too."

I had been out for at least a local day. I had missed the retreat.

"Did we capture 'Li?"

"They got quite a start. Then there was the bad weather. If Old 'Li hadn't left when he did, he might have been stuck here." The soldier twists the kepi in his hand and leans in. "If you ask me, I don't think General Deame wanted to follow. I think he was relieved he won."

My heart sinks in disappointment. Edelli had escaped - he was probably back on Virgis by now - and I would no longer be able to chase him.

He clears his throat. "I'm Private Eyron Daine."

There's no point in fancy titles or rules or regulations anymore. I will be honorably discharged and returned home with little ceremony or care. I had seen it happen to others. Now it will happen to me.

"Santi."

He wants to exchange war stories, to ask what happened to me, but I shift my attention back to the two soldiers packing boxes across the room. We sit there for a standard minute in silence.

"We saw your fire from Rust Hill. Did you see ours?"

I tip my chin in a slight nod.

"Well, the rebs started climbing and we heard the booms from your slingers. So then the officers told us to get our slingers ready, to keep a crossfire going, so the Secesh couldn't storm Ginger Hill. Heard they got up there anyway."

The horrible events are still too fresh, too painful to recall.

"They didn't make it up Rust Hill. But we could see all the flashes of cuff fire and the artillery blasts at the top of your hill. With all that commotion, the officers argued about whether or not they should break position to reinforce you."

I press my lips together. Even if a hundred troops from Rust Hill had come to our rescue, would that have helped Hucks? Would it have helped me?

"We fought clear into the middle of the night - for six whole standard hours. There wasn't a scratch on me. And then yesterday some Secesh cuffed me good, right in the chest." He opens his shirt and shows me the jagged scar. "While I was down, an artillery explosion blew off part of my arm. Funny thing, huh, Sarge? I heard the same thing happened to you."

My eyes harden and my mouth turns downward into a deep frown. *Funny* is the last word I would use to describe what happened to me. To him. To any of us *unlucky enough* to be here.

Yet here he is, eyes bright with a wide, joking smile. He's without regrets, frustration, self-pity and I cannot bear it.

"Go away, Eyron."

"But, Sarge - "

Clearly he needs some convincing. "Go away, Private."

Still holding his rumpled kepi, the boy hoists himself up and returns to his own cot across the room.

Without another word, I slide into my cot and pull the blanket over my head, trying to find a comfortable position with only one arm.

It's a lot harder than it looks.

***

"Psst. Hey, Sarge."

Fact: It's Eyron.

I know.

His voice is committed to memory, whether I want it to be or not.

He tries again. This time, I detect an urgency in his voice. "Sarge."

I draw the blanket from my face and give him a cranky glare. "What do you want?"

Eyron brushes aside my sour mood and lowers his voice so that the others around us can't hear. "The Fixers sent me. Someone asked for you."

I am torn between suspicion and interest. "Who?"

"You know a Nyrie?"

I fling back the blanket and hop out of the cot. If any of my crew had made it through, it would be Nyrie. "Where is he?"

"This way."

Pausing to grab my blanket and wrap it around me, I follow obediently behind. The blanket is a vain attempt to hide my broken body from Nyrie, whose only concern right now should be the Fixers and his own injuries. All that matters is that he's here and not in a little box like Hucks or the thousands of others. The Fixers will Fix him. He'll get better. Our cots will be moved next to each other. We'll exchange battle wounds and share war stories. We'll return home together.

"This Nyrie was part of your crew, huh?"

I'm too busy searching for Nyrie in cot after cot to respond. I don't see him anywhere.

Eyron leads me through a maze of neatly stacked crates with the Union seal. My grip on the blanket around my shoulders tightens as the boxed plates of my suspended brothers and sisters interact with my own. Here, they are not begging for mercy or pleading to pass along a message or two - they speak as though we march together through the fields of Nova Penn or seated on the next transport, bound for home.

```
[...we sent them running!...]
[...and I didn't run, not even when those
bunch of cowards next to me did...]
[...and we'll keep marching on!...]
```

At the corner, we turn into a darkened section blocked off by large strips of fabric stinking of earth and blood and static. I stop, rooted at the junction.

I hope Eyron will take me through another partition, to a well-lit room where Nyrie will be standing in full uniform with a bandage across his plate. He'll smile at me and I'll smile back because we both know he'll be going home, just like me.

"Here?"

To my dismay, Eyron pulls back the curtain and motions for me to enter.

But I can't go through the curtain. If I do, I will learn the terrible, unfortunate truth about Nyrie - that's he's not going to be standing there in full uniform and smiling broadly with only his plate bandaged - but that he will be too broken to be revived.

```
Directive: Go through the curtain.
Fact: It is the only way to learn the truth.
```

"It's okay, Sarge," Eyron says. "I'll be right here."

I scrunch up my face in a nasty glare. I don't want this kid to be *right here*, telling me it's going to be fine when I damn well know it isn't. Screwing up my courage, I force myself past the fabric barrier and into the tiny rooms on the other side, divided only by lengths of woolen fabric.

[*Sergeant?*]

[*Nyrie?*] I plod along, peering through openings in the curtains and studying the bodies within. Every single one has severe burns, smashed-in plates, and multiple missing limbs. My hold on the blanket has caused my knuckles to go white. None of these soldiers will go home, even with a Fixer's help.

Does Nyrie know this, too? Is this why he asked for me?

I hesitate when he calls for me again, now knowing on the other side of one of these curtained walls is a Nyrie so different from the proud and dedicated Nyrie I served with.

My heart aches at the recollection of Nyrie standing at the rock pillar on top of Ginger Hill, so gruff and immaculate and perfect in his blue uniform, his lips twitching into a rare smile once he spots me. He was immovable, a mountain of a man.

I can't face him like this.

Speculation: If you desire the truth, then you must.

I had always promised my crew I would be there for them, through every single impossible battle, through all of the endless marches, through the good times and bad. To abandon Nyrie now, to leave him in the company of the Fixers and the soon-to-be suspended soldiers in the cots next to him would be taking the coward's way out. I cannot do that to a man so faithful and brave.

His voice appeals for me again, leading me to the end of the row. Taking a deep breath to steady myself, I step past the fabric barrier.

A Fixer is hovered over a motionless figure, the fingers of one hand splayed across the soldier's battered, unrecognizable forehead. She's the same Fixer who was seated at the end of my cot this morning. Upon sensing my arrival, she releases the man and with a calculated motion of her hand, she slips my hand into the soldier's on the cot.

The moment our hands meet, I recognize Nyrie's calm detachment and serious demeanor. Breathing heavily at his disfigurement and dazed at the sight, I lower myself onto a chair at his side and tighten my grip. His hand is cold, but his bond is warm.

[So it's true,] he says. [*The Fixer told me you were the only one left.*]

[*Am I?*]

Looking over my shoulder, I peer up at the Fixer who nods once in dispassionate affirmation.

I edge closer to the cot, to my burned and beaten brother in arms. I want to know what happened to him, to the others, but mostly to me - but at what cost to Nyrie's peaceful tics before his suspension?

Nyrie wheezes and gasps. His eyelids flutter.

Through the smoke and haze, he stands on top of the hill with Bokay, panting and exhausted. The surviving Secesh lead a call of retreat as a small band of Union reinforcements pour in.

[*Bokay and I survived the rush. We knew that Ceska and Dai were nearby. I sent Bokay to find them.*]

Bokay finds Ceska and Dai surrounded by smouldering cartridge boxes and the torn up bodies of soldiers dressed in grey and blue alike. Bokay informs Nyrie he's found them.

[*They were fine, minor burns and scratches. They had held their own during the charge.*]

Nyrie picks up Pari's threader, covered in blood and guts and mud.

[*I knew it was you who had done it, Sarge. You'd fight to the end.*]

Only younger soldiers, soldiers like Hucks and Eyron, ever called me *Sarge*, not Ceska or Dai and certainly not a hardened career military officer like Nyrie. He's always designated me *Sergeant* or *Sergeant Metizon*. I squeeze his hand to encourage him to keep going.

Nyrie kicks over grey-clad bodies and calls my name, but the bond we share isn't there, it's not anywhere. He panics. A musty stench settles upon the hill. Nearby soldiers begin to compare their battle wounds. Fixers are summoned to gather up the wounded.

[*I found the rest of Pari.*]

With astonishing strength, Nyrie throws these pieces aside as if they are pebbles, shouting my name louder and louder, his cries echoing in the night. The smoke pricks his eyes, sending tears running down his cheeks - but he's too hard to cry, isn't he?

Others scramble to his side to help him. Pieces of Pari tumble down the hill, kicking up loose stones and ungrounded energy.

[*We couldn't find you. We thought you had been cuffed in the confusion. Or lost, like Hucks.*]

Dai spots me first, under the rock pillar. I'm staring into the dark sky, body battered and eyes glassy, parts missing.

[*I screamed for a Fixer, but my voice was lost among the others. Everyone was shouting for a Fixer, for someone to help their fellow officer, their friend.*]

Nyrie picks me up and carries me. I droop against him, still warm, still breathing, even though my right side has been blown away. He runs with me sagging in his arms, hot tears drop into my hair. Blood, my blood, smears the front of his blue jacket, a permanent black stain.

The extent of my injuries is suddenly so terribly clear: my hapless right stump hanging down from my arm socket, the burning flesh and fiber, the facial skin which had been ripped away. I looked as Nyrie does now, a hollow shell of a person, unable to be identified.

[*I brought you to the officers' tents and demanded a Fixer be brought immediately. They assured me one was on her way.*]

The officers order Nyrie to return to his post, to help bring the remaining injured from the field. He presses a hand to my forehead before walking back to the top of the hill, following orders - as is so quintessentially Nyrie.

[*I hoped that our paths would cross again,*] he says as the memory drops from sight.

I reprocess our shared vision, replaying it over and over again in my mind. Nyrie had not suffered more than a few scratches and a dirtied jacket that night. His injuries must have happened the next night, when the Secesh stormed the hill a second time.

The blanket slips from my shoulders, revealing the stump. I don't let go of Nyrie's hand to hide it. There's no point. He already knows.

[*What happened to you, Nyrie?*]

[*The next morning, we saw General Edelli repositioning his artillery units, but the Secesh waited for some time before attacking Rust Hill again. When they finally did, the ground shook with the amount of artillery that rained upon us poor bastards on the hill and I couldn't get the smell of ozone out of my nose. I can still smell it now.*]

I smell it, too, I want to tell him, but I don't. There's so much more I need to know first. [*Were the others with you?*]

[*Our superiors felt it prudent we stay together, so we were moved to another Sergeant's crew. He could have done with some additional training.*]

[*Not good enough for you, huh?*]

I feel Nyrie's amusement, even if I can't see it on his face.

[*No one ever was,*] he responds. [*But he did okay. He kept the slingers going, even through all of the rebel artillery fire.*]

I smile. That's high praise from a perfectionist like Nyrie.

[*Since those damn rebs didn't care to repeat what happened the night before, we weren't directly part of the fighting. But the ridge got a good pounding. We tried to keep the heat on the Secesh, but they broke through anyway. Lost a lot of good men and women over there.*]

I think of Eyron, his scar, and his arm. [*And your injuries?*]

[*Enemy artillery. A canister shot in just the right place.*] Nyrie's body quivers up and down once, as though he's sighed as he passes me a flood of memories of his experiences on the ridge. [*I wish I had a happier story for you, Sarge.*]

I laugh uneasily and clutch his hand. [*Oh, Nyrie. You'll be fine. The Fixer told me you'll be fine.*]

[*Have you actually seen me?*] I sense his amusement over my desperate statement, but it quickly fades away. Nyrie gasps for another breath. [*I need a favor, Santina.*]

My breath hitches. *Santina.*

He knows his body is almost at its last physical breath.

[*Of course. Anything.*]

Nyrie cracks open his right eye and wheezes. [*You'll take my plate to my Osco, won't you? I couldn't stand for my Osco to receive my plate from some random soldier. Who better than someone who went through the same thing?*]

When I accepted Adahi's plate, would it have mattered that I received the plate from someone who had fought with him? Or would I have been upset - angry, even - at seeing a fellow soldier who survived the battle when my Osco had not?

[*It would do me a great honor if you agreed to this.*]

I do not have to be reminded that Nyrie fought for a united Union. I do not have to be reminded that Nyrie and the others found me and brought me to the Fixer. I do not have to be reminded that Nyrie deserves this last rite to be conducted by someone who knew and respected him.

But the sad truth is: I don't want this burden. I don't want the responsibility of this promise. I don't want to be the one to have to say those words to his Osco. But mostly, I don't want to be reminded of my neglected duty to Adahi.

[*Please, Santina.*]

Out of the corner of my eye, I catch sight of the Fixer eavesdropping, her judgemental frown concluding I am the worst human being she has ever had the pleasure to meet.

I glower at her. *Fuck off, Fixer.*

The Fixer flinches, her features stony, but it's enough to give Nyrie what he wants.

Tears slide down my cheeks. [*I'd be happy to.*]

Satisfied at my promise, Nyrie takes one last breath and I feel the bond between us declining. I squeeze his hand one last time but his energy has disappeared.

The Fixer escorts me from the room to the hall where Eyron is patiently waiting.

[*You are doing the right thing, Santina,*] she murmurs.

I spit on the ground in front of her in childish defiance.

*** *

Fact: A promise is a promise.

It's been three local hours since my visit with Nyrie. I haven't moved since returning to my cot, not when Eyron invited me to play cubes with him and not when the Fixer placed a box in my lap. The box is identical to all of the other boxes stacked on the other side of the room, but the Fixer assured me that this box belongs to Corporal Yoan Rommen Nyrie.

The sight of it sickens me but I can't bring myself to push it off my lap.

I can't do this.

Fact: A promise is a promise.

My eyes wander across the basement to Eyron, laughing and joking with a group of soldiers as they toss the cubes. As soon as he feels my gaze upon him, he looks up and catches my eye. I respond with the meanest glare I can muster before tearing my face away. Dropping Nyrie's box on my cot and reaching for my jacket, I navigate the cramped basement to the stairs leading outside. Eyron's eyes tail my every movement.

Without the shriek of slinger fire or the howls of fallen soldiers or the smell of ozone in the cool air, the nearby fields have transitioned from a place immersed in confusion and frenzy into a place hallowed with struggle and blood. I trudge toward Rust Hill - the recollections of the rock pillar on Ginger Hill too fresh to revisit - while Setta's Burden hangs mockingly low in the clear sky. My left hand settles in my jacket pocket, but my right sleeve just hangs there. I don't know what to do with it.

I'm in no hurry, but as I near the top of Rust Hill, I catch sight of more and more broken slingers, pieces of shrapnel, and discarded packs strewn about. Swallowing hard with determination, I pick up my pace and focus on locating the horizon when it finally appears over the top of the hill.

Fact: You cannot shut out this scene forever.

I perch on a mound of slinger parts and stare out at the blushing daybreak. At any other place, on any other day, I'd find solace in Tol rising.

All That's Good, I could really use a drink.

Fact: Or two.

Three. Yes, definitely three.

Observation: He approaches, ten paces from your left.

I know who it is before he says a single word.

"Nice of you to take that soldier's plate back to his Osco."

I shrug. "Why do you care?"

Eyron plops down beside me and points at the neighboring hill, gesturing to the rock pillar. "You were right there, Sarge. I would have greeted you, if I knew where to look."

His words are meant to be kind, but glimpses of images flicker through my head, all of them unwillingly recalled: the gutted Secesh, glints of silver in the moonlight, Hucks's wide brown eyes, Setta's Burden, the rebs' call, the whistles of shot above the battesite, the dark patch on Nyrie's uniform.

One by one, I capture these images and bury them as far away as I am able. "So?"

"So, Sarge, we've gotta stick together. It's the only way we'll end up in a good place after all this."

I clench my teeth together. I jerk my left hand to Ginger Hill which is covered in the rotting grey bodies of rebels. The Secesh packed up so fast they left their suspended behind. Nobody knows what to do with them. "Good, bad - what's the difference? We're all in the same place, Private."

"But there's a reason for it, Sarge. There's always a reason."

"Ha!" The anger in my chest bubbles over and I grab onto Eyron's jacket and pull him close. He does not struggle to free himself, so I shake him to break his composure. "What is the logic that Nyrie and the others are suspended and I am not?"

When he does not respond, I shove him to the ground and wave my stump in his face, the empty sleeve flailing about. "What's the point of this, huh? What's the damned point?"

I want nothing more than Eyron to get up because I want to cuff him in the face. To my furious disappointment, he lies there motionless, like he's one of the reb bodies in the field.

So I kick him in the gut. His body crumples satisfactorily under the force of my foot.

"There is no damn reason, Eyron, no fucking reason at all!" I rage into the night as I storm down the hill.

CHAPTER TWENTY-ONE

With Edelli's defeat and subsequent retreat, the trams to and from Gerin-Bue are running again. I am at liberty to leave at any time, but I find myself reluctant to return home though everyone I served with has either moved on with the war or are returning home in little metal boxes. I am wistful for the closure of one or the other because now, I exist in an uncomfortable limbo. I was a soldier for so long - what do I do with myself now?

There's only one local hour before I leave. I pack up the few things that are mine - a comb, some crackers, extra socks, and a clean shirt - and pause. Nyrie's box sits on a nearby ledge.

Eyron saunters over and sits on my cot without asking. "Almost ready, Sarge?"

He speaks to me with the tenderness and faithfulness of a good friend, as though my outburst last night didn't happen, as though we had served together and laughed together.

Observation: Although you did not serve together and you do not care for his company, he is a friend nonetheless.

I grab Nyrie's box and shove it into my pack. Hefting the bag onto my left shoulder, I brush past Eyron. "Let's go."

Despite my foul attitude earlier this morning, Eyron accompanies me to the station. He chatters incessantly on the way, informing me the Fixers asked him to stay behind a while longer to help them remove, clean, and organize the plates of the soldiers still laying in the fields and hills. Even though the battle's over, the three Fixers who traveled to Gerin-Bue to assist the two already here can't do it all.

I do not understand why Eyron agreed to do this work. How is he able to remain impartial to the suspended rebel soldiers side-by-side our own? How is he able to process body after decaying body without reflecting on his own brokenness?

Fact: Eyron has chosen to look toward the future and not wallow in the past.

A part of me wants to tell both Eyron and my plate to shut up - but another part of me admires the way he holds his head high and hums a marching song. It's as though he hasn't a care in the world.

Eyron slows his pace to meet mine and grins. "Almost there. Ready to go home, Sarge?"

No. I'm not ready.

I'm not ready for my part in the war to end.

I'm not ready to deliver Nyrie to his Osco.

I'm not ready to return to my apartment, where Adahi's plate is waiting.

Worst of all, I'm not ready to see Nauru again.

Fact: It does not matter if you are ready or not. You must return home.

"No. Not really," I grumble.

"Ain't there anything you're ready to do?"

"I'm ready to leave *you*."

I meant it as a slight, the worst I am able to come up with, but Eyron shakes his head and laughs, unbothered by my rude comment. "You're really something, Sarge."

"Don't you care about what's happened to you?"

Eyron shrugs. "Sure. I can't work on the farm anymore and I know Pa was counting on the help. But, I'm the same person I was before - even if I don't look it - cause I got my plate."

Fact: His logic is sound.

His logic is not *sound. I have only one arm now. Therefore, I cannot be the same person I once was - even with my plate.*

Fact: You -

Shut up. I don't want to hear your counterargument, you horrible piece of tin.

At this outburst, my plate quiets and I realize what Nauru had meant when he said becoming a Freeman meant having a head full of silence, a head full of nothing but your own reflections.

It sounds wonderful.

Directive: Shut up.

Eyron leads me through the mess of crumbling buildings, heaps of rubble, and piles of debris. Except for groups of Cyborn and Freemen civilians working separately to unearth the streets and walkways, very few are out doing much of anything.

As we pass an apartment leveled by artillery fire, a Freeman child approaches us boldly, hands outstretched, gaze demanding. I recall the Freemen children I played ball with back home. The boy stares at us - two soldiers, each without an arm. Eyron ignores his very existence.

Remembering the crackers in my pack, I dig around Nyrie's box and my clean shirt to fish out four packages of nourishment and pile them into his open hands. The child grins, clutching the crackers tightly against his chest, then tears one open with his teeth and devours it. When I hoist my bag back onto my shoulder, my left arm brushes against my pants pocket. I recall the small, sticky shattered lump of sugar within.

I hold out the largest pieces of candy to the boy. "Here. This is for you, too."

The boy's eyes shine with gratitude as his hand snakes out to accept the small pieces of sugar. He shoves half into his mouth before offering me the other half.

I shake my head. "It's all yours."

The boy stuffs the candy into his mouth and tears across the cleared street, waving at me in what I have come to recognize as a farewell.

A sharp whistle escapes Eyron's lips. "You're really something, Sarge."

"No." I watch the Freeman boy disappear behind the apartment building. "I'm just doing the right thing."

"You ain't afraid of Freemen?"

I heave my pack over my shoulder and press on. "Should I be?"

"You're scared of going home, but you ain't scared of Freemen." He smiles carelessly as he meets my pace. "Shouldn't it be the other way around?"

***

Home is two local hours away. The tram ride is smooth, without incident, but as we draw closer and closer, dread weighs heavy on my shoulders.

When we pull into my station, I watch Freemen and Cyborn exit, greeting their families and friends on the platform. A part of me hopes Nauru is there, too, somewhere in the crowd.

Fact: Of course he isn't. He doesn't know

you've come home.

Children chatter with their parents and grandparents. Oscos and Oscas reunite. Freemen exchange affection with a meeting of lips. I clutch the stump with my left hand, a powerful misery settling in my chest.

Will he recoil at the sight of me?

Speculation: Nauru will say nothing to hurt you. He bears his own scars.

[Please exit the tram.]

I jump at the tram's unexpected, chastising announcement and blink away my confusion. I don't know how long I've been sitting here.

[Exits are located at the back of the tram.]

A quick glance out the window reveals I'm the last one off. The platform is empty; the families, the couples, the friends have all disappeared. I snatch up my pack and hoist it over my shoulder without a second glance.

Grasping the strap of my pack with my left hand and taking a deep breath to steady myself, I disembark the tram onto the wide open space of the platform. I stop, rooted in suspicion and calculation. Tol's light illuminates the platform. There are no shadows, no places to hide. Except for the stone benches lined up at the waiting areas and the station doors in front of me, there is nothing here.

Yet as I twist my gaze in one direction and then another, as I take step after halting step, as I challenge myself to focus on the double doors of the station entrance, I envision the place crawling with ambushing Secesh who dash into concealment whenever I turn my head.

When a shriek rends the air above me, I duck at the sudden whistle, so similar to artillery fire.

Fact: It is only the departing tram.

My heart beats wildly, my eyes dart back and forth, my palms dampen with sweat as the tram at the adjacent platform screeches to life and leaves the station. An embarrassed laugh bubbles inside me and quickly morphs into shameful, choking gulps. I wipe a stray tear from my cheek and leave the station with my head held high. No one will see the chink in my armor.

As I walk along the street, however, I find myself unsure of my next move. I can't face Nauru and I can't return to my apartment to add Nyrie's box next to Adahi's.

I had his plate for two standard months, but there had always been an excuse. There was always time to do it later.

Directive: You must fully process the consequences of your negligence.

Why bother? There's nothing I can do now. I reluctantly retrace the steps to my apartment, pausing to inventory every item in each window display on the block.

Four glass trinkets, five cracker tins, eleven bolts of cloth...

I catch my reflection in a particularly large window. The sight of my pinned up sleeve mocks me and, disgusted at my broken self, I avert my eyes to an older building across the cobblestone street. Advertising images of happy, carefree people sipping their fancy drinks flash through my plate. I scowl at the images.

A drink is not a necessity, not at all, but as I cross the street, the temptation to escape draws me inside under the guise of making one final toast to my fallen brothers and sisters. The bar door swishes open at my approach and I creep inside, less confident than I had intended to be. Only five other people sit scattered at various tables around the room. All eyes on me, I pick my way to the bar, the only sounds my footsteps and the soft music playing in the background.

> *Ten standard months have passed, Lemita,*
> *Since your hands remained in mine*
> *As up the cliffs we climbed*
> *To witness Tol's sweet ascent*
> *Your hand never leaving mine...*

Despite the appropriate, unfortunate words, I drop my heavy pack onto the floor and take a seat at the bar. The bartender glances up at the *thunk* and stares at the vacant sleeve which used to house my missing right arm.

Observation: This is a bad idea.

Shut up.

"What can I get you, soldier?" the bartender asks, resting his gaze past my face and pretending that my brokeness doesn't bother him. I know better - he won't look me in the eye.

Directive: Leave now.

Don't tell me what to do.

"Full Frontals," I say. "Six of them."

His eyebrows twitch upward in surprise. "Six?"

"Six. I want them lined up right here." My finger slides across the counter in front of me.

Without further argument, the bartender lines six tiny tin cups along my imaginary line, then reaches behind the bar and pulls out a large earthenware jug. He uncorks the top and pours the sweet-smelling amber liquid into each cup.

My left hand flounders for the faithslips in my right pants pocket. I collect a few and drop them onto the counter, cheeks burning and muttering my thanks. It isn't necessary for me to carry so many faithslips - my plate can easily handle these sorts of transactions - but I needed them at camp, for the sutlers.

Fact: Not anymore.

Without a word, the bartender eyes the little pile of faithslips and scoops them into his hand. He retreats to the other side of the bar to take another customer's order. I'm glad to be rid of him and his belittling stare.

Observation: This is a bad idea.

Six drinks, one for each of them.

I lift the cup on the far left and hold it up.

"To Private Yoan Hucksley," I whisper. "A root-raised country boy and the best damn gunner I've ever seen."

Down it goes in a single gulp. This stuff's meant to be sipped after a meal, not thrown back, and my sinuses sting from the liquor as it slides down my throat.

I set the first cup upside-down on the counter and lift the second cup.

"To Private Hoa Dai. You could have been my sister. I was more courageous with you nearby."

The liquid burns my throat and belly, filling the numbness inside with a welcome warmth I haven't felt since before Gerin-Bue.

Fact: With Nauru.

The second cup is placed upside-down next to the first. I reach for the third cup, raising it high.

"To Private Nan Bokay, a loyal and easy-going companion. Your jokes were my favorite."

I toss it back, ignoring the tears sliding down my cheeks and the rawness of my throat from the alcohol. I pick up the next cup.

"To Private Vilissa Ceska. You were the most insightful and hardest-working soldier I ever had the pleasure to meet."

My body tries to reject the potent, sweet syrup because I cough when the liquor hits my tongue. Somehow I manage to choke all of it down. I've only two more cups; what good would it do me to quit now?

Directive: You must stop this behavior.

Who cares? I'm not a soldier anymore, remember?

My voice is scratchy, barely a whisper. "To Corporal Yoan Rommen Nyrie. A most disciplined soldier with the highest honor and sense of purpose."

I drain my cup and lower it onto the counter upside-down beside the others. My stomach churns dangerously in protest, so I take a deep breath to steady myself. A happy, dreamy fog settles in my mind, wrapping me up in a delightful trance - till I realize I'm down to my last cup, the cup I dread most to toast.

Directive: Stop this.

My left arm shakes as I grasp the cup and bring it to my quivering lips.

Stifling a sob, I stumble over these hopeless words, slurring them, my tongue too thick for my mouth. "Here's to Lieutenant Commander Adahi (Metizon) Bashe, the bravest naval officer of the Union and my Osco whose memory I have betrayed because of my foolishness."

I drink, then immediately lift my left arm, signalling the bartender over with a lazy motion of my hand.

The bartender returns and clears the tin cups from the counter. "Anything else, soldier?"

Fact: You've had enough.

"Six more," I say, sliding my finger in a crooked line across the counter.

He obliges, as is proper protocol.

***

Fact: You've consumed twenty-one cups. You've had enough.

Not enough. Not nearly enough.

I pick up a cup, repeat the words.

To Private Vilissa Ceska. You were the most insightful and hardest-working soldier I ever had the pleasure to meet.

I drink, pick up the next cup, and repeat the same damn words again and again and again and again - but none of them are enough for Nyrie or Hucks or Bokay or Dai or Ceska or Adahi, no matter how many times I say them.

I fucked up, Adahi. I'm sorry.

Fact: Sorry can't make this right.

Shut up.

"Santi?"

I almost leap out of my barstool at the sudden mention of my name. My drink sloshes out of my cup. It oozes down the countertop and onto my lap.

I shake the liquor off my fingers. "What the fuck are you doing?"

The man beside me says my name again with a gentle voice. He's right next to me, so close I can smell the outdoors on his clothing and the shaving soap on his neck. It's all so familiar, as though I should know this man. I squint at him, trying to place him, scrutinizing his coveralls and dark hair and kind eye and the scars on his face -

Fact: It's Nauru. The Freeman.

Fuck. Nauru!

He says my name again. He asks me when I got in. He asks me how long I have been in this bar.

Directive: Answer him with something intelligible.

Observation: He is waiting.

I need to finish my drinks - just two more drinks.

Fact: You're stalling.

"*To Corporal Yoan Rommen Nyrie -* "

He tells me it's time to leave.

" *- A most disciplined soldier with honor and purpose.*"

He says my name again and clasps my right shoulder. I balk and shrug it off.

Fact: This Freeman will help you.

No one can help me.

"Go away, Nauru."

He drops into the seat next to me. *Please,* he says. He wraps his arm around my shoulder and tugs me away from the counter. He offers to take me home or to his home - it does not matter.

I can't go home, not with Adahi's box waiting for me.

Directive: You must go home and face the consequences.

I can't go home.

Directive: You must.

"Fuck you!" I wail. I don't know who I say this to. My arm smashes into the row of cups. They clatter to the floor. The spilled liquor drips onto my shoes. I shift in my seat and shrug away from him. "I can't go home. I made a mistake!"

He says everyone makes mistakes. He says he wants to help me. He says he wants me to tell him what I need. He says these words - all of these wonderful words of relief and devotion - but I don't deserve them. I will never deserve them.

"Stop it." I stumble out of my seat backwards.

He reaches his arms out to support me. I bumble back and away. He says my name over and over again. He tries to smile. I recall the way he used to look at me. He pleads that there must be something he can do. He says there must be a way to fix my mistake.

Directive: Be honest with him.

"Go away!" I dodge tables and patrons, desperate for the door. "Don't you see? *Nothing can be done!*"

He follows behind. I force my buckling knees to keep walking. I stumble over my feet. His strong hands catch me from falling. He says he wants to help me.

No one can help me.

Fact: He will try, whether you want him to or not.

"I didn't do what I was supposed to do. I didn't open the box." I wave the stump under his nose. I mix words and sobs. "I didn't follow proper protocol. I didn't even *try.*"

He says he's sorry. He apologizes over and over again. He says he didn't know. He says he never asked because he never wanted to know. He says he never wanted to hear the answer. He opens his arms wide to embrace me. I can't let him. I don't deserve that kind of forgiveness.

Not after what I didn't do.

I shove him away to keep him at a distance. "Go away, Nauru."

He says a Fixer - *another fucking Fixer* - will help. I don't see how. The Fixer at Gerin-Bue said she couldn't Fix what wasn't there. A Fixer here will only say the same.

The deep anguish and hurt in his eye is too much. It's too much. I throw myself out onto the street. I stagger away. "Leave me alone! There's nothing that can be done!"

He calls for me to wait. I keep going. He wants me to listen to what he has to say. I clutch the stump and keep going.

He whispers my name.

CHAPTER TWENTY-TWO

```
    Directive: You must return to your apartment.
    Directive: You must fully process the
consequences of your negligence.
```
As reasonable and logical as my plate's arguments are, I do not listen.
```
    Directive: You must return to your apartment.
    Directive: You must fully process the
consequences of your negligence.
```
Not only do I avoid my apartment, I also avoid the cliffs, the park, the docks, the streets leading to the Freeman Quarter - anywhere that reminds me of Adahi, Nauru, and my old, unbroken life. I spend my days endlessly and aimlessly wandering around while drinking the hardest stuff I can buy. The images bleed into one another. I cannot escape.
```
    Directive: You must return to your apartment.
    Directive: You must fully process the
consequences of your negligence.
```
My plate repeats these demands in a non-stop, angry barrage -
```
    Directive: You must return to your apartment.
    Directive: You must fully process the
consequences of your negligence.
```
- but the guilt and restlessness and disgrace and despair outweighs the nagging from my plate. I steel myself against this chant with a large bottle of liquor, draining it till I'm numb inside.
```
    Directive: You must return to your apartment.
    Directive: You must fully process the
consequences of your negligence.
```
Even what little sleep I need offers no protection against the constant orders and the images of shiny metal boxes stamped with the

Union seal.

    `Directive: You must return to your apartment.`

    `Directive: You must fully process the`
`consequences of your negligence.`

I believe I am doing the right thing - the proper thing - by staying away. My plate is obsessed with bringing me back.

    `Directive: You must return to your apartment.`

    `Directive: You must fully process the`
`consequences of your negligence.`

I know the number of local days I've been nowhere in particular, bottle in hand, too exhausted to cry, too numb to feel, so sorry for myself. I know the number of local days I longed for Adahi's stories, for Nauru's kind smile, for Nyrie's encouragement to keep it together. I know the number of local days I've sat propped up against a stone building in a nameless alleyway at the bottom, the absolute bottom.

    `Directive: You must return to your apartment.`

    `Directive: You must fully process the`
`consequences of your negligence.`

"Hey. Plate-face."

Her voice hovers above me, gruff and severe, but with an underlying kindness. I blink again and again till my eyes focus on the scars upon her face and the cross, drooping eye. I've seen this Freeman before.

She bends down to meet my eye. "What a state you're in."

In a sudden burst of clarity, I recall her. The party. The red dress. The stone stairs. The scowl. "Anma?"

"Nauru's been worried sick."

Shame is sprawled across my broken body, in my tangled hair, on my dirty plate. I cannot hide my recent activities from Anma even though I try.

I get up and the world sways around me. I huddle against the wall. "Get lost."

Anma rises next to me, her arms outstretched, ready to catch me if I fall. "No way, plate-face. I'm not leaving without you."

She reaches for my arm but I slap her hand away. "You don't care about me. Why are you even here?"

"You're right. I don't like you, plate-face." Her features remain careful and measured, but the resentment in her eye disappears. "But Nauru does."

Though I've been eluding him, I am quite desperate for news of Nauru. "How is he?"

Anma's stiff smile freezes upon her face. She leans against the building next to me. "He has the whole Freeman Quarter looking for you."

"He does?"

"Yeah." She shrugs. "He was never a very good listener."

At the realization that she knows of my outburst at the bar, I stare at the bottles of liquor on the ground. Seven. There are seven bottles. "Where is he now?"

"At your apartment, waiting for you."

"Has he been there long?"

"Ever since you've been doing this foolishness, plate-face."

Groaning, I slide down the building and bury my face into my knees, my good arm cradling my shins. What's left of my right arm comes up automatically, completely useless.

"You've got to go home," says Anma. Her voice contains both concern and exasperation.

My forehead weighs against my knees. "I can't."

"Sure you can." She drops to the ground next to me and settles her hand on my right shoulder. I flinch at her light touch but I don't edge away. "You know how I know?"

I don't look up, I don't answer.

Anma keeps going anyway. "Because you have Nauru waiting there for you. And he'd do anything for you."

She rubs my back. It feels strangely pleasant to have her fingers there, channeling her support - however small and forced it is.

"Nothing's going to be exactly the same anymore, Santi, but it's going to be better than you think it is because he'll help you through it."

I look up, into Anma's clear blue eyes. "Did he tell you what I did?"

"He said he wanted you back." Anma's hand perches on my shoulder again. "So I went looking."

Her words knock me back into reality. I recall the nasty, hateful words and the swearing. I recall the whisper of my name on Nauru's lips as I stomped away. My head sags between my slumped shoulders.

Behind Anma's wistful smile are her own feelings of love and loss, but she speaks with urgent honesty, as though we are becoming friends. "Nauru loves you. He's not going to leave you, not when you need him the most."

"Really?" I tilt my head to get a better look at her face. When her brow isn't furrowed, her features are actually quite friendly.

"Yes!" Anma huffs. "Look, plate-face, Nauru has been sitting outside your apartment for two local weeks. He hasn't worked, he's barely eaten! All he wants is to know you're okay."

Tears brim my eyes and I wipe them away with the back of my left hand. "But I'm not okay."

"No. You're not okay, not yet." Anma rises and extends her hand out to me. "And maybe you'll never be okay. But I promised Nauru I'd look for you and now that I've found you, I've got to take you home. I'm not doing this again."

The tension of the situation drops. I giggle and Anma joins in.

"Come on, plate-face. Let's go."

I grasp her hand and allow her to help me up. She settles an arm around my shoulders. This time, I do not flinch.

"Nauru's going to be so relieved to see you."

Anma coaxes me down the path, half-carrying and half-leading me back to my apartment. A one-armed soldier and a Freeman. Together, we must be quite a sight.

Nauru is waiting at the gate with my pack, exactly as Anma said he'd be. Thank all That's Good! I had left my bag at the bar and had been too embarrassed to retrieve it.

Once he spots us, his face - so lined with exhaustion and worry - sighs in relief. He wraps me up into his arms and clutches me, afraid to let me go, afraid I will disappear again. The faint, familiar scent of bath soap and washing soda lingering at his collar causes me to sob. Tears streak my dirty, filthy face.

Fact: You have finally returned.

Directive: Now you must begin to process the consequences of your negligence.

I feel Nauru's lips crinkle into a smile. "Thank you, Anma."

I don't hear her response.

The gate to the apartment building swishes open and Nauru hoists me into his arm. I let him carry me inside, all the way upstairs, all the way into my apartment. He lays me upon my cot and settles down next to me, combing my hair with his fingers and singing a nameless song with an unrecognizable melody into my ear.

I fall asleep well before the second verse.

CHAPTER TWENTY-THREE

Nauru's chest rises up and down in a rhythmic pattern, his breath slow and deep and heavy. He's still fast asleep, his fingers entwined mid-stroke in my snarled hair.

I twist my head to peek at the window. Tol's light colors the walls in a bright, mid-morning gold.

How long have I been sleeping?

Fact: You've been asleep for two local days.

I snuggle closer to Nauru, my fingers curling around the collar of his dock coveralls, the same ones I vaguely recall from the day I returned, the same ones which are now infused with several weeks worth of sweat and worry. He stirs, but does not awaken.

Will Nauru be fired again because of me?

Fact: You could wake him, of course, in order to find out.

I admire the dark hair tousled across his forehead and the thick growth of his facial hair. Nauru looks peaceful but unlike his usual self - I had always seen him well-dressed, without a hair out of place. As I nestle in his arms and stare at his serene, scarred face with affection, I reach out and caress his prickly cheek before rising off of him. A slight smile tugs at his lips.

It's not easy to balance myself up and over his body with only one arm, but my plate adjusts for my inconsistent movements. Somehow I get up without waking him.

At the strange rustle under my feet, I pause. Empty cracker wrappers litter the floor next to the cot and surround a neatly-folded bundle which sits on my nearby pack. I quietly ball up all of the wrappers within reach and stuff them into my pocket.

Poor Nauru. Even Cyborn hate these things.

Among the familiarity of my things, my apartment, my old life, I had not expected to feel so safe with Nauru here. I had anticipated being overcome by restlessness and anxiety, guilt and failure even with his presence. Lowering myself to the floor, I remove my kepi and jacket from my pack and open it, dreading what I will find - or *not* find - inside.

The silver corner of a metal container glints in the sunlight. Nyrie's box is still there, nestled inside my extra shirt.

I exhale, relieved. There would have been no forgiveness, no coming back had the box been missing or stolen or damaged. Clearly, I had been lucky.

Lucky enough.

Drawing the box into my lap, I bring myself to the edge of the cot and trace the Union symbol with my thumbnail. The plate within this box is the only thing left of Corporal Yoan Rommen Nyrie.

"Santi?" Nauru's hand rests on my right hip and I start.

"I didn't mean to frighten you," mumbles Nauru, removing his fingers from my thigh and tucking his other arm under his head to prop himself up.

I look from him to the box. "I was just..."

"Is this Adahi's box?"

"No, it's...it belongs to one of my crew. Corporal Yoan Rommen Nyrie. I've been tasked with taking it to his Osco and...." I pause, uncertain of the right words.

Seeing the doubt on my face, Nauru straightens himself up and swallows me into his arms. The sturdiness of his chest against my back, his smell - I close my eyes and drink in his comfort.

"And...I don't know if I am able to do it."

"Of course you are, Santi." Nauru's chin rests on my shoulder. His stubble tickles my ear. "I'll go with you, if you'd like."

The thought of Nauru's presence at my side relaxes me. "You will?"

"You don't have to do any of this alone. I will be here for you - as much or as little as you want me to be."

Anma had been right. With all that had happened to me, with all of the terrible choices I made, Nauru is choosing to be with me.

I place Nyrie's box on the windowsill next to Adahi's. I lean into Nauru, resting my left hand on his crossed arms. "I would appreciate that."

Nauru's lips press against the junction between my neck and shoulder and I laugh at the tickle of his scratchy cheek.

"Hmm...this could present a problem," he teases, his voice hushed and low as his lips trace an imaginary trail along my neck and shoulder. "I suppose it's time for a shave. And a bath."

I reach up to touch his beard and smile, my first real smile in two local weeks. "I need one even more than you do."

"Nonsense." His hand cups my cheek and tilts my face to meet his, grazing his lips against mine. "You're perfect."

"But I'm not perfect." All of my actions over these past local months have proved that.

"You're perfect for me." Nauru's lips curl upward into a teasing grin. "Even when you callously giggle at me when I share my deepest emotions."

I make an indignant face at him. "I've never done that!"

Nauru laughs and climbs off the cot. When he extends a hand to me, I accept and he pulls me up. Then he fetches the clean shirt from my pack and holds it up so that I can slip the stump through my right sleeve.

"Normally, Santi, I wouldn't suggest this, but..." His eyes flit to my face and then back to the top button. "...but it's about noonday. The Freeman bath should be empty, or mostly empty. I'd be happy to ask Anma and Udarah to help you bathe."

He stops, nervousness in his eye, worry on his brow, unsure if he's crossed some kind of line. Avoiding my eyes, he quickly attends to his own fastenings on his coveralls. "But only if you want me to."

I'm tempted by his offer. At this time of day, the Cyborn baths will not be private. The pool will be packed with excited children who will question me about my missing arm. There will be lines for the shower stalls, too, so I will be standing in the open, unable to hide from anyone.

"Wouldn't I be intruding?"

"After everything you've done, you are always welcome in the Freeman Quarter." Nauru shrugs. "Besides, you'll be with Udarah and Anma. No one will argue with them."

"Okay. Yes. I'll go with you, but first - " I pull the wide-toothed comb from my pack. "Will you braid my hair? I can't do it myself."

"Of course." Nauru takes the comb and settles behind me. He starts to pull it gently through my hair but the comb snags long before he gets through the entire length. It surprises me more than it hurts.

I wrench away. "Ow!"

Nauru leans in, ready to lecture me on the importance of mindful drinking and of sleeping in a bed with a familiar glint in his eye. "Sit still, Santi. You wiggle like a child."

He tries to draw the comb through my hair again but it only snags.

This will take all day.

"Just braid it. Please. I don't care if it looks silly. Just plait it and tie it up."

Nauru sets the comb on a nearby table. "Are you sure?"

"Yes."

He does as I ask, braiding my tangled hair into one long plait and then pinning it into a bun at my neck. It does not look so terrible when he is done.

Everything used to be so easy. Now I'll have to relearn it all. Will I ever be able to braid my hair or fasten my shirt by myself again?

`Fact: Your functionality is what I make of it.`

True. I cannot live in a pit of self-pity forever. My plate has already started to make adjustments to my balance and coordination, even distributing weight into my right shoulder so that it feels like I have a right arm.

But I have no right arm. It's all an illusion, nothing more than a trick.

`Fact: It is more than a trick. It is your new functionality.`

Nauru's voice brings me to the present. "You'll want a change of clothing."

I recall the clothes in my closet - all woolen, all blue, nothing but military wear. I will need to shop for some new clothing soon. It is a prospect that fills me dread.

"I don't have any civilian clothing."

Nauru's lips meet my forehead. "Don't worry. I'll ask Udarah or Anma to bring something for you to wear."

"That's kind, but - "

Nauru's eye pleads with me to humor him, just for today. I bite my tongue to keep from finishing my thought and nod once. Relying on Nauru, on Anma, on Udarah - relying on anyone! - makes me feel even more helpless than I already am.

We walk arm-in-arm to Anma's apartment, unconcerned about the opinions of others. I make eye contact with everyone I pass, daring them to find fault in walking with a Freeman and - even worse! - *touching* a Freeman. Five in seven people avoid my stony stare, but no one says anything to contradict what I am doing.

Anma is home and agrees to take me to the Freeman baths, as well as lend me a towel and a change of clothing.

"I didn't know I needed a towel," I say to Nauru when he rejoins me at the bottom of the stone stairs.

"The Freeman baths are more...rustic than the ones you're used to. We don't have a lot of the perks you'd expect to see at a Cyborn bath," Nauru explains. He glances at the door of Anma's building. "I'm going home to get my things and to find Udarah. Anma will be out in a few tics. Just wait for her here."

"Okay."

"I'll meet you on the steps of the Freeman bath later, though you won't recognize me without my beard."

I take the bait. "How will I find you, then?"

Nauru's smile crinkles his scars and hides his eye. "Just look for the handsome, freshly-shaven Freeman."

The door opens and Anma exits with a large bag slung over her shoulder.

Nauru offers her a kind smile before taking his leave. "Thank you, Anma."

"No problem." She grins after him and then turns to me. "You ready, plate-face?"

Those once-hated words have become affectionate and I nod.

She pulls the bag's strap higher onto her shoulder. "C'mon. Let's go."

Anma and I walk side-by-side through the Freeman Quarter in silence, but it isn't tense or angry. It's contemplative, reflective, and even friendly. The reservations we once had about each other are gone, replaced by a tentative friendship.

Her loyalty and stubbornness would have made her a good soldier, I reflect as she waves to a man across the street. He waves back and flashes her a brilliant smile.

We turn a corner and head toward a crumbling building with peeling green paint. Udarah sits on the cracked stone steps waiting for us, a large bag on the step beneath her. She greets Anma with an embrace and me with a large, toothy smile.

"Nauru's already inside. He said to take as long as you need to. I promised him you'd be in good hands," Udarah says.

I respond with an apprehensive smile. "Thank you."

The inside of the building is set up exactly like the Cyborn one I usually attend, with two large rooms containing shallow pools in each - one for the men and the other for women and children. Unlike the Cyborn bathhouses, the ceiling is open to collect rainwater. There is no other lighting, no lockers, no changing stalls, no heated pool. The tiles on the floors and walls are chipped, dingy and in desperate need of a cleaning. It is just as rustic and empty as Nauru claimed, but I don't care about my shabby surroundings because we are the only people here.

"Do you need help undressing?" Udarah asks me, setting her bag onto a nearby bench. Her voice echoes throughout the room. Anma puts hers on another bench and reaches in to grab two towels - one for her and one for me - and a bar of soap.

No soap - another amenity found in a Cyborn bathhouse.

She tosses one of the towels to me. I catch it easily in my left hand, pleased that my reflexes work just fine.

"I can manage," I say, noting the ease with which I am able to unfasten my shirt.

Is fastening my shirt just as easy?

Fact: It will be. It is your new functionality.

I vow to attempt it the next time I wear something with so many buttons.

My undershirt is a bit harder to remove. I have to wrestle it clumsily up over my head and around my braided bun. I don't have any such problems with my pants or shoes.

Anma and Udarah are already undressed and in the pool by the time I finish, shrieking and giggling at the temperature of the water. I step into the pool and inhale sharply, shivering. The water is freezing.

How can they stand it without a plate to make the necessary adjustments?

"Sit with us, Santi!" Udarah waves me over. "I'll wash your hair."

I wade through the pool to Udarah. She picks out the pins and carefully undoes Nauru's braid. With gentle persistence, she combs out my hair with her fingers, untangling the snarls and - to my great embarrassment - pulling out sticks and brambles and other evidence of my outdoor adventures. When she's finished, she lowers the back of my head into the water.

"Here," Anma says, handing Udarah a bar of soap. It smells like Nauru's skin.

Her strong fingers massage my scalp and neck and I sink into the compassionate caress of her hands. How strange it is that I don't shy away from another's hands like I used to! It is as if I no longer have a reason to avoid another person's touch.

I've changed more than I intended to by befriending Nauru.

Udarah's voice cuts through the silence. "I'm going to rinse your hair now, okay?"

"Okay."

She dips my head back into the water and runs her fingers through my hair till all of the soap has disappeared. With a little nudge of my shoulders, she lifts my head and twists my hair into a high knot.

What will I do when I have to wash my hair again? I can't invite Udarah or Anma to the Cyborn baths and I certainly can't return here, even at Nauru's insistence or permission.

Fact: There is only one logical solution to this problem.

I must cut my hair, short enough so that I can take care of it myself.

I don't want to cut my hair. It's been long for most of my life. I've loved playing with it, plaiting it, but the thought of all of the maintenance - washing it, brushing it, braiding it - overwhelms me.

Fact: This single action will help you live more independently.

Therefore, I will do it.

"Udarah?"

"Hmm?"

"Will you cut my hair?"

Udarah can't disguise the shock on her face. Even Anma seems uncertain of my request.

"Oh, Santi." Udarah strokes the back of my head. "Are you sure?"

"Yes."

"How short?" asks Anma.

"Short. As short as Nauru's, if you can manage."

The two of them exchange nervous glances.

"I know it's an odd request, but my life's gotten so...complicated. Things are harder than they used to be." I glance at the stump. "Does that make sense?"

Having extracted her plate, having lived a life without a plate, Udarah understands. She turns to Anma.

"Get my razor."

Anma retrieves the razor and a couple of towels from Udarah's bag while Udarah directs me to a spot near the edge of the pool. She hauls herself out and wraps herself in the towel that Anma has fetched for her. Anma spreads the other towel on the floor next to Udarah and gives her the razor.

Udarah ties my hair at the base of my neck and pauses. "Are you sure, Santi?"

"Do it." There is no regret in my voice. I close my eyes and control the nervous excitement of my breath.

THE LAST FULL MEASURE OF DEVOTION

With several quick swipes of the razor, the weight of my thick hair is gone, the ends skimming the tops of my shoulders. Udarah slides the razor through chunks of hair and with every *scratch-scratch-scratch* of the razor, I am shaped into someone new.

Finally, Udarah lowers the razor. "Okay, Santi. I'm done."

I open my eyes. A mound of hair is piled on top of the towel. My jaw drops at the sight.

"Was it too much?" Udarah takes in my expression and explains in a hasty rush of words. "I didn't think a cut as short as Nauru's would look right."

There aren't any mirrors on the walls, so I study my reflection in the pool. As I run my fingers up the back and through the sides, I am pleased to find no tangles or knots. My hair falls at an angle around my face, high in the back and low in the front. It's a no-fuss haircut that I'll be able to care for by myself.

"It's perfect. Thank you."

Udarah gathers up the hair and razor. Anma helps me out of the pool and into a towel. The three of us sit together on the closest bench, sharing the heat from our bodies. Their teeth chatter as they share a funny story about the last time they visited the baths.

As they remove the clothing they brought for me from their bags, however, I frown slightly. For an unknown reason, both chose to bring me dresses. Though I am grateful, it's clothing I rarely wear.

I rub the fabric of Anma's blue dress and then Udarah's green one. Both fabrics are soft, but Udarah's dress is less form-fitting and would be more comfortable to wear. "It's been awhile since I've worn an everyday dress."

Anma winks at Udarah. "Too bad, plate-face. Nauru likes dresses."

"You brought these on purpose, didn't you?" I realize. "Both of you?"

They giggle. I choose the green dress and giggle, too.

"Here. I brought these for you, too." Anma takes some light undergarments out of her bag and offers them to me. "They're lighter than your woolen ones."

I shrug into them and then Udarah's dress. The skirt barely covers my knees and the short sleeves expose the stump. It's odd to wear clothing so unlike me, but a part of me is excited. I am a civilian now, liberated from my soldiering life and reborn into a different person.

"I'll give it back once I get some civilian clothes," I promise.

Udarah shakes her head and waves her hand dismissively. "Keep it. It looks better on you than it does on me." Then she reaches into her bag and pulls out a pair of slippers. "These go with the dress."

There are no words to properly thank them for their kindness. I simply slip on the shoes and bundle up my shirt and woolen pants.

Anma and Udarah towel-dry their hair and dress hurriedly, Anma in the blue dress that had been meant for me and Udarah in a set of plain denim coveralls, identical to Nauru's.

`Speculation: Udarah works at the docks, too.`

How does she manage those heavy crates on her own?

The wet towels and dirty clothing are packed into the bags.

We find a clean-shaven and freshly dressed Nauru outside on the steps, exactly where he said he would be. His eyes widen and his jaw drops when he sees me, but he quickly regains his composure.

"I can't leave you alone without these two causing mischief, can I?" Nauru frowns severely at Anma and Udarah, but his eye shines. They laugh.

I giggle, too. "Apparently not."

Udarah brushes the hair from my eyes and wraps her arms around me. "Please visit us again, Santi. You're always welcome in the Freeman Quarter."

Anma embraces me as well. "Take care of yourself, plate-face."

Nauru walks me home. He does not say anything more about my haircut or the dress.

"Will you stay?" I ask him when we reach the gate.

"Only for a little while. I need to see if I still have a job."

"I'm sorry."

"Don't be. There's always something else I can do."

He follows me through the gate and up the stairs. Halfway to my apartment, my downstairs neighbor calls out to me. He studies Nauru with suspicious disdain.

"Santi? Can I talk to you? Alone?"

"Go on up. I'll be right there," I tell Nauru, who continues up the stairs and into my apartment. The door swishes shut behind him.

With Nauru gone, my neighbor is no longer so reluctant to speak. "Santi, I need to talk to you about the..." He breaks off, unsure how to phrase his next words. "...Freeman situation."

I recall my aunt's hateful words at the clothier's and this time, *this time*, I will not allow myself to cower when such obvious prejudice slaps me in the face. I will not allow myself to back down when my neighbor speaks ill of Nauru.

I blink at him innocently. "What *Freeman situation*?"

My neighbor frowns and lowers his voice, speaking slowly and carefully so that I can't possibly misunderstand him. He points upstairs, as if to further illustrate his point. "*That* Freeman. He's been hanging around outside and it's making people in the building very...nervous."

"It's not *my* problem their views about Freemen are distorted. It's *their* problem."

The man's eyes bulge in disbelief. "Santi, be reasonable. He isn't supposed to be here."

"He's always welcome here. He's a dear friend. Besides, there is no specific clause in my lease stating Freemen are not allowed here. I've checked."

My neighbor folds his arms across his chest. "If he continues to come here, the other tenants and I will contact management and have him removed. By force, if necessary."

"Go ahead. But you'll have to get through me first."

He shifts from one foot to the other uneasily, in obvious conflict about whether or not he should pursue the matter any further. Now he knows with certainty I will not be intimidated by him, by the other residents, or by management. He knows with certainty I will not be swayed by false niceties. And he knows with certainty I will not admit that I am in the wrong.

My neighbor mumbles a few more words I cannot catch and ducks into his apartment.

Nauru is standing just inside my apartment. I am barely through the door frame when he tugs me into his arms and crushes his lips against mine. My body melts delightfully against his.

Speculation: He heard the exchange in the hallway.

When we separate, Nauru runs his fingers through my hair. "Your haircut suits you."

"That's not what that was about, was it?"

Nauru responds with the intensity of his happy gaze and I sag into him again, curling my left arm around his neck, drawing the stump against his side. My hand dips below his shirt collar and my fingertips gently draw the same light, playful lines over and over against his skin.

I relish in the crisp scent of his shaving soap and the touch of his smooth cheek. "I can't stay here. I'll be kicked out."

I sense Nauru's lips twitching into a soft, upward arc. "Then move in with me."

"Really?" I break away. "Are you certain?"

Nauru doesn't say a word. He merely closes the distance between us, pressing his body against mine and leaning in to put his mouth upon my own.

CHAPTER TWENTY-FOUR

Finding a new place where we could live comfortably was surprisingly simple.

Less than a local week after the confrontation with my neighbor, Nauru spotted a couple moving out of an apartment above a dock merchant's office. He inquired about renting the space and the owner, Faarin, an ardent Abolitionist and Freeman supporter, was happy to show him around, despite Nauru's curious circumstances. Faarin even promised to replace the broken window and apply a fresh coat of paint on the walls as a gesture of welcome. A day later, our things were packed into boxes and crates. Extra furniture was sold or given away.

Today, we're ready to move in.

Faarin meets us outside the apartment the morning of moving day and greets Nauru with some words of welcome and a quick shake of his hand. I catch Faarin slip a notched, metal item into Nauru's hand which Nauru then slides into his coveralls. He does it so effortlessly, as if the exchange never took place.

While Nauru, Lem, and Gailen carry the few pieces of furniture upstairs, Faarin helps me shuffle boxes into the arms of waiting friends to be hauled upstairs and stacked against the wall. For a Cyborn, Faarin is unusually talkative and warm to everyone. He asks general questions about my experiences in the military without fishing for details. Meanwhile, I want to know what Nauru had been given.

Once the last box is handed off, Faarin offers me a polite smile. "It's a good thing Nauru spotted the empty apartment when he did."

"Oh?"

"More young people are moving in around here. They like the docks. It's full of adventure."

A strong truth. As a child, I spent hours at the front window of my parents' office watching the interactions between Spacers. I deduced what goods these men and women transported and where they had arrived from, my only clues the look of the crew, the ships themselves, and the contents of the crates - if the boxes were opened. My mother, who was quite good at the game, often sat next to me and provided me subtle hints by pointing out the clues I had missed. Till I was much older, it had not occurred to me that she already knew 87% of the passing Spacers and recognized a fair number of their ships with nothing more than a glance.

Faarin turns to leave. "Let me know if you need anything else, Santi."

My words tumble out before my plate can chastise me for being forward and rude. "I saw you give something to Nauru. What was it?"

`Observation: You are being forward and rude.`

Faarin chuckles. "It was only something to get him into the apartment."

His odd, cryptic answer confuses me. "But how can a lump of metal open a door?"

At my expression, Faarin laughs. He waves his hand as he walks away. "Ask Nauru. He'll show you how to use it."

It doesn't seem possible that a little piece of metal is able to open a closed door. Life is full of surprises, isn't it?

`Query: Don't you mean contradictions and inconsistencies?`

I trek upstairs, resolute to study the door, but it swishes open in one smooth motion when I approach and refuses to close till I step through. I walk out again, this time pausing on the top step several paces from the entrance. The door is not fooled and upon detecting my plate, the entry remains unblocked. Disappointed that the door will not reveal its secrets to me, I lean against the frame as Nauru discusses some recent changes at work with Lem and Gailen.

When I finally catch Nauru's eye, he thanks the two for coming.

Gailen reaches for his hat and steps to the door. "I guess that's our cue to leave, eh, Lem?"

Lem finds his jacket among a stack of crates and shrugs it on. "It's nice to have you back, Santi. Udarah wants to know when you'll be ready for visitors."

"Soon, I hope." I motion to the disaster of furniture, crates, and miscellaneous items stacked wherever there happened to be room and grin wearily. "But not too soon."

Lem shakes Nauru's hand. "Well, let us know if you need anything."

Nauru winks at him. "As long as Udarah brings dinner, she's welcome to visit whenever she wants."

"I'll let her know." As he passes me in the doorway, Lem stops to give my hand a little squeeze. "See you, Santi."

"Farewell," I say. I have gotten used to the words which at one time had been so foreign.

The door slides shut behind them, leaving Nauru and I to stare at each other from across the room.

"So," Nauru begins, navigating piles of stuff to reach me.

"So," I respond, arching my back and shifting my body nearer to his.

Nauru edges closer and trails his fingers up and down my left arm. "It's all a bit surreal, isn't it?"

"A bit. But I enjoy finding out more about you."

He leans in to nibble my ear, his breath hot and intense. "And what have you discovered so far?"

I reposition my body so that the wide collar of my dress drifts down my arm, exposing my bare shoulder. "A lot, actually."

"Really?" Nauru draws his tongue down my neck with gentle laziness. "Name one thing you've learned about me since moving in."

I slip my fingers into his pocket and produce the shiny piece of notched metal. "That you use *this* to get into doors."

Nauru laughs and shakes his head. Then he takes my hand, crushing the object between our palms, and motions to the door. "Come on. I'll show you how it works."

He leads me into the stairwell and halfway down the hall. The door slides shut behind us. It's now secured - no one is able to enter without the proper clearance.

Nauru points to the door. "Look at the very center. Do you see it?"

I squint, searching for whatever Nauru is referring to, but find nothing unusual. "What am I looking for?"

Nauru's eye twinkles. "I'll show you."

Returning fixedly to the entrance, he points to a tiny slit in the center of the door, exactly where he said it would be. It's so impossibly tiny that a person would completely miss it unless they knew it was there. "Do you see it now?"

"Yes!" I stare in amazement. "Do all doors have those?"

"No, not all. Only the ones both Freemen and Cyborn use in very public places."

"Why?"

Nauru's smile is frank. "Freemen generally go through the back door."

"Of course." With no other words, I am only able to give Nauru a grim smile. Although we have spoken of these inequalities before, I am still uncomfortable with his blunt talk.

Nauru inserts the metal object in the slit and turns it to the right. The door clicks open as readily as if I had been standing there myself. He pockets the notched metal and holds out his hand, beckoning me back inside.

This place is tinier than my old apartment and appears even smaller because of the stacks of crates and our choice pieces of furniture clustered in the middle of the room. The lighting is poor and only one of the windows is brand new, but the fresh paint smell reassures me. Despite the shabbiness of this place, it offers us something we can't get from living in the Freeman Quarter or in my own neighborhood.

A quiet existence, together.

I study the bustle of activities out of the new window. Ships come and go. Freemen unload cargo. Merchants greet business associates. Spacers invite old friends to the bar around the corner for a much-needed drink. It's the perfect place to observe the world around me, exactly as I had done as a little girl.

Distracted by the recollections of my past and the observations of the present, I wrap my left arm around my front, resting my hand on the stump before sliding it to my waist in disgust. My plate calls the stump "new functionality" - an ironic statement at best. My current look is new, but definitely unfunctional.

Fact: You are still functional.

I am nothing more than a broken Cyborn.

Fact: Put together, those two words do not exist.

Nauru steps behind me and encloses me in his arms. His cheek rests against mine and I revel in the familiar touch of his smooth skin, the stability of his body, and his warm breath at my ear during this moment we share together. I brace myself against him, stroking his forearm with my left hand and keeping the stump as unobtrusive as possible. My body is broken, but my heart is full.

"Shall we unpack?" Nauru asks.

I nod, curious about the contents of Nauru's crates, though I am in no rush to leave his embrace. "Your boxes or mine?"

Nauru shrugs, his arms still secured around my waist. He makes no move to actually reach for a crate and open it. "You choose."

"How about one of your boxes? I want to learn some of your deep, dark secrets."

I feel his lips twitch upward into a smile against my shoulder. "Hmm. I seem to have left all of those boxes at my old apartment." Then Nauru releases me and pretends to frown. "How unfortunate."

I pretend to pout. "But surely you'll tell me one? Or two?"

Nauru entwines his fingers with mine as he considers my request, his thumb rubbing against my palm, his expression unreadable.

Observation: He is taking your demand seriously.

I made no demand -

But my plate has become more adept at interpreting Nauru's strange looks because he simply asks, "What do you want to know?"

"I didn't - "

"Ask me anything, Santi."

I pause. *What do I want to know about Nauru that I don't know already?*

Directive: Ask him about his aspirations or fears. Ask him about his failures or successes.

Before I can stop myself, I blurt out the only thing I truly want to know. "What's the worst thing you've ever done?"

"*Worst* is completely subjective." Nauru pulls me away from the window but does not let go of my hand.

"Stop being such a lawyer. What did you do?"

Nauru grins wickedly at me and studies his stack of boxes. When he finds the one he's looking for, he drops my hand and chooses a small box which he sets on his *dining table* - whatever that is.

Fact: A table meant for dining.

Whatever that Is.

He rummages around inside, removing a few scraps of fabric and smoothing them out onto the table. I scrutinize them, these square pieces of white flax with beautiful embroidered designs around the outside, but I don't understand why these little pieces of fabric are so wicked. I glance at Nauru, who raises his eyebrows, urging me to keep searching the patterns. His reaction suggests there's something more in these treasures I don't yet see.

"Look closer at the embroidery."

Fact: There is nothing but stars and the lines connecting them.

Nauru wouldn't ask me to look closer if nothing was there.

`Fact: There is no logic to a Freeman's`
`request.`

I don't doubt Nauru, but there's nothing on this fabric I recognize. "What is it?"

"What do the patterns look like?"

I study the lines and stars and finally understand. I recall Adahi weaving his stories, the stories that connect the lines between the stars in the sky above the cliffs. "Constellations."

"These are sky symbols." Nauru's eye sparkles. "They are patterns that Cyborn Abolitionists paint onto their doors or around their windows to show their home is a safe place for Freemen. Spacers sympathetic to our cause will use these symbols to fly Freemen to safe locations around the system."

But there's more to these sky symbols, something in them Nauru finds humorous, something he has not yet told me. "That's nice, but there's more to it, isn't there?"

His smile broadens and his eye twinkles. Nauru rotates the fabric so that the design is inverted. "Some sky symbols have a double meaning if they are turned backward or upside down."

"Like?"

Nauru points out three tiny stars with bent points. "Turn it this way and it means you're on the right path, the path to safety. When it's turned upside down, it means someone is unable to perform...sexually."

When I do not say anything in response, Nauru quickly folds up the scraps of fabric and shoves them back into the box. "I often sewed these designs into clients' clothing when I worked for the clothier as a joke for other Freemen to enjoy. The crueler they were to me, the more patterns I sewed into the embroidery."

"People like my aunt."

Nauru does not avoid my eye but his gaze is guilty. He acknowledges his actions were hurtful, even if his clients deserved it. "Yes."

There are no words to describe the conflict I feel over this revelation. While I understand Nauru is only trying to assert power where there is none to be had, it is wrong to label another person, just to amuse others.

"What would you have embroidered in my aunt's clothing?"

For four tics, Nauru struggles over how forthcoming his answer should be. "If I knew she was your family, I would not sew any of these designs into her clothing no matter how rotten she was to me - out of respect to you."

I curl my fingers around his in a gesture of forgiveness. "Let's say she wasn't family, she was another terrible customer. What would you sew for her then?"

Nauru brings my hand to his mouth and presses it firmly to his lips. "I would sew her an upside down Union symbol."

"Which means?"

"She is a closet Confederate sympathizer and Freemen should spit at her back when she passes them."

"Oh, Nauru. That *is* terrible."

"You asked." Nauru strokes my cheek with one hand and circles the other around my waist, drawing me into him. "I am not so kind now, am I?"

I blush at the gentle pressure of his hand at my hip and the intense stare of his brown eye. "I'd still hold your hand."

Nauru's hand slides from my cheek to my left hand. He hums a nameless tune as we sway back and forth. I don't know what to do with the stump so it just hangs there. I do not yet know how he feels about my missing arm and I am afraid to touch him with the stump because I am afraid he will recoil.

Fact: You know him better than that. You are afraid to admit you have new functionality.

Stop saying that.

Directive: Then touch him. He will not cringe.

Now you're the expert on Freemen?

Directive: Touch him. He will not cringe.

I rest the stump on Nauru's shoulder. "Is this okay?" I ask, my voice trembling.

Nauru's response is firm, decisive, and unpatronizing. "Of course, Santi. I'd never shy away from your touch."

While my plate is smug with the satisfaction of being right, I nestle into him, committing his words, his pine-scented shaving soap, and his acceptance into memory.

"Santi?"

"Hmm?"

Nauru breaks away and sits on the dining table, still holding my hand. His smile has become stiff, frozen. "There is one thing I should have told you about earlier. It's about Anma."

I tighten my grip on his hand. "She loves you."

"Yes and I thought I loved her, too, but...it didn't work out."

All I really want to know is whether or not the same thing will happen to us, but I put on my kindest, most sympathetic face. "What happened?"

"Remember when I told you Freemen don't have one person in their life - that sometimes they may have connections with multiple people?"

I nod, recalling the face I made upon hearing that revelation.

"Sometimes when Freemen finally guess right, they may decide to form a union."

"Like Lem and Udarah."

"Exactly." Nauru squeezes my hand. "Anma wanted to be exclusive but I couldn't. I didn't love her as much as she loved me. So I left."

"But..." I pause. How do I ask a question I would rather not know the answer to? "Will the same thing happen to us? Will you someday end it?"

"The connection I felt with Anma didn't grow like I hoped it would, so I ended our relationship. I don't envision that happening to us. I see our connection growing stronger and stronger with time. Perhaps someday we'll be bonded as Lem and Udarah are."

`Fact: You already have an Osco.`

Yes. I had an Osco.

`Fact: You have an Osco.`

I have Nauru.

Nauru takes a deep breath and offers me a kind smile. "I wish I could say with certainty that we will always be together, but everything about our relationship is just a guess, Santi."

`Fact: Cyborn do not guess.`

Though Nauru and I have a natural understanding and appreciation for each other and a bond that transcends the social relationship we are supposed to have, there is no certainty in his explanation. "I am not satisfied with your answer."

Nauru laughs. "Neither am I, but it's the best I can give you right now."

Despite the uncertainty, despite my guilt over Adahi, right now Nauru is the only one I want. I lean in, grazing my lips against his.

CHAPTER TWENTY-FIVE

In less than one local week's time, I receive advertisement upon advertisement for cybernetic limbs.

[Our artificial arms are worn freely and gracefully as soon as they are surgically attached!]

At first, these announcements are little more than an amusing coincidence; the government just promised all broken soldiers a credit toward the purchase of one of these limbs. All of these companies must be working overtime to sell their products to mangled ex-soldiers like me.

[Our limbs provide the greatest degree of comfort and durability, enabling our clients to return to the rest of the world without betraying their loss.]

As I am inundated with more and more messages, I begin to consider what life would be like with a cybernetic arm. Though I cannot quite believe that a miracle limb would solve all of my problems, I still toy with the idea of a new arm, wondering which would be more noticeable: a tech arm or no arm at all?

[This widely celebrated artificial arm is so natural in appearance as to defy detection.]

As the days progress and the advertisements don't stop, the enchantment of a cybernetic arm wears off. The constant commercials make me feel inadequate and cross, and remind me of the darker side of this war, the part I recall with a stunning regularity I do not care to admit.

It is the part in which I cannot reconcile my entire crew had been suspended for nothing more than a series of bloody days which resulted in fields of blue and grey bodies - 48,632 bodies, at last count.

It is the part in which I survived a war, celebrated not for my sacrifices but for my expendability. *I* had protected Nova Penn from invasion. *I* had sent those damn Secesh running back to the Inner Colonies. *I* had lost an arm for my part in this war, but the brutal truth was it doesn't matter what I did at Gerin-Bue. There are always more men and women to recruit, either willingly or not, in order to continue this war for duty and for patriotism and for the United System. What did my sacrifices mean, then?

It is the part in which I am exhausted from balancing the person I was and the person I am now. Having witnessed some harsh truths and endured some terrible things, I am not the person Nauru fell in love with because I am not the same Santi I was before.

It is the part in which I am so obviously marked as different, leaving the system to process my appearance however they choose: by looking past me, by staring at me with confusion or pity, or by offering unkind and insensitive remarks. I shut out the world, watching from the safety of my apartment window.

It is the part in which I recall having made promises, promises I have not kept. I had pledged to keep Adahi's memories alive through our Merge, but I had not. I had also agreed to deliver Nyrie's plate to his Osco, but I have not.

I do not tell Nauru about the cybernetic ads or my time spent at Gerin-Bue or any of these dark thoughts. I don't know how he will react. I don't know he will understand.

Instead, I brood over it all, letting the tension and frustration build inside me while I stare out the window day in and day out, watching the world move along without me.

Till one day, Nauru arrives home from the late shift. He drops his lunch pail on the table and steps behind me, wrapping his hands around my left arm and the stump.

I recoil, shaking off his hands and maneuvering away. "Don't touch me."

This outburst doesn't phase Nauru. He immediately backs away, keeping his hands where I can visibly see them. "I see you've had a bad day. Do you want talk about it?"

I suck in my breath and clench my fingers into a fist. "You won't understand."

There are no words to describe the howls of the approaching rebels; the shrieks of the slingers; the thick smell of ozone; the black ground, slick with blood; the detached limbs and body parts piled onto a hill; the loss of my crew. Without an oscos, there are no words for the images I've recalled today from my perch at the window.

Without an oscos, there is no way to share my recollections with Nauru.

Nauru grips a chair and smiles encouragingly. "I won't understand, but I am able to listen. What's bothering you, Santi?"

He's too kind, too patient, and in my blinding anger, I am desperate for him to hurt as much as I do. "Shut up, Nauru! You're always trying to clutch my hand! Leave me alone!"

Nauru's voice struggles to remain level. He's been wounded by my surprise attack. He wants to retaliate, but he's too stubborn to let me pick a fight with him. "Please, Santi - if you won't talk to me, then talk to Udarah. Talk to Anma. Talk to Lem. Just talk to *somebody*."

I snatch up my jacket and shrug it on, then head for the door. Nauru's by my side in an instant, but he makes no attempt to reach for me, no attempt to touch me. He remains respectful of my space, though I see the worry in his eye.

"Where are you going?"

I don't answer. I push past him, fleeing down the steps and through the busy docks. From the apartment doorway, Nauru's panicked shouts ring in my ears, torn between allowing me space and following me to who knows where.

[All of our limbs are guaranteed to completely compensate the loss.]

It won't matter where I end up...

[An amazing 92.67% of our clients resume their vocations after our patented implant surgery.]

...I will be pursued by the distractions in my head.

Fact: You need a means of escape.

I need a drink.

Fact: Another means of escape.

There are plenty of places to meet my need at the docks.

As a child, I knew how to sneak a treat from my parents' merchant friends. I knew where all the best climbing crates were stacked. I knew all the Spacer songs - including the ones with dirty words. I knew all the corners at which I could sing those songs in the hopes that someone passing by would drop a few faithslips my way.

But since my enlistment, since my travels throughout the system, since Adahi, since my parents' suspension, the docks became less and less important. Now, here I was, in a place at one time I knew so well, yet a place so obviously changed, remodeled, expanded, modernized.

Wishing I brought my kepi to hide my face, I rush around a corner and plow into three drunk Spacers ambling away from the row of bars and clubs along Drinker's Paradise. One laughs and salutes me while the other two swear at me good-naturedly, warning me to watch where I'm going.

With its rowdy patrons and free-flowing alcohol, Drinker's Paradise was absolutely off-limits as a child, but I was fascinated nonetheless. I liked to watch the people walk in and stumble out two or three local hours later, sometimes propped up by a friend or two. I did not understand what was so terrible about people having a good time; now I know places like Drinker's Paradise are not meant for good times, but meant for losing oneself in a Full Frontal escape.

I trudge along the walkway, glancing at each of the bars as I pass, deciding which to enter. I settle on the bar at the end of the block - The Fly-By. Unlike the other businesses in the row, it's nondescript, dim, and quiet. The door opens as I approach. I hover in the doorway.

`Query: Is this what you want?`

I don't know what I want.

There's no one in the bar, no one except for the bartender stacking empty glasses under the counter, whispering to a woman wearing navy coveralls and a ratty olive-colored vest. She sits in the seat opposite him, four empty shot glasses lined neatly between them. Their conversation is intimate, private, and I feel as though I am intruding. I am about to retreat when the woman nods for me to join her.

She taps her index finger on the counter as I approach and I am certain she's a freighter because Adahi did the same thing whenever we went out. "Drink's on me, soldier."

"Thanks." I fumble into the seat next to her and pull my blue jacket closer to my body to hide the stump.

The bartender slides the shot in front of me and raises an eyebrow at the woman, but she only waves him away and refocuses her gaze on her cup. "Where were you stationed?"

"I was with the 73rd Nova Penn. We went all over the Inner Planets. Virgis, mostly."

"Hear about Gerin-Bue?"

My left hand grasps the tiny glass. "I was there."

She tilts her head, her gaze watchful and steady. "No wonder you need a drink."

I like her direct, gruff talk and her country accent that's even stronger than Hucks's. It puts me at a strange sort of ease. I gulp down the shot and wince as it burns my throat. "Where are you from?"

She swallows her shot, too, then signals for the bartender to pour us another round. "Vori. Left as soon as I could. You?"

I kick back the second round. "Nova Penn. I stayed here."

She drops more faithslips on the counter and taps it again. The bartender pours her another and is about to do the same for me when I reach out with the stump to cover the cup. I quickly pull it back and settle my left hand over the cup, but it's too late.

Catching a glimpse of my missing limb, the woman offers me a funny little smile. "Any regrets?"

I stare at her, dumbfounded. "I don't know."

Fact: You were hasty in admitting you liked her direct talk.

"Gonna get one of those new cybernetics?"

"I don't know." I shrug irritably and scoot the cup closer to the bartender. He pours me another.

The woman traces the rim of her own cup with her index finger and passes me a sidelong glance. "Seems like they'd be a good idea for someone who needed it."

"Why do you care?" I ask, deflecting her comment.

My mouth drops open as the woman twists her head, revealing canyon-like scars across her plate. She ignores my stare and simply turns over her cup, lining it next to the others. "Been there, done that. Just like you, soldier."

Observation: With that much damage to her plate, it is not possible for her to function.

As a Cyborn, you mean.

Statement: As a Cyborn, yes.

"How?" I study the profile of this unlikely kindred spirit. "How did it happen?"

"Minding my own business at Osarro." The woman's mouth twists into a wry smile. "Could blame a whole lotta people, but in the end it ain't a story worth telling, really."

Observation: Her explanation elicits more questions than it answers.

She's allowed her secrets.

"But you're...fine?"

"Yeah, everything works. Just looks like I went through a ship's engine." She tilts her head, her cool eyes on the stub. "You?"

"Slinger explosion." I did not expect to find the words so readily. I haven't been able to tell Nauru what happened to me yet.

We settle into silence. I sip my drink.

She still functions. And as a Cyborn, too.

`Fact: She received new functionality. As did you.`

The woman plays with her row of cups. "Get the impression you hain't been so fine."

The words which came so readily a few tics ago have been lost again.

The woman folds her arms across the countertop and looks away, allowing me my privacy. She knows my hurt and my pain. She understands my predicament because she has lived it, too. "Was it worth it?"

Since my return from Gerin-Bue, I have been asking myself that very question.

Was it worth it?

I left my crew, my arm, my means to Merge with Adahi, my self-worth at Gerin-Bue. I sacrificed the life I knew for something else entirely, but I do not know what my new life is supposed to be. I have no direction and nothing to drive me. I have no goals and no aspirations.

"I'm lost," I choke out. "I don't know what to do now."

The woman motions to the bartender for another drink. This time I let him pour me one, too. "You don't let a Freeman lead a ship."

`Speculation: This sounds like a phrase Adahi would have said.`

I reach for my cup and pull it close. "What does that mean?"

"Do what you're good at." She tips back her drink and gives me a hard stare. "Believe it or not, I was a soldier till there came a point I couldn't be a soldier anymore."

"Your...accident?"

"Nah. My principles." She taps the bar and offers me a knowing smile. "Tend to get into a lot of trouble for my damn principles."

Despite feeling sorry for myself, my lips twitch in response.

The woman swallows her drink. "We're all lost at some point, soldier. Best to suck it up and move on."

"I've made some bad choices."

She shrugs, unimpressed by my issue. "So what? We all make terrible choices. Own up to it, then let it go."

"I can't let it go."

The woman snorts and places her cup on the counter upside-down next to the others. She fishes through her pockets for a few faithslips. "Then find a way around it. Solve it. Don't let it define you or your sense of self-worth."

"But I can't do anything about it. It's too big."

She tosses the chips on the countertop and passes me a sympathetic half-smile before stepping away from the bar. "Well, do *something* about it. Your problem ain't gonna go away on its own."

The woman brings two fingers to her forehead in salute. "See you, soldier."

"Yeah. See you." I watch her leave, her hands in her pockets and humming.

Without a word, the bartender collects the empty cups. He offers me another but I shake my head. For nearly a local half hour, I sit there, alone, staring into my glass at the amber liquid, the drink unappealing. As much as I do not want to admit it, the woman is right. None of my problems are going to disappear on their own, especially without an effort on my part.

Is there a way to Merge with Adahi after all?

Fact: Such a means does not exist.

With more determination than I've had in five local weeks, I leave the bar, my head held high. My drink remains on the counter, untouched.

It does not matter if such a means does not exist - I have to try.

I owe that much to Adahi.

When I arrive home, Nauru is pacing the apartment. At the swish of the door, he rushes over, but catches himself before embracing me. His uncertainty is endearing and my heart softens with affection.

"Santi!" His voice cracks with worry. "Are you all right?"

My jacket falls to the floor as I sink into him, my left arm and my stump wrapping around his back. His arms envelope me in a tight embrace and as our cheeks touch, I feel his jaw soften.

"I'm so sorry, Nauru. I shouldn't have left like that."

When we finally part, Nauru sets a troubled gaze in my direction. "Santi. I know you're suffering. More than anything, I want to be able to help you."

"I know."

He takes a deep breath, reluctant to say his piece, but acknowledging the necessity of his next words. "I meant what I said - you should be talking to someone about what happened to you, even if it isn't me."

I hesitate. Since my return home, Nauru and I had been in silent agreement to never bring up the confrontation at the tram station. Now, of course, I had to.

Through dry lips and hoarse throat, I find the words. "I have to talk to Adahi."

Nauru hangs his head and stares at a spot on the floor three paces away. It's clear that my problem has been weighing on him, too. "When we met at the park and at the cliffs, I meant only to be polite because it seemed you needed someone to talk to. I had not intended to keep you from Merging with your Osco. I'm sorry to have played a part in this."

I attempt a forgiving smile. "It's not your fault. It's mine. I didn't use the time given to me for its intended purpose."

"But I never asked. As the local weeks went by, I should have asked." His fingers brush strands of hair from my eyes. "Had I known, I would have left you to your purpose."

"I could not have let you do that, Nauru. You've become an important part of my life."

"I would have understood." Nauru clutches my left hand, his face bright and optimistic, but I catch the doubt in his eye. "How will you Merge with Adahi?"

"I don't know yet," I say with as much conviction as I am able to muster. "But I have to try."

CHAPTER TWENTY-SIX

I am glad Nauru has a double shift at work; I do not think he would appreciate the amount of swearing I've done today.

Once I have calmed from my latest attempt, I pick up Adahi's plate and curl my fingers around the cold, curved metal - exactly like the fifty-seven times before.

The fifty-eighth attempt, however, is no different. There's nothing - no smell of static, no words of encouragement, no Adahi. I squeeze his plate harder with my left hand in frustration and disbelief.

What would you say to me? Right now, what would you say?

Fact: Adahi would tell you to stop trying so hard, then illustrate his point with a story.

I groan and set his plate back into its box with disgust.

My plate's right. Adahi always knew what to say and exactly how to say it. He never once gave me a piece of bad advice in all the standard years I had known him. We shared an oscos once - surely I could figure out what he would say to me right now as he witnessed my struggle.

I gather up his plate and turn it over in my hand.

What would you tell me, Adahi?

Fact: Adahi would say, "You are different; therefore, do things differently."

I screw up my face. I thought I *had* been doing things differently. I had held Adahi's plate to my own, between my hand and stump, and even touched his plate to my heart - anything and everything I could think of to initiate the Merge, but still, nothing.

Fact: You lack two hands. The Merge will not initiate without two hands.

I frown sullenly. "I don't have two hands. Just two feet."

But what if...

Fact: It is a ridiculous thought.

With a pounding heart and a trembling hand, I sink onto the floor. I take a deep breath, close my eyes, and gently place his plate between the soles of my feet.

When I open my eyes, Adahi is crouched in front of me, wearing his freighting coveralls and the fringe vest with the Union pin I so admired. His long hair is braided and his brown eyes twinkle. He is exactly as I recall.

[*Adahi?*] I whisper in utter disbelief. He's here. He's actually *here* with me.

After fifty-eight failed attempts, I hardly believe it worked! It *worked*!

Adahi reaches for my left hand and as his fingers entwine with mine, he knows everything - of my failure to Merge with him, of my return to the front, of the loss of my crew, of my missing arm, and of Nauru. With a single touch, he knows it all.

[*Santi. You are forgiven.*]

My Osco's words are soothing, understanding, but they are words I cannot accept.

Adahi's lips twist upward in a crooked smile and he runs his fingers through my hair. [*Why so hard on yourself?*]

I have no words to describe my guilt, my shame, my embarrassment. Tears stream down my face and I choke out a sob, undeserving of his absolution.

He tilts his head to the side and leans in close. [*You are my Osca, my one and only. I will always forgive you, no matter how many times you are wrong.*]

Adahi says this with his usual directness, with the words I have wanted to hear since my return from Gerin-Bue. I blink back tears as I exchange the rush of affection I felt as he spoke my name, the oneness I felt when we were wholly bonded through our oscos, the completeness I felt during our time together. Without any words of my own, I apologize for disappearing. I apologize for finding myself in Nauru's arms.

[*Does this Freeman make you happy?*]

I blush and the words rush out. [*I enjoy his company very much.*]

[*Then don't apologize, Santi - never apologize for finding happiness. We often find peace in ways we least expect.*] Adahi settles next to me and I rest my head onto his shoulder, snuggling next to him. He cradles my hand against his heart. [*Be happy, even if you can't be happy with me. It's the only thing I've ever wanted for you.*]

[*How can I be happy when I've changed so much?*]

Adahi's thumb rubs against my fingers. [*You're still here, Santi. That's what matters.*]

[*There's so much I can't do anymore - and what I can do isn't nearly as easy as it used to be.*]

[*True, but surely you've noticed that your plate is able to account for your failing abilities.*]

I recall my successes and sigh. [*Yes, some of them.*]

[*Then do what you can now. Learn the rest later. You have time to take the rest of your breaths, my Osca. Don't burden yourself with self-pity.*]

It is that word that stirs in me the only memory of Adahi's I want to know. [*Adahi?*]

[*Yes?*]

[*Tell me her story.*]

Adahi's grip on my hand tightens, as though he means to protest like he always did when I asked him to tell me Setta's story. After a lengthy pause, he clears his throat. [*You will not like this story. It is not like the others I've told you.*]

[*I will learn this story through our Merge sooner or later. I would much rather hear it from you.*]

For several tics, we cling together. When Adahi speaks, it is with great reluctance. [*Once walked a woman of many talents. Many spoke of her kindness, her intelligence, her bravery. Her name was Setta and she was like you, I think.*]

I give him a little smirk.

[*Setta lived in a time of drastic change. Her people were forced into endless migration from one planet to another. They had been displaced by the ones who had crossed many systems and chose to settle in the Nomads' territory. Her people tried to protect their children from conflict with these invaders, but eventually, there was nowhere left to go.*]

Adahi pauses to control the edge in his voice and the grimness in his eyes. [*They decided the Nomads were unfit to raise their own children in the ways of their ancestors. Setta and her brothers and sisters were taken to new camps, far from their families. They were taught to become new people.*]

I shift my face toward Adahi. He does not look at me. [*That's terrible.*]

[*One day, Setta and her brothers and sisters returned, for they were* not like the invaders, but they had become unrecognizable to their kin. Who were they now?]

Adahi grits his teeth and I fear he will stop. [*Keep going. Please.*]

[*When Setta saw the tears of her people and realized she would never be one or the other, she could not bear it. She tore herself right down the middle. She became two people: her past and her present. Setta could never be the person she used to be, nor could she be the person she had become.*]

My breath leaves me in a sudden rush. [*Like me.*]

He nods. [*Like you. Once, you used to be a proud and dedicated soldier; you were my dear and devoted Osca, but now, there are other possibilities before you. How should you exist now? Who is it you want to be?*]

[*I don't know.*] I find myself unable to respond to Adahi's questions. [*I can't return to the army and even if I were able, I don't want to go back. What else do I do?*]

[*That is your struggle, your burden.*] Adahi frowns, though he gazes at me with fondness. [*Promise me you'll someday become the person you choose to be. I don't want you to suffer the same fate as Setta.*]

[*But how do I redefine who I am? Where do I even begin?*]

Adahi shrugs. [*There's no one way to find yourself, but you will, my Osca. You are determined. You are a fighter. You will find yourself someday.*]

Fact: He is right.

My eyes well with tears. I close them, basking in the touch of his heavy hand in mine and his familiar energy surrounding me. [*Our time together was too short. I wanted another fifty standard years with you.*]

Adahi's half-smile is faint. [*I will always be your Osco, Santi. Remember that.*]

[*My hands are empty without yours.*]

[*As are mine.*]

[*Adahi...*]

I'm alone. Adahi has disappeared, the only evidence of his presence the odor of thin static in the air. With care, I rise from the floor and place his plate back into its metal box, then close the lid.

Gratitude. Contentment. Forgiveness. I am lighter now, unburdened by Adahi's compassion and filled with renewed hope and courage.

I am no longer lost. I have direction. I have Adahi's guidance.

Without jacket or shoes and grinning like a fool, I race through the docks toward Nauru's platform, dodging Freemen and Cyborn alike and ignoring their protests as I sprint past. I spot Nauru laughing and joking with Lem and other Freemen I do not know, swinging his lunch pail at his side.

His eye meets mine. For a tic, he's concerned, worried - then he sees my triumphant smile.

We race to each other. He catches me in his arms and swings me around, narrowly missing an unsuspecting man. I clutch onto him, my arm secured around his neck.

"Nauru! I did it!"

CHAPTER TWENTY-SEVEN

Before Nauru, before Gerin-Bue, I was only a soldier, only an Osca to Adahi. I led a simple life, one in which I asked few questions. I blindly accepted the status quo because that's how it was supposed to be.

Now that I am able to see the path so clearly in front of me, I no longer accept the labels that exist within the system simply because that's how it has always been. I no longer see Freemen as broken because I am broken, too. I am no longer a Cyborn because I am broken, but I still possess a working plate, unlike a Freeman. What is my label? How am I defined?

To the Abolitionists, it does not matter if I am broken or not. I attempted to exterminate an immoral ideology which suppresses 12.76% of the Nova Penn population. I am a hero.

To my own family, I am no longer a Cyborn. I am disgraced for choosing a Freeman over my own flesh and metal.

To the civilian population, I am an oddity - my body broken, but my plate intact. No definition of what I have become exists.

To acquaintances, I am only a broken ex-soldier, deserving of pity and sympathy, but not always receiving either one.

To Freeman friends like Anma and Udarah and Lem, I am like them, but not like them. We are broken, yet not broken, entities.

To Adahi, I will always be his Osca, his one-and-only.

To Nauru, he is mine and I am his. I do not have a proper label for him and he does not have a label for me, at least none that convey what we are to each other in a satisfactory way. Nauru claims he does not need a label, but he no longer recalls Cyborn know their world best through the distinct labels we are assigned. It is not so with Freemen - their labels are adaptive and fluid.

How do I define what we are so that other Cyborn understand?

I cannot call him my Osco - a Freeman cannot be an Osco or Osca because they cannot share an oscos. Besides, Adahi is my Osco and always will be.

I cannot call him my love - Cyborn do not understand the concept of love. Affection, yes, but not love.

What a burden it is to properly name someone!

I don't know what else to call him.

Thus, Nauru remains nameless - well, mostly nameless.

While Nauru is at work, Adahi and I speak daily. We have initiated the Merge and I have enjoyed our time together so much I feel foolish for not doing so when I had the chance. My plate reminds me that had I initiated the Merge with Adahi, I never would have met Nauru and I would not be the person I am today. For this reason and this reason alone, I am grateful I did not follow protocol.

As we've Merged, I have indulged very little information about Nauru to Adahi, and, following my cue, Adahi has allowed me that privacy. He has never specifically asked about Nauru and always refers to him as "your Freeman" whenever he is mentioned in our conversations. It is a label that works for our purposes, yet a label I would not have chosen for Nauru on my own.

Since both of us have been officially discharged, we bond over what we did during our absences from each other. He relays images and funny stories of his naval adventures and I recall images of the battles at Fick's-Bue and Gerin-Bue. I speak of them as much as I am able, always falling back to a touch of Adahi's hand when I don't have suitable words to express myself.

Everyday, Adahi tells me I can't keep running from my duty.

I know exactly what he is referring to.

[It's been six local weeks since you've returned,] Adahi hints. [What of Nyrie's Osco? Doesn't he deserve the right to Nyrie's plate?]

I know bringing Nyrie's plate to his Osco is the logical course of action. I know it's been cruel of me to have denied him the right to Nyrie's plate for so long. [Of course.]

[Then let him.]

Like every day we've had this discussion, I nod without commitment.

Today, however, instead of immediately fading away, Adahi sighs. [If you will not listen to me, Santi, then talk to your Freeman. He will say the same thing.]

I balk. [How do you know?]

[*He is quite logical, for a Freeman.*]

[*He used to be a lawyer.*]

His face screws up in dislike and I laugh. [*Your choice of Freeman is questionable.*]

Adahi fades from sight. I return his plate to its box and close the lid. [*Until tomorrow, my Osco.*]

Considering Adahi's stern words, I stare out the window and watch a group of Freemen hauling crates and large boxes onto a medium-sized freighter. Nauru isn't with them; he works at a dock three platforms down.

Nauru had not broached the subject since the day Anma brought me back to my old apartment, though he had agreed to accompany me to Nyrie's home whenever I chose to deliver his box.

`Fact: He is simply following your lead.`

In disgust, I turn away from the window. Six local weeks have gone by. I have not yet kept my promise. Nyrie's box is here, tucked safely away in a drawer. Have I not learned anything about keeping my word?

I slide my fingers over the top of an end table and a drawer pops open. I remove Nyrie's box and run my fingers over the lid. There's a warmth to it I had not detected before.

I made a promise to you, Nyrie. It's time to see it fulfilled.

The box vibrates in agreement.

When Nauru returns home, he greets me warmly, pressing his lips to my forehead, but his brow lifts when I don't return his smile.

Nauru pockets his key and sets his pail on the dining table. "Is something wrong, Santi?"

I fix my gaze on Nauru and fight back the tremor in my voice. "Adahi says I shouldn't be holding onto Nyrie's plate anymore. He says you would agree with him."

Nauru leans against the table and puts his hands in his coverall pockets, choosing his words with great consideration. "I don't disagree."

`Fact: Always the diplomat.`

I carry Nyrie's box to the table and place it next to Nauru. "I know he's right. It must be done."

"But you are afraid."

I exhale and reach for the bottom of my stump with my left hand. "Delivering Nyrie's plate means I'll have to face what happened there, but I am not certain I am able to do it."

Nauru removes a hand from his pocket and trails his fingers up and down along my spine in a gesture of comfort and encouragement. "Do you really want to know what I think?"

"Yes."

"I think Adahi's right. Nyrie's Osco has waited long enough." He cradles me against him. "But ultimately this is *your* decision, Santi. If you need more time, I will go with you whenever you are ready."

"Tomorrow," I say into the warmth of his cheek. "Let's go tomorrow."

***

"Last one," says Nauru, his fingers fiddling with the final fastening of my uniform, the one under my chin. With his help, I had spent all of last night scrubbing out the stains and repairing the holes. My uniform was not perfect, but proper enough to fulfill this one last promise.

"How do I look?" After going so long without an identifier, I feel out of place wearing it again.

Nauru brushes a piece of lint off my jacket. His hand trails down my arm and squeezes my left hand. His fingers are warm and sturdy wrapped around mine and my heart flutters in my chest. "You're doing the right thing, Santi."

I push away the nervousness sinking into my belly and pick up Nyrie's box before I change my mind. While I am grateful Nauru offered to come with me today, I am still uncertain of what is to come. I do not know how I will be received. I do not know what is expected of me. I do not know anything about Nyrie's Osco.

The hopper we arranged to take us to Nyrie's home is uncertain about us, too - a Cyborn who travels so willingly with a Freeman - and only agrees to our destination when the fare is doubled. I don't argue. The only other way to that part of the city is by tram, and trams - though cheaper - remind me too much of slinger fire.

Nauru and I don't speak in the hopper. He stares at me, offering looks of reassurance when I breathe out too heavily. I stare at Nyrie's box and rehearse what I am going to say to his Osco, but nothing I prepare sounds exactly right. All of my words sound like poor excuses.

The hopper stops in front of a neatly-groomed home in the outskirts of the city. I study Nyrie's house, the one he and his Osco lived in together. It's the perfect size for two people, with a red brick foundation and unchipped yellow paint, large windows in the front and flower-shaped stained glass inlaid in the front door, a grey cobblestone path leading to the porch. The outside greenery is overgrown, but not enough to blemish the happy scene.

I'm about to order the hopper to turn around when Nauru reaches for my hand. "You can do this, Santi."

I study the house for any flaws I am able to exploit. I nod at the windows and raise my eyebrows at Nauru. "Is anyone home? It's dark inside."

Nauru shrugs. He will not let me retreat now. "Let's check anyway. We've come all this way."

As soon as we exit, the hopper zooms away, relieved to be rid of us.

Nauru and I walk up the cobblestone pathway. Nyrie's box is heavy in my hand. I drag my feet. I'm sweltering in my woolen clothing though it is not hot today.

When we reach the halfway point between the street and the front door, Nauru stops and adjusts my kepi. "Do you want me to accompany you to the door?"

I balance Nyrie's box between my side and my stump so that I can trace the delicate parade of sky symbols on Nauru's new green vest. He's been embroidering it for several local weeks. "This vest is my new favorite."

`Fact: You are avoiding the reason you came.`

Nauru brings his lips to my forehead. "I'll go with you if you want me to. All the way to the door."

I eye the house again. "I know."

Like a good soldier, Nauru stands there, waiting for my direction, waiting for me to give him an order. In this moment, he is like Nyrie, dedicated and strong, fearless and loyal.

Pull it together, soldier.

They were Nyrie's words.

`Fact: Today they are yours.`

"No." I turn toward the door. "I've got this."

"Yes." Nauru's fingers graze my chin and fall down my arm to my hand. He strokes the back of my hand with his thumb. "You do."

Squeezing his hand once, I pass Nauru an uneasy smile, then trudge down the rest of the path and up to the door. Shifting my weight from one foot to the other, I glance back at Nauru. He only nods, urging me on.

I bring my stump to the door in one muted knock, but there's no answer, so I beat my stump against the door again, this time a little louder.

The door opens just wide enough for me to see a sliver of a man's face inspecting me through the crack. He glowers at me as his eye roams over my blue woolen uniform.

"What do you want?" His rough voice is haunted from irregular use.

"I am Sergeant Santina (Bashe) Metizon. I served with your Osco at Gerin-Bue." I clear my throat, grasping for any of the words I strung together in the hopper. "He was part of my artillery crew."

"My Osco?" The door widens slightly. "Yoan, you mean?"

"Yes. Corporal Yoan Rommen Nyrie. This is his home, isn't it?"

The man throws open the door and advances onto the porch, into the sunlight. He is older than Nyrie by several local years, with silver-grey hair and wrinkles along the outsides of his eyes and mouth, but the creases at his left eye are far more pronounced than his right.

`Fact: Nyrie's Osco is a Freeman.`

Dumbly, I stare at the scars at his left temple, but my confusion doesn't register with the man - he hardly acknowledges it. He studies his yard and then the street in hopeful anticipation. "Where is he?"

I lift the metal box etched with the Union symbol, the one containing Nyrie's plate, and extend it to him. The man's face drops into the same forlorn expression I wore so many local months ago when I received my own Osco's plate. With trembling hands and without any words for me, he accepts the box, tears flowing freely down his cheeks.

"Nyrie - Yoan - was one of the bravest soldiers I knew - disciplined, with the highest honor and sense of purpose," I say, but my words sound hollow, empty, without conviction.

Clutching the box, the Freeman shuffles to an aluminum porch swing and pats the seat next to him. I remove my kepi and sit. He sets Nyrie's box between us and rests his hand on top. There is nothing but the creak of the swing and the man's sniffles as he slowly pulls himself together.

When he finally speaks, his voice is empty and his expression blank. "What happened to him?"

This is the moment I've dreaded since bringing Nyrie's box home. I stare at the ground, hating the awful words I will speak.

But I am too slow - the Freeman glares at me. His mouth twists into a frown and blinks away his tears. He does not understand why I hesitate to tell him - why I won't tell him - though it is obvious I had shared a moment with Nyrie before his plate had been packed into a box.

`Fact: You made a promise.`

I made a promise and I intend to keep it.

I force away my nervousness and doubt. I am here, bound to my word to Nyrie. Unclenching my sweaty hand and setting it on my knee, I turn to the Freeman. "You really want to know what happened?"

The Freeman wrings his hands together. "Yes. I need to know."

I recall Nyrie at the top of Ginger Hill, his blue uniform flawless and shining with brass buttons. I recall taking his hand in greeting. I recall his stiff smile, though his eyes were pleased I made it through the city.

"After my...accident, Nyrie pulled me from the earth and rubble. He carried me to the Fixers and returned to his position on Ginger Hill. The next morning - the third day - he was transferred to another crew on Rust Hill."

I recall Nyrie's uninspiring words about the new crew he had been assigned to. I recall the proud gleam of the row of slingers shining in Tol's morning light. I recall the line of rebels approaching in the distance.

"The Secesh attacked the hill, sending showers of cuff fire into their ranks. Nyrie and the other soldiers returned their own bombardment of slinger fire."

I recall Nyrie's watchful eyes fixated on the row of rebels, intent and alert. I recall the shrieks above him and the stink of ozone. I recall the billowing haze clouding the bottom of the hill.

"They fired round after round to push the rebels back, their ears ringing from the echo of artillery shot. The rebels kept going, relentless in their barrage. Nyrie and the others ducked from the showers of rock and metal that rained overhead."

I recall the flashes of shrapnel and energy fire that strike from the sky like lightning. I recall Nyrie's pounding ears. I recall the weight of the threader in his hand.

"An errant shot caught a nearby cartridge box and it erupted into an explosion of fire and hot metal. Nyrie and the rest of the artillery crew were trapped in the blast."

I recall the screams of nearby soldiers, their cries blurring into the raging flames. I recall the intensity of the searing heat melting the jacket from Nyrie's body. I recall his attempts to stand without the use of his legs.

"His plate was smashed in. He had lost his legs and an arm. His body was so burned I would not have recognized him without our oscos. It was determined later his injuries were too severe to Fix."

I recall the impassive gaze of the Fixer. I recall Nyrie's burned and shattered body on the cot. I recall his halting breaths.

"We exchanged words and he requested I bring you his plate." My voice cracks as I grip my itchy pants leg at the knee to focus. "And...I agreed."

I fear the Freeman will demand to know what has taken me so long to bring him Nyrie's plate, but he only removes his hand from the box between us and settles it on mine. The heaviness of his hand and the warmth of our physical contact calms me.

Speculation: The Fixer in Gerin-Bue knew of Nyrie's predicament.

Having Fixed Nyrie, having Fixed me, she knew about our odd choice of partners. She knew I would understand.

It was a simple, logical decision for her, but not for me. I had not wanted to take Nyrie's box. I had not wanted to be burdened with the responsibility.

She was right. The Fixer had been right.

For four local minutes, we sit on the bench in peaceful silence, rocking back and forth as we inhale the air heavy with the sweet scent of flowers, both lost in our respective thoughts.

Did Nyrie and his Freeman often sit here together before the war? Did they landscape the yard with rocks and gravel they found at the cliffs? Did they plant the flowers along the walk together?

As though he can hear my thoughts, the Freeman removes his hand, bringing it back to Nyrie's box. His eyes are glassy and sad, reflective and full of tears.

I look to Nauru for a bit of guidance, but he is no longer on the path. *Where on Nova Penn is he?*

Observation: He has asked you a question.

My focus returns to the Freeman next to me. "What?"

"Have you an Osco?" he repeats.

"Yes. He was aboard the *Kaigaa* during the attack on Chule." I peer around a large potted bush with bright pink flowers in an effort to locate Nauru. "He is suspended now."

"I'm sorry for your loss."

But I am too distracted to give a response and glance around the porch swing in the opposite direction.

The Freeman's face shifts into an expression of wariness. "What are you looking for?"

At that moment, Nauru suddenly appears from behind the house!

As Nauru crosses the front lawn to the porch, the Freeman's eyes narrow in distrust. He's ready to order Nauru off his property.

"Forgive me for intruding." Nauru joins us on the porch, his mouth in an apologetic smiles. "But I noticed the garden in back. It's spectacular."

The Freeman is confused. "Do you know him?"

"This is Nauru," I tell him. "He's my...Freeman."

"A pleasure." Nauru extends a hand to the Freeman, giving me a playful glare of contempt at his new label, an added means for Nauru to tease me.

His guard no longer up, the Freeman grasps Nauru's hand in his and shakes it once. "I'm Gan."

The Freeman motions to an empty seat across from the bench with his left hand and Nauru sits down. "I saw a lemon tree back there. I didn't think this was the right climate for citrus."

Gan's thumb runs back and forth against Nyrie's box. "Yoan found a way to keep one growing."

Nauru smiles politely. "Oh?"

Gan chuckles. "Yeah. It's been a real pain in the ass to deal with."

Nauru's eye twinkles. "I'll bet."

Then Gan clasps his hands together and sighs. "I don't know what to do with it all now. I'm not a very competent gardener. I told Yoan what I liked to eat and he grew everything himself."

I've never had an interest in gardens before - even flower gardens at the local parks did not captivate me - but knowing Nyrie had created an area especially for his own Freeman piqued in me an eagerness. "May I see it?"

Gan cradles the box in his hands and stands up, leading us around the front lawn and behind his house. "It's become a bit overgrown since Yoan's left, but I'd be happy to show you."

Nauru takes my hand and passes me a secretive grin as Gan leads us to a large, red gate. He unlatches it and throws open the door. My jaw drops in wonder.

The view is more stunning than the rolling hills of Virgis and more breathtaking than returning home to Nova Penn via transport after a lengthy absence. There are no words to describe this scene, no words beyond *beautiful*, *lush*, and *green*.

From one side of the fence to the other, a jungle of flowers, herbs, and greenery pour out from raised boxes and clay containers. The plants boast a kaleidoscope of colors and dangle an array of swollen fruits - bulging yellow orbs from the well-established lemon tree, shiny purple globes, bright red lumps, yellow and green zig-zag patterned rounds, long navy pods whose ends skim the ground. The air vibrates with insect wings. The air is thick with floral perfume.

Regardless of the time it would have taken to clean under his dirty fingernails, Nyrie would have spent hours out here digging and planting. This place was his sanctuary.

Nauru squeezes my hand. "Isn't it amazing?"

But there are no words to describe what is actually here.

`Fact: This is love.`

This is love in its purest form.

Gan hands us two massive straw baskets he's fetched from under the back porch. "Take as much as you want. I can't eat it all."

Nauru accepts his basket gratefully and stoops to pick the purple globes. I open my mouth to protest, but Gan stops me.

"Please," he says, holding out the basket. "It's the least I can do for you."

I accept the container. "Are you certain?"

"I am grateful you came all this way." Gan's mouth twists into a tight-lipped smile and his eyes shine. "And I would be doing Yoan a disservice if you did not take something home for your troubles."

Mindful of the trailing plants spilling from the boxes, I shuffle toward Nauru who is quietly picking the purple globes from under the fuzzy leaves.

As I approach, he holds one out to me. "These are excellent stewed."

I don't know what he means - Cyborns do not consume nourishment in this way - but I nod as though I do, in fact, understand.

One local hour later, Nauru and I say our grateful farewells to Gan, hefting the heavy baskets filled with enough food for a family of six Freemen. Nauru cannot eat all of this himself; I have already decided to split my basket's contents with Anma and Udarah. I owe them for the kindness they showed me at the public baths.

Before stepping past the gate, Gan positions a potted plant against a bunch of pods which had been tied together with a length of string. It sits precariously on the top of the basket, its golden leaves veined in a shade of pink the exact color of the morning sky.

"These were the first flowers Yoan planted for me. With enough water, they bloom frequently," he says. "I can't think of a better way to remember him."

I offer Gan a warm smile as he grasps my hand. "Thank you."

He and Nauru shake hands again.

We cross the front lawn, our arms weighed down with produce. Nauru whistles a happy tune, but my thoughts are focused on Nyrie and Gan. Their commitment to one another is proof that I cannot be the only Cyborn on Nova Penn who chooses a Freeman as a companion.

    Fact: It is highly improbable at best.

CHAPTER TWENTY-EIGHT

The revelation Nyrie had a Freeman companion consumes me, though no one else is as interested in this discovery as I am. Nauru politely listened to my one-sided dialogue for a local week before tiring of the subject and Adahi simply shrugged and replied that companionship comes in many forms - even for Cyborn, regardless of what our logic dictates.

Although both Adahi and Nauru are unconcerned by my obsession, I continue to process this discovery when I should be asleep at night, wrapped in Nauru's arms, my head on his chest and his fingers tangled in my hair.

Adahi and I existed through an eternal bond, our oscos. When we were apart, we were able to maintain that connection, our link. Nauru and I have no such attachment to one another, no means to contact each other when we are apart. How could I have communicated with him, with no system for sending and receiving tangible messages?

Fact: You do not share an oscos with Nauru; therefore, a message could not have been sent.

But Freemen use symbols and images on canvas or scraps of fabric. Couldn't I do so as well?

Fact: Cyborn do not use symbols and images to communicate.

I could. With practice, I know I could.

Fact: To communicate through such a means is inefficient.

Query: How would one find trusted messengers?

Fact: Civilians are not allowed near the battlefields. Soldiers cannot obtain leave to deliver messages.

But what of the washers, the sutlers?

```
Fact: They must be given the symbols, then be
able to accurately interpret their meanings in
order to pass the message along. It is not
possible. Such a network does not exist.
```

"Nauru?" I ask, tracing the contours of his chest with my fingers and listening for his heartbeat.

"Hmm?"

I tilt my head to look at him. "The sky symbols - do Cyborn Abolitionists like Faarin know them all?"

He shifts his body and rests his chin on my head. "I don't want to speak for Faarin, but like any good Abolitionist he knows they exist."

"Does he understand their meaning - even when they are turned upside down?"

"Surely he knows what many of them mean." Nauru runs his fingers down my spine. "Why?"

"How could I have sent you a message from the march - a message you would have understood?"

He lifts an eyebrow and considers my question, the scenario unlike the typical family dictations passed from Freemen to their distant, exoplanet families by Spacers or couriers. "It's not possible. The usual messengers couldn't get near the front."

"No. No, they couldn't. Not unless they had help from *inside* the lines."

For two local minutes, Nauru runs his fingers through my hair. "You're thinking of soldiers."

"Exactly." I cock my head and peek at Nauru's interested face. "Then the message could be transferred from one trusted soldier to another - Cyborn or Freeman - from all over the system."

"How would your idea work?" There's an underlying excitement in his voice.

I shrug. "I don't know. To be honest, I am not certain it will work."

Nauru sits bolt upright and I find myself vertical, too. He tears open a nearby drawer and pulls out a scrap of cloth and a black stick.

```
Fact: Charcoal, he called it.
```

Nauru leans against the headboard and scratches marks into the cloth, but these marks do not form an image. These strokes are separate images, combinations of dots and lines, waves and shapes. He mutters to himself as he creates row after row of marks, his eyes bright and wild.

I settle next to him, resting my cheek on his shoulder. "What are you doing?"

He presses his lips against my forehead. "I'm drawing out all of the sky symbols I know. I'll ask Lem if he knows more tomorrow morning."

I knit my brows together and frown. "Why?"

"So we can integrate them into your syllabary."

"But I don't *have* a syllabary!"

"Not yet." Nauru's lips meet mine. "Tell Faarin we need to speak with him. Midday tomorrow, if he his able."

"About what?"

Nauru's eye shines. "About your idea. He'll be as excited as I am."

***

Faarin, having no other engagements, comes exactly at midday. After our greeting, I invite him to take a place at the table. He looks confused at my request, but does as I ask.

`Fact: He believes you contacted him about an issue with the apartment.`

Nauru gives Faarin's hand a quick shake, but does not join us at the table. He paces the length of the kitchen, too excited to sit still.

Faarin looks from me to Nauru, then back to me again. "What can I do for you, Santi?"

I rest my elbow on the table and curl my hand around my stump, leaning in toward Faarin. "I have an odd favor to ask of you."

He leans in, so eager to hear my next words he does not say anything.

"Nauru and I are able to communicate when we are together, though he does not have a plate. We are able to use our words and bodies to express ourselves. It is not always easy, but we are able to manage."

Nauru's hand falls heavily on my shoulder and I grab onto it with my own, but my voice does not falter. "I was a soldier. I had to leave, and when I did, our ability to communicate no longer existed. There was no way to tell Nauru what I was doing or where I was going."

`Fact: There was no way to tell him of the misfortunes you suffered.`

Ignoring that dark thought, I press on. "While it is true couriers and Spacers will often deliver messages for Freemen and their families, they are not allowed at the front and within the ranks of the soldiers.

197

Therefore, it was not possible for Nauru and I to send and receive messages while I was away."

An encouraging smile settles on Faarin's face and he nods. "And this favor?"

"Nauru and I have developed a means for people like us to communicate with each other over great distances, but we need people like you to inform other Abolitionists all over the system - especially within the Inner Planets - about it. These Abolitionists would inform Freemen of this new service and also act as a network to connect soldiers with their partners while they are gone."

"I see." Faarin leans back in his chair, tapping the fingers of one hand against his chin. "How will the process work?"

"The exact system has not yet been perfected."

"Understood," Faarin says. "But let's say you had been called to duty and Nauru wanted to send you a message. How would he have done it?"

"Well...Nauru would have heard about a new service enabling him to pass messages to me at the front."

Faarin taps his chin again. "From who?"

"From a co-worker or friend, a Spacer at the docks, an Abolitionist acquaintance - anyone who has heard and is willing to pass information about the network to Freemen and Cyborn who need it. For the purposes of this example, he heard it from you."

"Of course. Go on."

"Nauru would record his message on a bit of fabric using a special, standardized syllabary which compliments the Freeman symbols already in existence. He could choose to speak his message instead and let you translate his words into syllabary symbols."

Nauru hands Faarin the fabric with his marks on it. "This isn't complete, merely a draft."

Faarin flips through the scraps, careful to keep his fingers from turning black. "And then?"

"You would send the message through a network of others - Abolitionists, soldiers, sutlers - who would then send it on till it finally reached me."

Faarin slips the fabrics back to Nauru with trembling fingers. "Next?"

"I'd decipher the message and send one in reply, directly to the original sender of the message - you. You would then pass the message on to Nauru, via words or fabric, whichever had been agreed upon. From that point on, our messages could be sent directly from myself to you."

Faarin gives me a wide smile and his eyes gleam. He is far more excited about the idea now. "How would someone identify your couriers - one of your network operators?"

Nauru pulls a small bundle from his vest pocket and places it on the table in front of Faarin. He unfolds the handkerchief, revealing two fastenings - one metal and the other cloth. Both are marked with the same two-toned nine-squared pattern: the first and third rows alternate between two triangles and one white square, while a dark square sits between two light squares in the middle row.

Nauru's words spill out in an eager rush. "It's an idea similar to the badges of marque the Confederate pirates use. Someone wearing this button or this symbol on their clothing would subtly show Freemen they can be trusted to give or receive messages."

"It isn't a perfect process - there are still a great many questions to answer," I point out. "We will also need to ensure our network is full of trusted individuals who can help vulnerable people and navigate delicate situations."

"I like it." Faarin snatches up the buttons and tucks them into his pocket. "I'll spread the word immediately."

He rises to leave, shaking Nauru's hand and nodding to me, as is customary.

***

By the end of the local week, Faarin tells me sixty-five of his Abolitionist contacts throughout the system have agreed to assist in the network. I am surprised - but pleased - he had found at least one supporter on every planet within the system, given the repercussions of Abolitionism on places like Virgis, Chule, or Auracania.

`Fact: Faarin is a most resourceful individual.`
Absolutely, he is.

The Inner Planets were where soldiers laughed and talked as they marched through the foreign countryside, where battles happened, where Union soldiers faced suspension. In order to send news from home and messages of encouragement, we must have access to the Inner Planets. I was fortunate to have Faarin's connections.

With Anma and Udarah's help, Nauru set to work sewing buttons and badges for each of our new volunteers while Lem, Gailen, and Sim etched the same pattern onto metal buttons. Once those were complete, Faarin sent them to each of his contacts, paying for the shipping with my pension money.

I personally contacted two hundred and seventy-three officers, artillerists, and infantry men and women who I had served with over the course of my many standard years in the Union army and discreetly requested their support. Of those, forty-eight soldiers stationed throughout the Inner Planets were willing to join our cause.

By the beginning of the second local week, three Freemen and one Cyborn approached Faarin, desperate for news of their soldier. Life became a flurry of sending and receiving messages, keeping contacts focused and on task, and sewing more badges. Marching through the fields of Virgis had been less exhausting than this!

Our efforts in only two local weeks time proved to be a good start; however, it was not enough.

We greatly needed a wider network of soldiers.

CHAPTER TWENTY-NINE

I enjoy the quiet walk along the yellow dirt path more than I intend to.

Nauru offered to come with me and though I would have liked his company on this lovely day - our hands entwined as we moved at a steady pace alongside the sweet-smelling fields of grass - I refused. I do not know how Eyron or his parents would react to me bringing my Freeman to their home.

Apart from our time together at the field hospital, I do not know Eyron well, but I owe him a visit for the kindness he showed me and an apology for my rudeness. He had tried to ground me, to recenter me, but I had been stubborn and uninterested, completely consumed by the fear of the unknown and all of the new challenges I would face.

I am no longer the same person I was when I left Gerin-Bue, but am I much different now?

Fact: No. You are not.

Has Eyron faced the same challenges? Has he changed?

I stretch out my hand to touch the tall grasses in the field. The coarse tops tickle my palm and fingers. I eye my stump, envious of his isolation.

Surely there's no one to stare at him here.

Fact: Isolation has its own problems.

I hear a cart behind me and raise my left arm in a friendly wave at the passing driver. The man lifts his own hand to me as he goes by and nods in acknowledgement. Though I am not dressed in uncomfortable shoes or itchy pants or a faded blue coat or my familiar kepi, he knows where I have been.

The man's three paces ahead of me when he pulls on the reins. His cart creaks to a halt. "You off to see Eyron?"

"I am."

He points to the back of the cart which is piled with stacks of pressed, dried grass. "Hop on."

Eyron's house isn't much farther, but I scramble onto the cart anyway. The man snaps the reins and the ancar clicks its mandibles as it heaves forward. The wagon lurches and I grab onto the side to keep from falling off.

As my destination comes into view, the man scrutinizes me from under his floppy hat. "You served with him?"

Not knowing what Eyron's relationship to this man is, I am uncertain about how much to divulge. "We met after the battle."

The man sniffs, and when he speaks, his voice sounds far away. "Lost both my sons out there."

"I'm sorry. This war has been hard on everyone."

The wagon grinds to a halt. I hop off and thank him for the ride. The man touches the brim of his hat and clicks his tongue. The ancar scurries along the dusty path which crosses the hills and valleys in the distance. I watch the dust cloud float away, hopeful the man is returning to the place he shares with his Osca, his one-and-only.

`Speculation: He has no Osca. He has no sons.`
`He is alone, left with only Merged memories.`

I stand at the juncture of the path and the overgrown gravel lane that leads to Eyron's property, wishing for a sudden inspiration, for an observation refuting my plate's claim.

But I have no final argument to make.

I trudge on to Eyron's shabby, two-story stone and mud-packed home, tucked away down the path, though I am far more interested in the smaller, dilapidating stone structures one hundred paces to the southwest, nearly hidden by the barn.

Homes for Freemen.

`Fact: A testament to the changing history of`
`the area.`

Curious about the stone houses, I wander toward them and find two men lifting bales into a large wagon behind the barn. The first is an older man, stocky and serious, with fading reddish hair and moist, brown eyes. The other is young and lanky, with calm blue eyes and a face lost behind his shaggy red hair - a face so familiar I am able to recall every freckle dotting his cheeks.

He knows I am thinking of him because he turns, pushing back his hair and smiling at my approach.

"Sarge!" Eyron waves a hand in welcome.

I catch a flash of shiny metal where his arm should be and I falter. He was so collected at the field hospital, so accepting of what happened to him at Gerin-Bue.

What made him change his mind?

Eyron motions me over to his father. "Pa, this is the Sergeant I was telling you about, Sergeant Santina Metizon. She helped me out of Gerin-Bue."

Without a single word, the older man dips his head, but his eyes speak, thanking me with silent gratitude for guiding his son - his only child - through crumbling buildings and artillery fire when he himself could not.

"I'm gonna show the Sergeant around, okay, Pa?"

Eyron's father removes his hat and scratches his neck, then returns his hat and shrugs. His pace is methodical and steady, as though he has nothing else to do today but move the sweet-smelling bundles of grass from one part of the field to the other. Eyron, however, moves on without permission, heading off behind the barn. I throw a gracious smile in his father's direction and hustle to catch up.

When I am within earshot to Eyron, I motion to his new arm. "You got a new fixture."

With a little flourish, he extends it to me. His cybernetic arm, though comprised of metal and wires instead of flesh and bone, could have passed for a real one. "Yup! Got it two local days ago. What do you think?"

"It's amazing."

"Yeah, I'm a regular machine now!" Eyron laughs as he clenches and flexes his hand. "I had to go into town for the installation. Pa wanted me here, but now he doesn't have to haul all the heavy stuff on his own."

"It works okay?"

With his cybernetic arm, Eyron snatches up his straw hat and throws it into the air, then catches it deftly. His demonstration proves the arm's joints and range of movement are natural, but this new piece will not hide Eyron's brokenness - it attracts far more attention than it deflects.

"It's heavy and clunky, but it runs alright with my plate." In one swift, deliberate motion, he plops his hat askew on the top of his head. "Where's yours, Sarge? I thought for sure you were gonna get one as soon as you got back."

I shrug. Thanks to the modifications my plate made, the familiar weight of my right arm is there, even if my right arm is not. "There hasn't been a need, not yet anyway."

Eyron rights his hat and cocks his head. He knows there's more to this story, but decides now isn't the proper time and proceeds to another topic. "Glad to see you well, Sarge. Crossed my mind more than once to check in on you, to see how you were getting on, but I wasn't certain you wanted to hear from me."

He leads me to the top of a hill fifty-three paces behind the barn. He sits, parking himself against a fence post and with a nod of his head, indicates I should join him. We stare out at the rolling hills blanketed in shades of soft yellows and partitioned by slender rows of black fences. Across the expanse of grassy field, his nearest neighbor's barn resembles a child's toy.

Nauru would like to create this image with his charcoal and fabric.

`Fact: You can describe it to him.`

My words will be inadequate.

`Fact: You can bring him to the country so he can see it for himself.`

Yes. Someday, I will.

Still absorbing the charming scene, I pluck a pebble from the ground and rub it with my thumb. "Eyron, I'm sorry for my outburst on Rust Hill."

Eyron picks up three pebbles and juggles them with his cybernetic hand. "Don't worry about it, Sarge."

"I was angry, so angry about what happened to me. I shouldn't have taken it out on you."

Still tossing the pebbles one after another, he lifts and lowers his shoulders in a quick gesture of easy forgiveness. "We all handle what happened to us in different ways."

I throw my stone away. It lands in a patch of weeds. "How were you able to get past it all so quickly?"

A tired smile falls across Eyron's face. "Truth is, Sarge, I'm still trying to get myself back to the way things used to be."

One by one, he aims for my pebble. The first overshoots the weedy patch. The second falls too wide to the left. The third lands a hand's width away from my stone. Eyron's swear breaks the silence.

I laugh at him.

He joins in, too, but when he sighs, it's sad and lonely. His brows knit together. "Most of the time, it's like I did wrong by leaving and more wrong by coming back." Eyron pauses. "Ever feel that way?"

The faces of my crew flash through my mind. "All the time."

Eyron grasps another pebble and takes careful aim, but it lands with a dull *thud* an arm's length away. He swishes his cybernetic arm and scowls. "Guess I'll have to find a Fixer to get this thing recalibrated."

This discouraged boy questing to be normal again is the *real* Eyron. I like this Eyron far more than that happy-go-lucky mirage from the Gerin-Bue field hospital - he's believable, human. My heart fills with genuine affection for him because he's not a champion or super-warrior. He's finding himself, like me.

I flash him a sympathetic smile and hold up my stump. "It's better than nothing."

Eyron passes me a toothy grin. "Yeah. Better than nothing."

He picks up another stone and flings it down the hill. This time, his pebble knocks into one he had previously thrown in an attempt to hit mine. Satisfied at last, Eyron licks his lips and whistles a passive, sleepy tune. I join in, my words hushed and low:

> *"No more can you recall the burden of your way,*
> *Too short of breath,*
> *Too weary and too worn! Still, we'll know you,*
> *Among the field of blue,*
> *As we gather up the plates of the soldiers good and true."*

We sit in the friendly noises of the sweeping wind and the grunts from the domesticated ancar in the barn.

Eyron turns to me. "You didn't come here to check on me, did you Sarge?"

His metal fingers snap off a long stalk of yellowed hay growing beside the post. He sticks it in his mouth and then rolls his head to look at me, tickling my nose with the end of the grass.

I giggle and wave the stalk away with my left hand. "No. I didn't. I came here because...I need a favor. An unconventional one."

Eyron raises his eyebrows, intrigued. "What is it?"

Fact: You are here for the countless other Cyborn soldiers and their Freemen - for Nyrie and Gan, for you and Nauru.

I do not know how Eyron will react to my request, but despite not knowing, I extend my hand to him. When he grasps my hand, I squeeze my eyes closed. My story tumbles out in a series of images and emotions.

I recall receiving Adahi's box.

I recall meeting Nauru.

I recall ignoring my duty to my Osco.

I recall my growing affection for Nauru, a Freeman.

I recall the return to my crew.

I recall the pain of my brokenness and being discharged from the army.

I recall the shame of my mistake.

I recall my attempt to Merge with Adahi.

I recall returning Nyrie's plate and meeting his Osco - a Freeman.

I recall creating a network of Cyborn and Freemen messengers.

Nothing is hidden from Eyron - not even my many mistakes. I recall my story boldly and without shame. When I am finished, Eyron's face is pale and his hand is slack in mine. He scrutinizes me from under his straw hat and frowns as though he thought he knew me, only to be seriously mistaken.

He has no words.

Fact: This cannot be good.

Eyron scratches his head and furrows his brow. "So, lemme get this straight: you want me to find soldiers who will pass messages to Cyborn soldiers from their Freemen."

"Yes. I need you to contact as many soldiers as you can."

Eyron slips his hand from mine. "I don't know, Sarge."

"What don't you know?" I demand, pressing him for a more specific answer. "You now know how this is a benefit for Union soldiers dispatched all over the Inner Planets. Freemen with Cyborn companions deserve to know how they fare, just as an Osco or Osca would."

But Eyron's face remains doubtful.

"Eyron, please!" I snatch up his flesh-and-bone hand which is now clammy with sweat. "My corporal had a Freeman companion. I had no idea. Though we were good friends, he never told me. I didn't find out till I delivered his plate to his Freeman."

I drop Eyron's hand. "If you won't do it for me, please do it for him. His Freeman would never have known what happened to him if I had not told him."

Without words, he presses his lips together into a thin line.

"Show everyone you contact my recollections in order to explain - I don't care. If I cannot fight for the Union anymore, then I'll fight for something else that matters just as much."

Eyron leans in, uncertainty in his eyes and the frown deepening on his lips. "This matters that much to you, Sarge?"

I draw Eyron's hand into mine again and focus on Nauru, on his enduring struggle for equality. I share his desperate fight with Eyron - the fight that has become mine, too.

"This Freeman matters to me," I say. "Therefore, his struggle matters to me."

"Okay." Eyron's eyes soften in defeat. "I'll pass on the message, but I can't promise anyone's gonna volunteer."

"All I ask is that you send my message."

He blinks once. "Done."

"Thank you, Eyron." I release his hand.

"No problem." Eyron passes me a shaky smile. "Ain't my place to judge."

Now, of course, there is nothing more to say, nothing more to do but wait. From the top of the hill we watch the fields turn from yellow to amber and then purple as Tol crosses the sky and sinks below the horizon.

CHAPTER THIRTY

Adahi always said: *with or without you, life goes on.*

He is right - life goes on, whether I choose to watch it through my apartment window or in the midst of the action on the dock platforms below. It is a lesson that has taken me far too long to learn.

Today, the Merge with Adahi will be complete. His memories will soon be my memories and I have a hard time admitting I will not miss our frequent interactions.

With or without him, my life will go on.

Tucking his plate between the soles of my feet, I open my eyes to his familiar face, embracing his scent of wind and weather and oil. My chest radiates warmth at the sight of him.

[*Santi.*] My name is affectionate on his tongue.

[*Adahi. It's time, isn't it?*]

Adahi reaches out to stroke my upper right arm. [*Yes, my Osca. Are you ready?*]

I nod, clutching the top of his hand with my left hand. [*My hands are empty without yours.*]

Although I have Nauru now, it is not a lie. Adahi is my Osco and that will never change.

Adahi's fingers glide through my hair. [*Be happy, Santi. It's all I ever wanted for you.*]

With a loud snap and crackle of ozone, Adahi disappears - but he is not gone.

Cyborn never say farewell.

He is embedded in my plate, along with the memories and recollections of his ancestors, all of the eternal stories of his grandmother, of her mother, and her mother's mother. I am able to see the world as Adahi would have seen it, with knowledge and passion, patience and humility. It's all now a part of me.

With or without him, my life will go on.

I bring his cold metal plate to my lips and place it into the box with the Union seal. The box is returned to its home on the sill.

The Merge is complete.

Scanning the apartment for something to do, my eyes rest upon the piles of different sized fabric bundles on the dining table, all recent creations of Nauru's. He always carried a stick of charcoal wrapped in one of these bundles while he was out.

I flip through the muslin bundles, hoping to find some of his images within them, but only one contains any at all - nimblemouse sitting, nimblemouse jumping, flower, vine, nimblemouse running, embroidery pattern...

At the end of the bundle are the existing sky symbols and the syllabary which Nauru designed. I trace a few of his marks lightly with my finger in order not to smear them.

Lines, dots, arcs - how hard could it be to make these images myself?

Inspired to try, I fish a piece of charcoal from a nearby drawer and smooth the smallest fabric bundle out on the dining table. I grasp the charcoal and hold it above the fabric as I had seen Nauru do it one hundred and two times before.

`Fact: You cannot undo the marks you make.`

My plate's observation is true - anything I scribble on this fabric will be permanent.

With quivering fingers, I copy the first symbol and frown at the crooked, uneven lines. I attempt the second image, then the third, fourth, fifth, and sixth. When I stop to compare my marks with Nauru's lines, my brows knit in frustration. His lines are beautiful, strong, and confident, while mine resemble bits of metal that had melted under extreme heat.

Gritting my teeth, I repeat the process, spending the next three local hours at the dining table duplicating the symbols in the bundle. I scratch row after row of black marks. I perfect the motions necessary to craft straight lines and rotund dots and curves. When I fill a bundle of fabric, I get another. Then another. And another.

"What are you doing?"

I jump in surprise, sending the charcoal heavily across the fabric. I glare at the ugly black mark through rows four and five, then at Nauru hunching over my shoulder, watching my struggle.

"Your syllabary looks pretty good, Santi," he says. "Except...I'm not sure what happened here." He points to the black mark that extends from one side of the fabric to the other.

"Shut up." I turn to a fresh piece of fabric and reposition the charcoal in my fingers. "You don't have to tease me."

"Last remarks aside, I wasn't teasing you," Nauru protests as I linger over the fabric bundle. "I'm actually quite impressed."

"But my symbols look terrible! They aren't nearly as nice as yours."

"Even I had to practice to get as good as I am now."

I sigh and scratch out another row of images, while Nauru observes my progress. As I painstakingly scribble symbol after symbol, his fingers slide my hair over my right shoulder and travel to the neckline of my dress. He slips the neckline down my left shoulder. I clutch the charcoal tighter and focus my attention on the symbols. I'm still annoyed with him and pretend to ignore him.

Nauru drops his lips to the junction of my neck and left collarbone, his breath hot on my cool skin. "Loosen your grip. You're going to break the charcoal."

I raise my left shoulder in mock irritation. "If someone stopped *bothering* me, I'd be able to concentrate."

Nauru's fingers pluck at the fastenings on my back, his lips tracing a path up and down my neck. "I'm not bothering you. I'm inspiring you."

I struggle to keep a straight face as Nauru flicks one of the hooks open. My hand rests on the table, unmoving, but I don't discard the charcoal yet. "You're unbelievable."

His lips meet my skin where the fastening was undone. "This isn't the first time I've been called unbelievable." His fingers tug at the next loop.

Though I force myself to keep both breath and voice steady, my skin prickles under his touch. My face flushes from the recollection of the last time Nauru played with the buttons on my dress. "I didn't mean it in a good way."

The second fastening falls, exposing my upper back. "Neither did I."

Dropping the charcoal onto the table, I leap out of my seat and grab Nauru by the collar. I sink my lips onto his and run my blackened fingers over his coveralls and through his hair. Nauru's fingers fumble with my next button and I scramble to unhook the fastenings of his coveralls -

Fact: There is someone on the other side of the door. Someone you know.

Tell them to go away!

Fact: It is Pella.

"Pella?" I squirm out of Nauru's grasp. "Pella's at the door."

He listens for a tic before edging closer to me. "Are you sure?"

I nudge him away and quickly secure the top fastenings of my dress, then lift the neckline from my shoulder to its proper position. When I am decent, the door opens and standing there is my cousin Pella, completely out of her element.

She takes a single step inside before catching sight of Nauru. She wraps her arms around her body, as though she is protecting herself.

I do not move from my position at Nauru's side. "What are you doing here?"

Pella evades the question and concentrates on me, ignoring Nauru. [You've cut your hair. It looks nice.]

Nauru shifts away from me. "Perhaps I should go."

"No, Nauru. Stay. This is your home, too." I glare at my cousin. "What do you want, Pella?"

Pella eyes her surroundings, showing a mild interest in the fabric bundles and the charcoal on the table, but she doesn't ask about them. [I thought the directory had made a mistake.]

I recall her unhelpfulness at the dress shop. I'm growing impatient. "What do you want, Pella?"

Still, she says nothing. She is fascinated by my missing arm and tries not to stare. I know she wants to ask about it but has the good sense not to.

[I feel bad about what happened between you and Mother.] She pauses, wandering into the tiny area that stores all of Nauru's cooking contraptions. She picks up one of the implements and studies it. [I want you to come to my oscos, Santi.]

My mouth falls open in surprise. "What?"

[I really want you there. You're like a sister to me...even with what had...happened.] She glances at Nauru and then back at me. [Please? It wouldn't be the same without you.]

"Are you extending this invitation to Nauru as well?"

Pause.

[Santi, I hadn't - what would everyone think if you brought a Freeman to an oscos?]

Nauru has no clue what my cousin has said, no clue what she wants, but this time I will ensure he is privy to my portion of the conversation. He will not think the worst of me. This time I do not deserve it.

I reach out and grasp his hand in mine. "I will not go if Nauru can't come with me."

Pause.

Pella's mouth drops open, like I've reached out and slapped her in the face. [*You're serious? You're actually serious?*]

Fact: She does not understand why.

"Nauru is like an Osco to me. I will not attend your oscos without him."

Another pause.

[*What would Adahi say?*]

"He said it himself: *Be happy, Santi. It's all I ever wanted for you.*"

Pella sucks in her breath. My choice defies all logic. How is it I am choosing a Freeman over my own flesh and metal?

She shakes her head in disbelief. [*Why, Santi? He's just a Freeman.*]

Just a Freeman.

The words are shallow and spiteful.

I could try to remedy her blindness. With a single touch of her hand, she would witness Nauru's patience and generosity, his dedication and commitment. She would know the simple truth: that I am what I am now because of Nauru.

Fact: But she has already made her decision and you have already made yours.

I agree. No matter what I do or say, Pella's heart will not change.

Instead of dropping Nauru's hand and reaching for hers, I entwine my fingers with his. "Nauru isn't just a Freeman. He's a good man, deserving of kindness and respect. If you took the time to know him like I do, you would understand why, too."

Pella merely stands there, agast, flustered, and upset.

I step closer to Nauru. "Give my kindest regards to Auntie."

This is a battle she will not win and she finally knows it. Pella's shoulders sag in defeat and she trudges to the open door. With a final disappointed glance at me, she steps through the doorway and the door closes behind her.

Nauru lets out his breath. I hadn't realized he had been holding it in. "You could have gone, if you really wanted to."

"Not without you."

Nauru furrows his brow. "Are you certain?"

"If you're not welcome, then I'm not welcome."

He balks slightly, but there's a pleased twitch forming at his lips. Nauru draws me in and I wrap an arm and a stump around him.

CHAPTER THIRTY-ONE

Tol's morning light shines in my face. Nauru and I are naked, tangled together in blankets and arms and legs. Nauru's hand cups one of my breasts and his soft breath tickles my neck. He's asleep and will be for another local hour or two. By living with Nauru, I have learned sleep is not a necessity for Cyborn as it is for Freemen.

Content in the security of Nauru's arms, my thoughts wander off, hunting for news of recent battles. Even though I am no longer an active soldier, I keep in touch with the 73rd Nova Penn - my old regiment - and map their journey around the system. I miss the camaraderie of my brothers and sisters in blue. I miss traveling along the endless flyways. I miss belonging to a cause and having a purpose greater than myself.

What of the regiment?

Statement: The 73rd Nova Penn has traveled through Auracania and are now on their way to Nessettie.

The seasons will change from one planet to the next - I will enlist some of the Freemen here to sew socks and mittens for them.

Statement: Nomad groups all over the Inner Planets have allied themselves with the Confederacy. They are involved in skirmishes with Union troops along the territories.

What would Adahi think of that?

Statement: There's been another raid on Cantis. The city of Lacren has been burned to the ground, 175 suspended.

Does that Spacer woman with the plate scar know anyone who was suspended in the raid?

Statement: The Confederacy is pushing into the

Outer Planets and the K-Cluster. Another battle is expected at the border as the Union sends reinforcements. There aren't enough Fixers already there to tend to the injured or suspended.

What of the Fixer in Gerin-Bue? Is she now tending the wounds of soldiers like Nyrie, Ceska, Dai, or Bokay? Is she preparing to send soldiers like Hucks home to their families?

Nauru stirs in his sleep, his arms tightening around my body. He buries his nose in my hair and blinks sleepily.

"How long have you been awake?" he mumbles.

I shift in his arms so we face each other. "Only forty-seven local minutes."

Nauru closes his eyes again, his lips upturned. "And what news from the front?" He knows of my fascination with the war and asks about it every morning. I remind him he doesn't have to humor me. He always claims he is not.

"My regiment's in Nessettie. They opened up a supply line along the eastern flyway of the planet. There's talk among the soldiers of another confrontation with the Secesh soon."

"Hmmm. Heavy losses?"

"Two-hundred twenty-one Union soldiers, last count." My tone is sober, reflective. How many more bodies will the Union lose to this conflict?

Nauru's lips brush against mine. "I'm sorry, Santi."

I shrug. I am not part of my regiment anymore; thus, their fight is no longer my own. I change the subject so I don't dwell on what was. "What are we doing today?"

"Lem and Udarah invited us to their house to share some food and wine. I think Anma and Caigh will be there, too." Nauru's mouth forms into a gentle grin. "We'd better bring you some of those moldy crackers you like so much."

I snort. "They're better than that stuff you call nourishment."

Nauru runs his fingers through my hair, his eyes playful and full of good humor. "Freeman food is delicious. You should try it sometime."

I make a face and nudge him away with my stump. "It's disgusting and much too strong for my delicate sensibilities."

"My poor, dainty flower."

I stick out my tongue and push back the blankets.

I have not been back to the Freeman Quarter since I had tried to find

Nauru by holding Anma captive in her apartment. I sat there, alone, till the children invited me to play with them. The recollection of their faces at the big, red ball causes me to smile, but it quickly fades with a swift glance at my right arm. The children know nothing of what I've been through.

What will they say about my appearance?

Nauru passes me a lazy grin from the bed. "I have a surprise for you."

"For me?" I glance around the apartment, scanning the room for anything out of place.

Fact: All items are where they should be.

"For you." Nauru, knowing what I am up to, sits up. "But it isn't here."

"Where is it?"

He lifts his eyebrows, but doesn't say anything. As far as he is concerned, the matter is closed. No amount of pestering will get him to talk; therefore, I don't even try.

Though the recent afternoons have been quite comfortable, it's grown rather chilly in the mornings, so I dress warmly and in layers: sweater, flax shirt, cotton pants. Nauru, of course, prefers to be well-dressed whenever he isn't wearing his work coveralls. Compared to him, I always appear too casual and a bit sloppy but, as a civilian, I have come to prefer function to form.

Nauru smooths out his vest, then extends a hand to me. "Ready?"

"Ready."

Hoping he's somehow hidden the surprise in his hand, I reach out and take it, fighting back the disappointment when there's nothing but my palm against his.

As we enter the quarter, I worry the children will ask about my arm. How will I be able to explain what I have been through in words they will understand?

It is the bouncy red ball I hear first, followed by shouts of impatience. I spot an older child rolling the ball to a little boy with dark hair in a long line of younger children. When the ball is within range, he kicks the ball as hard as he can. The ball flies wildly to the left, bouncing over the raised median full of garden boxes. The dark-haired boy runs to the other side of the street while the older child scrambles for the ball - trying not to squish the colorful globes under the plants - and tries to tag him with it before he reaches the sidewalk. The boy leaps to the sidewalk, safe.

It's a new game with new rules.

Nauru directs me to an empty median where Lem and Udarah are already watching the game. They're sitting on a blanket, Udarah's head upon Lem's shoulder, fingers entwined. I recall the day at the cliffs when Nauru and I sat on his homemade blanket and shared a bottle of wine - the same day I realized I had grown rather fond of Nauru.

It was the day I hoped he had grown fond of me, too.

Lem motions us over, sliding closer to Udarah to make room. He shakes Nauru's hand before Nauru joins him on the ground. "We didn't expect to see you till later."

"Santi insisted we get an early start," Nauru says, his eye teasing.

"Nauru has a surprise for me." I glare at him. "But he won't tell me what it is."

Lem chuckles when Nauru shrugs.

Udarah elbows Lem in the ribs and rolls her eyes. She smiles at me, tilting her head toward mine. "Will you help me gather up the fruits? I've been asking Lem to do it for days now."

Lem throws her a look of pretend protest. "I've been busy!"

"Yeah, right." Udarah gives him a sideways glance as she hands me a canvas sack. "You've been lazy!"

Lem drops backward onto the blanket and slides his hands behind his head. "But I'm so tired from working so hard at the docks!"

Udarah's false stony exterior cracks and she giggles, grabbing another sack. "Come on, Santi. These poor, tired men need a break."

I follow Udarah to the far end of the neighboring median where she plucks bright green and red globes from the plants and then sets them in her bag.

[Nauru: Choose the largest and the most perfect.]

That is what Nauru said in Nyrie's garden.

Without much else to reference, I settle across from Udarah and copy her movements, always mindful of Nauru's advice as my fingers skim over the smooth skin of the fruit.

"These gardens are nice," I tell Udarah as she scoots down the row. These plots in the middle of the street aren't as lush as Nyrie's backyard and they're oddly placed, but they'll provide the families around here with nourishment nonetheless.

"They've been here a while now. Hoppers won't come to the Freeman Quarter. It seemed a waste to not use the medians for something."

"But if they were not necessary, why build medians in the first place?"

"This whole quarter wasn't always for Freemen. Cyborn lived here, once."

"Cyborn?" I process her words. "What happened?"

"What usually happens." Udarah drops a handful of blue fruits into her bag. "This area is a good place to live because it's central to other areas of the city. You don't need transportation to get to and from most jobs, so Freemen chose to live here. When they started moving in, the Cyborn moved out."

I sit back, staring at the crumbling cobblestone medians. I have lived here my entire life. This is my city, and yet there are parts of its history I do not know.

Udarah attempts a comforting smile. "It is the way of things."

I used to be ignorant, too. Before I met Nauru, I thought my knowledge about Freemen sufficient enough, but in actuality, I didn't know much about Freemen at all. Though I don't understand all of the nuances that separate us, I know that Nauru and I are more alike than we are different.

I respond with my own painful frown. "It doesn't have to be."

The hollow sound of rubber bouncing against stone grows nearer, accompanied by the pounding footsteps of a group of children - at least five that my plate is able to differentiate. The red ball bursts into view and bumps into my leg. I gather the ball up and stand, left hand outstretched and ready to return it. The children stop short when they see me holding the ball. Their eyes grow wide, mouths gaping in confusion.

One of them shrieks and claps her hands together. She dashes over and throws her arms around my middle. "Santi's back!"

The girl's cries alert the other children in the street. They come pouring over the gardens and around the median in a mad rush to my side, clutching my hand and legs, wrapping their arms about my waist. They tug on my clothing and bombard me with enthusiastic questions, causing me to nearly drop the ball.

"Where have you been?"

"Is it true you were at Gerin-Bue?"

"How come you haven't visited us yet?"

"Why aren't you wearing your uniform?"

"What was the Fixer like?"

"Did you bring us another present?"

"Do you really know how to shoot a slinger?"

"How come you cut your hair? I liked it long!"

"Will you play ball with us? We have a new game!"

Question after question is lobbed at me in rapid fire succession, as though I am back with Pari and my crew, hurling shot after shot. None of the children ask about my missing arm. None of them care I am no longer who they recall. They are only excited I have finally returned.

I catch Nauru's eye. He's seated beside Lem at the next median, but his smirk tells me my appearance was a surprise for the Freemen children, too. Doing my best to hide a broad smile, I simply shake my head at him - this tricky, irresistible, wonderful man who does his best to make me happy.

His surprise was a success: I am delighted by the attention.

From across the median garden, an older boy with a slim scar on his temple lifts his hand. He had been the one rolling the ball to the line of children. He plays it cool, but his eyes are glad to see me, too.

I toss the ball to him. "I'm up."

The children release a deafening cheer and race to the street to line up behind me, bumping and pushing each other to secure a place next to me in line. Even the older children on the steps of the nearby buildings venture over.

The boy holding the ball is a natural showman, alternating between carefully taking aim and bouncing the ball from one hand to the other. "Bet you can't kick it over the building!"

"You'll never find it if I do!"

Along the line, the children exchange awed whispers.

The boy flashes me a grins and rolls the ball, but it isn't a gentle lope like his previous serves. This one flies toward me, bouncing in great leaps across the street and up the sidewalk. I kick the ball, sending it flying straight up, up, up! The children crane their necks and stand on their toes to search for it, but it's only a tiny red speck against the sky.

I run to the other side of the street, clearing the median garden in one great leap, and then back before catching the ball neatly in my arm and stump without dropping it.

The stunned silence is broken by the children's impressed glee, their frenzied clapping and wild stomps indicating this is entertainment at its best. It's a stunt no one in the entire Freeman Quarter is able to do.

"Do it again!" someone begs. Heads in the crowd nod in agreement.

I shake my head to hush the children. "I'll serve so I don't lose your ball."

The children scramble back in line from shortest to tallest. Four older boys - including the boy with the slight scar on his temple - ignore the unspoken rule and push toward the front, thrilled for an opportunity to go head-to-head with a Cyborn. The stubborn little boy at the front manages to hold his place from the older ones with a few choice words about fairness.

`Observation: He is clever and argumentative, like Nauru.`

I see it, too.

While clearly giddy to be part of the action, the boy at the front is visibly hesitant. He sways his body weight from one leg to the other and his hands shake with nervous energy. I roll the ball at him and it bounces with a slow and steady gait, one he is sure to be able to kick.

He gathers his courage and kicks the ball as hard as he is able. It spins on a wild trajectory to my left. I scoop up the ball easily and chase him, pretending he is too fast and I am unable to catch him. He reaches the other side of the street and waves triumphantly at his older sister standing in line. The other children cheer.

I send the ball to child after child. In the spirit of fairness and good sportsmanship, I always allow a young child to cross the street and back no matter how effortlessly I am able to tag them out. In contrast, it's all-out war with the older children. I chase them down in a mad fervor. They attempt impossible leaps and tricks to dodge the ball, but I tag them out every time.

I am so focused on strategy that when the next person steps up, I am surprised to see Nauru there, his vest removed and his clean white shirt untucked. It's the most disheveled I've ever seen him and I can't suppress a grin.

His eye gleams. "Let's see what you've got, plate-face."

I bounce the ball with my left hand. "I've got enough for five of you, Freeman."

A showdown! The children squeal in delight and settle on the sidewalk to watch, nudging each other and whispering back and forth as they declare a winner. My plate analyzes their murmurs as I prepare to roll the ball to Nauru.

`Fact: The odds are good: 80% of the younger children favor you. All of the older children back Nauru.`

He studies my every move with a critical eye as he waits for my serve. I bounce the ball three times before flinging it to him. It curves in a wickedly wide arch to Nauru's right. He kicks out but completely misses. The crowd groans.

"Is that all you've got, Freeman?"

Nauru collects the ball and tosses it back to me. "Just getting warmed up, plate-face."

I bounce it again before hurling it at him, but this time he's prepared for my tricks. As the ball skims the street, Nauru successfully estimates the ball's path and strikes it with such effort that the ball sails over my head. He runs to the other side of the street and the children leap up and down, yelling and applauding for him.

I catch the ball on the second bounce and tear after him, my feet pounding against the pavers in rhythmic strokes matched only by the heartbeat in my ears. I quickly gain on him, extending the ball to Nauru's back, lunging at him in an attempt to tag him out. He dodges my reach and dives at the designated safe zone on the sidewalk. I throw the ball at his back, but he suddenly turns and catches the ball. Nauru falls onto the street, half of his body on the sidewalk and the other half on the pavers.

A whoop goes up as the children crowd around him in a burst of chatter and confusion. Did Nauru win? Did he lose? Does it even matter?

I press through the crowd and pause at Nauru's feet. Still clutching the ball, he blinks up at me and I extend my hand out to him.

"Draw?"

Dropping the ball, he takes my hand in a firm grasp. "Draw."

When I pull him up, Nauru cups my face and leans in. Right there, in front of twenty-seven pairs of intent eyes, his lips meet mine. I am only vaguely aware of the howls of approval as I tug him closer.

CHAPTER THIRTY-TWO

As the local weeks go by, my production of symbols slowly improves. Nauru compliments my strokes, saying they are noticeably bolder and clearer than a local month ago.

Though Nauru encourages me to practice, he also wants me to leave the apartment, to get out, to do other things. Twenty-four percent of the time, I do make an effort to venture out - I bring Nauru his lunch pail during his noonday break, I go to the park and watch people, I scale the cliffs with one arm and a stump - but the remaining 76% of my spare time is spent hunched at the table, charcoal in hand. My fingertips are perpetually black now.

Today, Nauru has convinced me to accompany him to the Freeman market where we'll be searching for yellow and green fabric scraps to sew into a blanket - a gift for Udarah because soon she'll be having a baby. He knows I'd rather be at the table, working on my symbols.

"Surely you don't need my help digging for scraps!" I complain on our way.

"Not at all. My reasons are entirely selfish." Nauru squeezes my hand and pulls me closer to his side. "I hope to find you some fabric to make you a dress."

"I need more practice, not a dress."

"Of course you need a new dress!" Nauru's lips draw upward into a teasing smirk. "Anything to get my hands on you."

I blush, our shoulders bumping together as we turn the corner into the Freeman Quarter.

Along the sidewalks, three dozen Freemen have constructed tables and arranged their items upon them. Nauru and I browse rows of colorful, hand-thrown pottery; racks of handmade clothing and jewelry;

mechanical and spring-loaded toys; neatly-folded squares of embroidered cloth; sweet and savory scented foods on sticks; and bins of old clothing.

Nauru greets a friend standing behind a table with a quick handshake. The two discuss recent events as the man hands Nauru a large basket of striped homespuns. Nauru bends over it and sorts through torn shirts and worn dresses, seeking the perfect colors and patterns as he converses with his friend. I hover above him, pointing out possible choices, but I remain disinterested nonetheless.

I catch sight of Anma bartering with another merchant across the street and give her a friendly wave. She puts down the blue and white painted pitcher she's holding and comes over, a smile for Nauru and a quick embrace for me.

"I need your opinion on a new dress," Anma says, reaching for my hand to tug me away.

I gesture to my own clothes - a plain shirt and heavy pants. "Why? I'm not fashionable."

"Who cares?" she huffs. "I trust your judgement."

I glance at Nauru. "Can you sort through scraps on your own?"

He sighs and makes a grand production of it. "I suppose, but it'll be rather boring without you."

"You'll survive." Anma grabs my hand and drags me away. "Come on, Santi."

Anma steers me through the disorganized crowd, careful to avoid touching as many people as possible, for my benefit - of this I am certain. Cyborn naturally fall into neat lines in large groups and tend to move at a regular pace, but Freemen wander from one place to another inconsistently. They stand in the middle of the streets and walkways. They bump into each other as they make their way from one vendor to the next. They idle next to tables, crowding around so that others have to elbow their way through. It is an inefficient and confusing system, but one I never tire of watching.

`Observation: She has already decided on the dress. She knows exactly where she is going.`

I had not considered this possibility, but my plate is right. Anma heads to a table, says a quick greeting to the vendor, and picks up a brightly-colored garment. She holds it up and lifts her eyebrows.

"It's nice," I say, shrugging.

She shakes the dress again and frowns. "Nice?"

`Fact: Obviously that's not the answer she`

wanted.

I scrutinize the dress further to find what Anma finds so appealing about it.

"It's...a...beautiful color."

"And?"

"And it...has a flattering cut."

"And?"

"And...it is perfect for you."

Finally satisfied with my answers, Anma gives me a toothy grin and turns to barter with the vendor. As they argue over the price, my eyes wander around the market. I study the facial expressions and interactions between vendors and consumers, trying to discern exactly what they are feeling. As skilled as I have become in deciphering Nauru's emotions and expressions, I am not so adept at reading other Freemen.

"Excuse me?"

My gaze breaks away from the two Freemen arguing across the street to the man next to me, his stare directed at me. I flounder for words of some purpose, but he appeared out of nowhere and I have no words of greeting to offer him.

At my dumbfounded expression, the Freeman hesitates a tic before removing his hat. "Are you Sargeant Metizon?"

At the mention of my name, I croak out a barely distinguishable: "I am."

The man exhales in relief and the grip on his hat loosens. "I wanted to thank you."

Without words, kind or otherwise, I stare at the Freeman who stands here, appreciative of some unknown actions I have taken. But why? I have never seen him before - why is he *thanking* me?

"My...partner...is away. On Nessettie, last I heard."

"Last you heard?" I repeat. Nothing he says is clear. "How do you know - "

Fact: The syllabary. He is using your syllabary.

Of course.

This Freeman is using the same symbols I have practiced everyday, the symbols that blacken my fingers, the symbols that enable long-distance communication between Freemen and their Cyborn. My heart softens to see him here, speaking to me so openly and honestly about such a private part of his life.

A faint smile graces the Freeman's lips. "I don't hear from her as often as I'd like, but it's good to know she's well."

"That's wonderful." I extend my hand to him and he accepts it with one sound shake, his calloused palm warm in mine. "I'm happy to help."

Without another word, the Freeman drops my hand, replaces his hat, and disappears into the crowd.

Once the Freeman is out of sight, Anma appears at my side, adjusting the bag on her shoulder and tilting her head in the man's direction. The dress is draped across her arm. "Who was that?" she asks.

I do not know his name. I do not know his occupation. I do not know where he lives. I do not know of his partner. I know nothing about him, except that we are like family, though we are not related by blood or flesh or metal.

"He's a dear friend."

Linking arms with Anma, I steer her towards the vendor where we left Nauru, who will be excited to hear of our success.

CHAPTER THIRTY-THREE

I am not certain how Nauru heard the news before I did, but one chilly winter day he tears into the apartment with an announcement.

"The president's coming to Gerin-Bue!"

I glance up from my lines and squiggles and wipe my fingers on an edge of the practice cloth. "Who said this?"

Nauru's eye sparkles with excitement. "Some of the dock workers. A few freighters told them last night during their shift."

With only a mild curiosity, I check the messages my plate's been trying to pass along to me and discover an official invitation mixed among advertisements and other junk. I've been so busy transcribing the personal messages of others I have not accessed my own.

[It is with great honor that Sergeant Santina (Bashe) Metizon is invited to the dedication and consecration ceremony at Gerin-Bue. Details follow.]

In two local weeks, the Union president is coming to Gerin-Bue, but I am not as enthusiastic about this news as Nauru.

I fidget with the scraps of cloth on the table and swallow hard. "I don't *want* to go."

Nauru's smile shrinks, then reappears - a mask, hiding his disappointment. He puts a hand on mine and brings his lips to my forehead. "Of course - how insensitive of me."

Observation: Nauru expected you to go.

Before I can explain, he slides a hand up my arm and through my hair. I lean my head against his hand. His thumb strokes my cheekbone. "I have an errand to do. It shouldn't take long. Would you like to come with me, Santi?"

"No." I pick up the charcoal and return to the cloth in front of me.

"I've got work to do."

Nauru presses his lips to my forehead again before he leaves. I take a deep breath and bring the charcoal back to the cloth, but as I draw those lines, those curves, those spirals and dots, I recall the path of Nauru's fingers and the gnawing invitation to the ceremony.

It is my choice and I am choosing not to go.

Fact: Nauru wants to go.

Yes, I know. But I have moved on. What is the point of returning to the past?

Correction: You would not be returning to the past - you would be sharing a part of yourself with him.

Nauru shared a piece of himself - he invited me to Lem and Udarah's party - and even though I was not certain I belonged there, I had a good time. I had formed friendships because of that decision. I had learned more about Nauru's life because of that decision.

Observation: But you are choosing not to reciprocate. You are choosing not to share this part of your life with him.

Nauru did not insist I attend, though I know he wants to go, very much.

Fact: You belong there more than you care to admit. That is the truth of this situation.

I fought there. I bled there. I drove the Secesh from there. I left my crew - and my arm - there. Pieces of my life and part of my story had been left behind on the hills of Gerin-Bue. However painful it is to recall those memories, refusing to go at all and ignoring what had happened there would be like spitting on what I had - at one time - valued. How could I spit on what Hucks had done? Or Nyrie? Or Ceska, Dai, and Bokay?

Fact: Casting aside your decision regarding Nauru, you owe it to your fallen brothers and sisters to visit one last time.

Though I still suffer, though I still live with sadness, I cannot refute the truth of this statement. As the last of my crew, I am obligated to pay my respects where we had once stood in blue, so dignified and so proud.

***

In preparation for the ceremony, Nauru made all of the adjustments to my uniform: the cleaning, the sewing, the patching, and the alterations to the right sleeve. When he pulls it out of the closet the morning of the dedication, I gasp in surprise. It looks exactly as it had before I left for Gerin-Bue.

Nauru holds up the jacket. "Do you need help with the fastenings?"

I shrug into it and deftly fasten the closures with my left hand. "I've got this."

There's a growing sense of pride in my chest at my adaptability, at my functionality. Adahi's words echo through my head: *Do what you can now. Learn the rest later.*

I place my kepi on my head and turn to Nauru. "How do I look?"

Nauru straightens my hat, then scrutinizes me as he taps a finger against his chin. "You're missing something."

"What?" I examine my uniform, puzzled. I'm wearing everything I'm supposed to, down to the itchy woolen underwear. It's finally the right season for it.

In a grand production, Nauru checks and rechecks his vest pockets and the pockets of his pants.

Observation: His actions are suspicious.

"What are you doing?"

Nauru picks up his overcoat and digs through the pockets. "I'm missing something. Perhaps you ought to check your jacket, Santi."

Nauru isn't fooling anyone. I roll my eyes and reach into my pocket, extracting a small, tightly-covered bundle wrapped in one of Nauru's handkerchiefs - the one with the stars and crescent of the Union around the edge.

"What is it?" I ask, but Nauru does not answer. He only responds with the same tricky smirk he gave me when I saw him at the park on our second meeting.

Dragging my thumb along the edge of the handkerchief, I find a blue and white Abolitionist badge inside. It's identical to the pins Nauru made for our network contacts all over the system, but the border of this one is fashioned of metal, not fabric. Alternating light and dark threads are woven through tiny, punched holes in the metal creating three rows of near-perfect squares and triangles in a soft, exquisite sheen.

"It's beautiful." I thumb the slick, rich strands. "But why? What is it for?"

"I felt compelled to make you something that symbolizes your work, both as a soldier and as an Abolitionist." Nauru pockets the

227

handkerchief and unfastens the clasp on the back of the badge. "May I?"

I nod, blushing as his fingers work the clasp, weaving it through the fabric above my right breast and pinning it securely. He straightens the badge and steps back, a satisfied expression on his face. "Now you're ready."

My fingers fondle the pin, tracing a row of blocks. Triangle, square, triangle. I had produced this image just last night when I practiced the syllabary. "Thank you."

"Shall we go?" Nauru holds out his right arm, an invitation for me to take it. "We don't want to miss our tram."

The tram was my idea because it's the cheapest and most efficient way to get to Gerin-Bue but, upon later reflection of my undignified return from the front, not the best means of travel for an ex-slinger operator. Today, I am determined not to allow my recollections to affect my peace.

I grasp Nauru's arm. He settles his other hand on top of mine. "I'll be right here."

"I know." I squeeze his forearm.

The day is cool and clear, perfect for a detour through the park on our way to the station. The transition from crisp fall to barren winter had always been my favorite time of year.

It will be an odd sensation to admire the snow without having to march through it.

I hear the squeal of the trams long before we arrive at the station, but instead of dread and fear, I feel only a sense of calm duty and determined commitment urging me forward. I am backed by Adahi's words, by the scarred freighter's encouragement, by Nyrie's confidence, by Hucks's playful humor, by Bokay's loyalty, by Dai's courage, by Ceska's diligence, by Eyron's conviction, and by the strength of my own recollections. Nauru is the only one with me, yet the others offer their invisible support, too.

My ticket is free - kindly paid for by the person ahead of us in line. When the man hands it to me, he tips his hat and says, "Soldier." He doesn't give Nauru a second glance. I consider passing the ticket to the woman behind me, but Nauru convinces me to keep it.

Without the rowdy songs or the rude banter of soldiers, the packed tram is relatively quiet, filled only with the whispers of children and the hum of plates. Nauru and I choose seats next to each other in the middle of the car and I watch for anyone who disagrees with this arrangement. No one does.

I catch a small child across the row staring at my stub, which is hidden under my folded sleeve. She tugs on her mother's coat. Although I cannot hear the exchange through their plates, the girl's mother pulls her out of her seat and to the only empty seat left at the front of the car. The girl peeks over her mother's shoulder and frowns at me.

Her mother's words had their effect. Ignoring the girl, I sigh and focus my attention at the barren countryside and never-ending fields of dried grass out the window, so sparse away from the city. Here, fall is not the beautiful season I know it is.

Nauru wraps an arm around my shoulder. I expect the child to gasp in horror and alert her mother, but when I glance at her seat, she is no longer looking at me.

Nauru and I exchange few words as the rest of the journey passes in an endless parade of fields and frost, hills and rocks. I rest my head on his shoulder, content to enjoy the view from the tram while my plate ticks off a silent countdown till we arrive at the station.

The Gerin-Bue station is packed with politicians, ex-soldiers, civilians, honored guests, and Freemen - more people than the soldiers and civilians present at my first arrival. They flood out of the station and to the battlefield in a neat, steady stream. Tens of thousands of pairs of eyes scan the area, desperate for a glimpse of the president.

Nauru secures a place in line and navigates us through the crowds. The people around him step away with as many paces as the cramped conditions will allow. Once we reach the front exit and the lines thin as people locate a place to watch the ceremony, I sigh, finally able to breathe. My self-imposed isolation copying the syllabary at the dining table did not prepare me for this.

"Let's find a good spot to stand," Nauru says, steering me toward the stage where hundreds of people have already gathered, surrounding the vacant platform in orderly rows. Despite such a large group, Nauru locates two empty places only four rows from the front. He ushers me into the empty spots, a happy smile tugging at his lips.

A lone slinger shot tears through the air, its piercing shriek reminiscent of the artillery fire. Nauru winces as I clutch his hand a little too tightly.

Fact: There was no shot.

I loosen my hold on Nauru. The crowd scans the area, searching for the direction of the noise, wondering where the shot had come from, but I know. The artillery unit is on Ginger Hill.

229

Slowly, the procession trickles over from the north. The military band in their splendid dress uniforms and the high-ranking military leaders arrive first, settling in their designated area. The government officials appear next - the president among them - their hoppers kicking up dust to announce their presence. As they climb the platform steps, the crowd releases a great cheer. They wave for silence and the first speaker is introduced.

The dedication has begun.

The audience clings to his every word, but he is long-winded and dull, without any particularly memorable words to say. Ten local minutes pass. Then twenty. I glance at Nauru who hangs upon his every word, completely entranced.

"I'm going to wander," I whisper to Nauru.

Nauru inclines his head close to mine, eyes still on the speaker. "Can I come with you?"

I hesitate. I had not expected Nauru to want to accompany me. "Do you want to?"

"Of course. Will you show me the hill?"

The hill - Ginger Hill - the place I fought, the place I bled, the place I became broken.

I offer Nauru my hand and he accepts, his hand a warm comfort as the winds pick up.

The hill is as steep as I recall, but cleaner. The debris from the shrapnel is gone - gathered up by the residents of Gerin-Bue or carried off by scavengers and souvenir hunters - and the endless stretch of grey and blue bodies are gone, too - removed by the Fixers. The bodies in blue were processed, plates were returned to families, their sacrifices represented in single blocks of marble with the Union emblem near the stage - one for every soldier suspended here.

What did they do with all of the Secesh?

They had been here, too, but not anymore.

I lead Nauru to Ginger Hill. For four tics, we stand there, together, before I release his hand and point to the top. "I ran up this hill, all the way to that pillar."

Nauru raises his eyebrows, clearly impressed. "Really?"

"Pari was already at the top. Along with everyone else."

"Pari?"

How is it I had never mentioned Pari to Nauru before now?

"Our artillery unit," I explain. "We designated it Pari."

As Nauru and I climb up Ginger Hill, my words spill out in a desperate rush.

"The Union line stretched from there - " I point to Rust Hill and bring my arm toward the row of hills and ridges to the south, " - to there. There were thousands of us, all lined up and waiting for the Secesh to attack our position. They broke through at the top, but we fought them off."

Nauru stops to absorb the view. I push on, keeping the rock pillar, the same one that marked Pari's position, in sight. At the top, tears forms in my eyes. Except for the echoing speech and an errant cheer or two, the hill is empty and peaceful, all remnants of Pari and empty canisters and bodies absent.

I lean against the rock pillar with my stubby right arm and weep, hiding my face behind my left hand. I do not recall when I become wrapped in Nauru's arms, his cheek resting against my temple. I sob freely into his coat.

"How does anyone know of our struggles or sacrifices, when there is nothing left here to recall?"

I feel the crinkle at Nauru's temple as he smiles. "Cyborn don't need such reminders."

"Don't they?" I peel myself away from Nauru. "When you were Cyborn, did you ever recall the memories of your ancestors? What do you know of your lineage?"

Nauru is silent. He has no words because he does not want to admit that the memories of his family's past no longer endure so vividly in his recollections.

"How can we be devoted to a memory, to our past, when there is nothing left to recall?"

"I don't know." Nauru's arms tighten around my shoulders. "I'm sorry, Santi. I don't have an answer for you."

I have no other words, no other questions, and certainly no answers. I have only sobs. Nauru is unfazed by my reaction and gently rocks me side to side, humming a dock song, then another, and then another.

As I regain my composure, my blurry vision rests upon the sandy-colored rock pillar at the top of the hill, less than two paces away from my touch. It can easily be seen from the outskirts of Gerin-Bue.

I break away from Nauru's grasp and lift a finger to scratch the grainy stone, leaving an indent in the pillar's face. I fumble to remove my Abolitionist badge.

"Give me a boost," I demand. Nauru kneels down, one knee up and one knee down in the yellow dirt, and I step onto his thigh.

For three local minutes, I carve deep lines and curves into the pillar with a metal edge of the badge, scarring it with the symbols I have memorized and practiced over and over again at the table in our tiny kitchen.

When I am through, I drop to the ground and admire my dedication:

HERE FOUGHT THE BRAVEST MEN AND WOMEN
OF THE 73RD NOVA PENN REGIMENT.
DESIGNATED:
PRIVATE VILISSA CESKA
PRIVATE HOA DAI
PRIVATE YOAN HUCKSLEY
PRIVATE NAN BOKAY
AND CORPORAL YOAN ROMMEN NYRIE.
MAY THEY BE RECALLED FOR ALL TIME AND ETERNITY.

Nauru squeezes my shoulder.

I hand him the badge. "Too much?"

He repins it to my chest. "Most Cyborn will not be able to understand what you've said here."

"But they'll understand something was done here."

We sit in the yellow dirt at the base of the pillar, my head on Nauru's shoulder and his hand on my knee, immersed in the distant, ongoing words of the orator.

"...we, the Cyborn patriots and Freemen across this great system, graciously acknowledge the survivors of this devastating battle. We are indebted to their service, their loyal hearts, and their dedication to our cause..."

Observation: You have finally found your place.

I am no longer who I was, but never have I seen my life so clearly.

I am Santi, the soldier.

Santi, the messenger.

Santi, the Abolitionist.

www.ingramcontent.com/pod-product-compliance
Lightning Source LLC
Chambersburg PA
CBHW031725170626
46808CB00005B/1888